INDULGENCE

Maurice Bouguerra

ISBN: 978-0-578-02287-1

Website: www.mauricebouguerra.com
E-mail: ashbenbay@yahoo.ca
Title: Indulgence
Publication Date: 04/2009
First Paperback Edition

All my life I have been surrounded by beauty. In nature, in music, in art and within everyone I have ever seen. I have tasted the bitter, the vile, the tender and the sweet. I understand it all, though it has taken growth to accept. It is what it is, in its full expressions, in its paradox and its parody. It is life and the Greatest Gift. It is the majesty of the creative will to share that little part of the universal need, to be simply … Beautiful.

CONTENTS

With Much Love to

Ashbenbay

Tony Flavell

Heather Leitch

and .... Her.

CHARENTON

Prelude of the Forth-Coming

Madness is a quaint genteel. Subtly protruding itself through the tiniest of facial gestures, unintroduced statements that seem like amusing gaffes and movements foreign to the situation, but thought of as the delightful peculiarities of the charming eccentric. Rarely understood for what it is: the shadows behind the reasonings.

That dark corner in the middle of the room where the carrier tends to be moved to by the piloting companion in the dance of insanity. For the center is the location where it can best hide itself, as it performs for the various circles of individuals, who unknowingly have passed the outward boundaries of their own tethers to personal beliefs of what defines itself as rationality.

From our perch on a branch behind we witness harmonious defiance in the stride of a black cloaked man as his boots kick aside the gold leaflets that gather beneath the late October trees on a boulevard approach that is the product of the Rue du Marechal Leclerc in the Paris of

1829. The sound of the stones that serve as the altars to every tempered boot step adds that baritone resonance to the soprano Chorus of the leaves as they, in turn, are in response to the tenor twirl of the wind through the branches. And, of course, the altos are ever present in a texture produced by the distant sounds.

All in the dark symphony of this moment that will be forever known as: Prelude of the Forth-Coming.

A spiraling fountain of leaflets and golden dust is cast in a surrounding whirlwind by the certainty of direction of the cloaked booted man as he walks away from our safe nest of witness. He reaches the far barrier of the tree-lined boulevard where in the light beyond the canopy he finally arrives at the fortress of sanity, where mental clarity sanitizes for the purposes of mental hygiene.

On the pinnacle above, the Cross of Jesus has been strategically placed at the joining juncture. Being reassured that God remains ever diligent in the defense of his own eternal soul and righteous worldly purpose he begins to scale the appropriate steps, the ones that ascend to the right. The ones that ascend to the left will remain forever ignorant to the choice that has just been made.

Once the ascent has been superbly accomplished he walks into the foyer being instantly greeted by a fawning administrative assistant.

"Monsieur Scherer, it is my honor to welcome you."

"Mechant's companion, where is she?" is the sudden response.

"This way, Monsieur."

The tempered boot steps begin to follow at a pace that symbolizes position at the top climax of authority. Slower than the guide's desire, forcing the one leading the main object of the procession to curtail to the timing of the boots' baton, as they move through the activities of this sleepless sanctuary. This is a place where one can continue to hear those distant echoes in the middle of the night no matter what time of day it is.

Again the dark symphony is added to by various voices. The keys in the locks of dominos of metal doors, the musicians of rust playing on their hinges, as the repetitive pitch of water dripping joins in with that confining substance that makes one aware their life has been enveloped by a black sunset at noon. Then there is the sound of far away screams, satanic laughter and crying in all its variations that wake up the internal fear inside the most resilient in our audience.

We look around and see portraits on the walls where cracks pass behind the frames like lightning bolts of warning. There are outlines of disposed paintings that cover our thoughts with shrouds of doubts about whether we should continue to follow the man who is now taking off his heavy leather gloves that unveil large hands with scars entrenched on the knuckles.

He begins to beat the gloves on the side of his thigh in mid counter to the tempo produced by his boots. Passing through a doorway that has been promised redemption by the cross of crucifixion that remains still at its post above like a brave sentry. Another hallway with casts of characters annexes their contributions to this production of hysteria.

This hallway is more animated than the first. There are the nurses, attendants and relatives of the victims who have been poisoned by ingesting too much abnormality, or perhaps too much normality. There are the rooms that are opened for quick inspection and the rooms that are closed in order to stop their occupants from inspecting outwards. At the end, the true triumph of this branch of the fortress is the large common area that is caged off so inspection can be neutral, both in and out.

Inside, there are faces of every possible expression glued onto heads that are worn by a forest of trunks. Some, able to move past those that sit stationary and then there are the others that don't appear to understand the meaning of erect balance. More than half have something to say while their companions seem utterly unaffected by the coherent ramblings and verbal rampages.

There are the few that stutter at the rims of the cage certain that they are the ones that are looking at the oddity. They laugh as their captors hurdle responses back like people do to the neighbors' dog that yaps profusely through the entire midnight.

This is the grandeur of the prelude's ballet, where all has been masterly perfected for the witnesses in the audience, who struggle with their role as the entertained in the violent patterns of sickness as it cores itself through the minds in order to nest and create more distortions. But the gloves continue their counter as their owner seems unaffected and also possibly entertained.

The commander leads the orchestrator through a side doorway that opens upon a patio where stairs up and down converge for the purpose of temptation. The flight down is the sin considered as we watch the two play the stairs in a finery of artistic expression. As they continue beneath the floor just entertained, the advance takes on the makeup of hesitant restrainment due to the location to which this particular sin will lead.

The appropriate landing is found at the heels of the structure above. Here below the fortress' feet, the ceiling can barely be seen as the lamps are dim and their numbers are un-abundant. The air is sparse because it is encased in the aroma of stale disgorge, recent fecal matter, as well as fresh and evaporated urine that overpowers the sweet smell of drying blood. The gloves are brought quickly to the nose for the futile hope of masking the vulgarity, as the end of this first step arrives at a door that is opened to reveal the second.

As the door is swung open a beam of sunlight is instantly exposed as it warms the room and the pathway behind with its ability to cast aside harsh darkness' lover, sterility. There is a kind breeze that the window above also grants making the reality below easier to lose grip of.

On a well used mattress on the floor by the corner a young lady lies comatose. There are unattended cuts above her eyes, welts under, stained blood on her face and in her hair, with slight movement the only sign that life isn't through with her.

"Will she survive, Mousseau?"

"Not if she remains here Monsieur, her destiny is about to be completed. There is no other place for her. Even the Sisters wouldn't want her."

"She is 15… 16?"

"Yes, Monsieur Scherer, perhaps even younger."

The assistant draws back the blanket to unveil the smooth body in one more final look for eyes that need the reassurance of the power they have behind them.

"Just another wayward whore who has served her purpose," Scherer determines.

The assistant drops the blanket on the girl fully aware her bruised neck and breasts along with more blood stains are left uncovered. The two men turn to leave her alone with the breeze, the sunbeam and her fumbling death. The door is closed, then locked, as the pair hurry for the staircase, chased away by the perfume of the forgettable.

As the two reach the landing above, Scherer lays four gold coins in Mousseau's hand,

"This is to help fortify your defenses against memories."

"There is no need; it has been taken care of."

"Needs are forever present, whether they be yours, mine or others, Mousseau. Now take me to Mechant."

Again the procession continues with a destination defined. Up the stairs to the third floor where the adjoining hallway finds an area that is in constant natural light, natural plants and calming artistic fixtures that have bright colors aside softening tones. Calamity may be close by, but for a few short moments those of us in the audience are reminded that every nightmare has its waking point.

The beginnings of the Romantic Era stumbled on a walk that was not designed for leisurely amble. Political and Religious power was well preserved by the wealthy who felt the high-wire act of the status quo kept balance in constant teeter. The privileged had all at their disposal, no matter what the substance was, be it flesh or thin air. Everything could be persuaded to serve a certain function. Naiveté is a welcoming whore and the starving recall their last meal and the cook, but not the dish it was served upon.

Among the privileged atrocities were indiscretions, but no matter the size, each could be trivialized. All was forgotten, be it blood letting, betrayal, or convenient absences. There was a large vacuum between the masses and the ruling class. Although the vacuum was populated with refined merchants, their immediate under-class, workers and other subordinates, for the most part there were peasants, whores, villains and vagabonds. Few could reach the class of being considered truly underprivileged.

Finally, Mousseau and Scherer stop at a door that is suddenly flung open by a woman who runs out.

"We've arrived."

"Yes, Monsieur."

Scherer walks into the room to see a man crawling on the floor, vomiting violently while a lady of obvious station crawls next to him, sobbing while clutching the man tenderly.

"My voice, my dear voice, you must stop this self-defecation. You tear your fabric to shreds while you leave my soul stained and shallow. There will never be a point to this constant loathing of your life."

Just as the woman that flung the door open reappears with water, cloths and a young nurse, Scherer in a much more tender voice…

"Dear Angelique, get up from the floor, let them attend to your husband."

He then bends over to pick up Angelique as the woman helps her also while tending to the vomit that has been cast upon her purple velvet dress and the nurse retains her duty next to the crawling wretch.

"Carl…," is her only response as she falls into his arms succumbed by her obvious dysphoria and heavy tears. The woman scents her employer with a small vial of perfume after removing the spew from the garment.

She is steered out of the room by Scherer to an awaiting davenport, leaving the two behind as they are joined by a male attendant and Mousseau. They sit close to each other as she begins to adjust herself. Almost instantly her feminine grace is restored fully as she looks passively at her companion who, in turn, has an empathetic look in response.

Quickly we are reminded that compassion remains intact. The grip of this opening lays back and the tension eases. On the outer-side of these walls the gold leaflets fall upon the ground as normality reassures us that it remains close by. All that is meant to be glides inside its purposes as we go unattended into our own capacities of comprehension. We are comfortable enough to remember the dish this particular meal will be served upon, and we acknowledge the fact that these morsels we are being fed are meant only to tease our palates.

We notice that time has shifted to a slower pace. This shift treats us to the features that are Angelique's. Her auburn hair is long and flows well past her narrow shoulders. She has light green eyes that soften you instantly. There are thin lines close to those sparkling eyes and her pale skin acts as a gentle receptacle to her full lips of the reddest rose. She is an incredible beauty. Her slim frame accents every well formed curve, and her fawn like movements serenade the moment.

There are stunning instances that compel us to still ourselves to notice them completely. We fall into their arms and are held there close to their existence. We are entranced by these glorious possibilities in our lives even though they remind us that these particular heavens are for us to notice but never to have dominion over. The foolish ones among us desire to squeeze these moments in order to extend their time and intimacy with them. But in doing so they will soon realize all they are capable of doing is to attempt to harness them while destroying their spirit.

One must stop themselves from turning their curiosity into the stare of discomfort. But we in the audience are perfectly located in order to stare in the delight of this experience to the point where we change our curiosity to gluttonous morbidity. We can do what we want, for we are just the observers, although we are beginning to understand we may be affected by this compelling opera. But the effects are why we attend such events. These effects garnish the boring aspects of our lives with tasty samples of distant delights and rude surprises.

The grip begins to tighten as we are made aware of the fact that our pause to reflect was designed to remind us that our control over our faculties has been entrusted to what continues to unfold upon the stage.

Again we turn our full attention to the lights at the front of the theater. Perhaps, we'll have time to readjust ourselves later.

Carl was a large man with blonde curly hair, blue eyes and a rugged yet distinguished appearance. He was born in Germany and his manner was due to the influence of the fatherland and his family's ties to the Austrian Hungarian Empire, the Hapsburgs. He was always equipped with fresh handkerchiefs, which he had a habit of constantly holding in his left hand, while it found itself touching his mouth and nose consistently.

"Oh, Carl, what happened last night? I thought the two of you were to be together," Angelique asked as she continued to use one of Carl's handkerchiefs.

"It began that way, but Gabriel started to over drink again. I tried to help him curtail his intake and as usual he was not open to any kind of reasonable suggestion," Carl offered.

"Were you with him for the entire night?"

"No. He disappeared shortly after the performance. I made the familiar rounds but he had not shown himself to anyone of our mutual acquaintance."

"The truth, Carl, do you know if there was another woman involved? I am certain he was whoring again."

"Angelique, no one has made me aware of what he did after he left me," Carl sincerely responded. However a slight look of disbelief was drawn upon Angelique's face.

She moved herself from Carl in order to gain space to complete her attempt at composure. The two sat quietly next to each other without a word for a while. There was a noticeable tension with them that neither seemed willing to sweep away. Carl excused himself and left her on the davenport alone.

She leaned back with a comfort that was not there before he left. She dropped her hands on her lap as a reflective tone replaced the stress on her face. Her eyes took her beyond the windows and into the branches where the song birds were performing soft renditions of favorite familiarities.

Winged folk songs that she remembered from the long hours she would spend in the gardens of her parents' summer home in Provence. She'd watch herself soaring on the back of a butterfly as it galloped in-between the flowers and their incredible colors. She enjoyed her childhood serenity within her imagination while atop the most brilliant butterfly of all.

There were other times by the lake when her stallion was a dragonfly of the most peaceful blue. It had a power over the water that could still it, so the lily pads could bask themselves in the afternoon sun without the threat of being cruelly splashed. Other moments had her on the still ground, sitting in the tall grass, hidden by her fantasies and her shyness.

"Excuse me," were the words used to bring her back to the davenport, "Madame Beauvie, may I have a few moments with you?" Mousseau requested.

"Most certainly, Dr. Mousseau."

The assistant sat down on a chair close to her and began. "Your husband will be fine, Madame. Again he is the victim of over indulgence. He may have also eaten an off piece of meat or such. He is through emptying himself and we have successfully transferred him off the floor and into the bed. When he stills completely he will sleep and that will terminate the majority of the physical crapulence.

"I must warn you however, he is becoming a more frequent visitor of our hospital. I am sure you are aware that, at this pace, soon his visits will have to be prolonged in order to help him save himself from tripping on his favorite sin, promiscuity, and never be able to be righted again.

"He is killing himself in the ugliest fashion possible. I can tell you, I have never found the answer to how a man of such internal beauty can have such a dark disposition? Without that knowledge, I think all we can ever do for you is clean him. We will never bestow on him the gift of sobriety."

"I understand, Doctor," Angelique agreeably said.

Mousseau then stood up and walked away leaving her alone again surrounded by her dilemma. She had watched her husband deteriorate for years and always understood that the eventual circumstances would arrive one day. It was a common practice among the entitled; all was simple in the hours of their lives. The only difficulty was how one could stay occupied. Boredom is the burden of the idle mind, and Gabriel Mechant found it a constant pressure to attempt to outrun boredom's charges.

She pulled him out of the fires in his mind over and over. She had lied to protect him from his self-hate, constantly reassuring him of his considerable abilities. But, he never believed he was an artistic genius even though it was those exact words that were forever being used throughout Europe. For over twenty years his literary masterpieces were enjoyed by the functional literates, thought of as required readings of the gentry, the scholarly as well as the common others that blessed on him enormous popularity as well as wealth on top of his family fortune.

Of course there were the critics, but Gabriel once wrote in reference to them, "Commoners confuse the profound with profanity." A remark so skillfully timed that he was bestowed the power of carte blanche and even thought of as the possessor of a personal saving trait, delightful boyish foolishry that was merely a characteristic source of balance for his incredible artistic mind's intensity. He had developed a soul that could never be forever stained.

Angelique, on the other side of his public mystique, knew the private man that no one else could imagine. But his frailties had been on display for years in the taverns, brothels, and drug dens that festered deep in the intestines of every major city of Europe no matter how glorious its outward appearance. His seduction of the noble women in these centers was not as known because secrets are better hidden when more than a few ropes of elegance would fall for public viewing.

His wife tolerated all. She had a compassion for Gabriel that could only be understood as devotion for his capability to enhance the lives of his readers. There could not be another reasonable conclusion one could come to. Because of her faith in the Catholic Church the thought of becoming a divorcé was not a spoken desire. Of course, she could leave him, but that had never happened before and she undoubtingly desired to remain his wife until death cut that blind bind.

"Madame Beauvie, the husband sleeps. He will rest away his evening's activities and his memories of his adventure," calmly worded the woman who was in Mechant's room helping earlier. She then sat next to Angelique while putting her palm on her lady's brow.

"Nana, you are a comfort," Angelique purred.

"Angel, you must rest yourself; there is nothing remaining to do here. He will take his time and you must now take time for yourself. Come let me take you to your abode."

At that moment Scherer reappears as the two women rise together.

"I'll be escorting the Madame to her residence, Herr Scherer; she needs to welcome her coming restful pleasure."

"I'll be back after noon tomorrow Carl, Nana is right. A rest from this annoyance will be welcome," Angelique says while walking with the aid of her childhood Governess towards the staircase that will lead the pair of them from this episode in their lives.

"Certainly Angelique, your attendant is the authority when your needs are in question," Scherer offers with a small tone of insincerity. "I will be here in the morning also."

The audience of this première looks steadily at the stage as Scherer goes into Mechant's room closing the door after him. The women have left and the opera falls on the strings of a lone violin as its master plays a melody of compliant resignation. A solo that speaks of the calm found in the turmoil when the clutched understand they must fully participate on the stage that presents the nouvelle, while we in the chairs of observation are left with our anticipations.

Every one of us sees this spectacle of human intrigue and interference in a manner that is filtered by our experiences in order to be receptive to the narration. We may have judged too soon or interrupted falsely, but that is how an audience participates in this kind of opera as it is in progress. That is our role as the ones the whole production was meant to entertain. We are the ultimate judges and we must realize these are only the beginning scenes of this extravaganza. With that in mind it may be too soon to determine where we will be led or where we will be left.

Through the night, Gabriel slept still enough not to force the attention of the attendants. They used the time to add their views to the gossip and speculation as to what dropped Mechant into their lives once more. Did he try to out-drink the military again, or could the size of his penis not equal the tasks he had given it.

After all, wine has more control on a man's erection than most women ever could. Continuous glasses of wine can easily outpace the continuous beds of a brothel. But control of the bottle means the right man will remain steadfast in his appointed tasks. Gabriel was believed to be that type of man. However, it was also known that the genie in the bottle was becoming more alluring to him than the high quality of his woman or the quantity of the rest.

More would come in the morning when he awoke to his entourage of believers, disciples and charmed delegates. The morning could give answers to us in the audience, or would all of us mentioned be treated to more hollow speculation due to the fact we have been placed in this theater by our fixation on moments such as this.

"Why do I awake alone in this bed? I must certainly have been used or I failed to please."

Gabriel mutters into his empty room as the light of the morning encourage the hands of his unconsciousness to pass the chain to the hands of his waiting stupor. Looking around the room as he moves himself to a sitting position at the edge of the bed, he begins to realize.

"The events of the last performance have brought me to the home of the Director once again; I'm in Charenton."

His matted black hair and his hands congregate on his face as he points it towards the floor in obvious disappointment that his drunkenness has put him behind the same walls that restrain the insane. He begins to smell himself and the disgust he feels passes the chain to the hands of guilt.

"They will inform me of my crimes soon. That is how this particular song is sung," he strangely reminisces.

He finds the chamber pot and quickly relieves the strain as he carries it in front of himself. He places it on the side table where another counter sits with water. Taking the container towards a table by the wall, he drinks from it. He then pours the water into a washing bowel and in turn splashes water on his face and neck in front of a mirror.

He is a man of dark features, with a pleasant poetic voice. His eyes are dark brown and his leanness allows his masculine frame to accentuate his muscle structure. He completely understands God has given him the appearance of the high priest of the aphrodisiac. This and his playful nature have cursed him with a love for the pleasures found in pleasant recreation and the aperitifs that lubricate the hold on inhibitions.

He is well schooled in the practice of charming conversation and quick repartee. His mind also houses a large library of interesting tales, dark secrets and other spellbinding material. He recites his poetry and performs his stories in a way that is not only entertaining but also artistically stunning.

He has accomplished the idealisms of the true courtier. He plays the violin, sings, and dances. He is a champion at the foils, so well respected that his reputation has never been offered a chance to prove itself in a duel. And as a horseman there are few that can parallel his talents. But his literary works are considered masterpieces. He is the mold of the Renaissance man.

Clothed in a provided linen robe he goes to the door and opens it to face the outcome. There is only one nurse sitting in a chair close by reading from the Holy Bible, she is young and that assures him that she hasn't learned how to perform the duties of the executioner yet.

"Sister," he asks, "Could I, please, have some bread and cheese?"

"You will need more than that, but for now food is all I can do for you," she says in a convicting tone. "Go back into your room and I will be back soon."

He closes the door after her command and begins to quietly laugh.

"It seems that the Church is now teaching disgust to their nuns before they even finish cutting their teeth. That little one needs a nip in retaliation before she loses all of her sense of feeling," he confides to himself.

"C'est la vie, that bite would be better administrated by someone in a more comfortable position than I find myself in, no matter how much I would enjoy the taste," he smiles.

The morning went by slowly as Gabriel took his punishments from the Sisters, and his warnings from Mousseau and shared his amusings with the attendants, who were laymen that bestowed on themselves the humor found outside the covers of the Sisters' favorite book. This was a trait that Gabriel had, although in him it seemed to have slaughtered every form of seriousness; at least that was how he portrayed himself.

He became agitated at certain times, but Charenton troubled him like nothing else. The reason for that was simple, he believed the rhetoric that if he carried on with his destructive pattern, this was the place he'd spend the rest of his life in. Of course that would mean he had successfully navigated himself through the gauntlet of assassination or the various execution techniques, including the ones that the public would most definitely attend because of their morbid curiosity: the gallows and the guillotine.

Just at the point of noon, Scherer came to visit and the two remained in Gabriel's room alone for over an hour. At 1:15PM Angelique and her governess appeared and just before they entered the room Angelique requested, "Marta, wait for me out here."

"The wife must remain controlled, dear."

"I will. Nana, wait for me."

Marta sat in a chair facing the door as she watched her Mistress walk into the room alone. Marta was a stout woman of some age, perhaps 55 or 65, although that detail was not as important as the plain fact that she was always close to Angelique, much like a net that caught the acrobat who only fell privately.

Marta produced her waiting companion, her crocheting. Her full face carried frail glasses, and the bun in her hair was perfectly woven with an expertise gained from many years of practice. Her close to forty year deployment as the caregiver and nurturer to her responsibility had deprived her of many personal satisfactions. She was given the appropriate first name, as duty to this graying woman was her self-assurance that she would be given the pleasures of paradise to entertain herself with for eternity.

Angelique closes the doors behind her as she softly asks, "Well, gentlemen, are we discussing excuses, alibis or escapes?"

"Your wife, Mechant, proves my point that directness is the quickest way to the center of any matter," Scherer casually says with his familiar smirk, from his leaning position in the corner.

"No Carl, she is displaying her gift of clairvoyance," Gabriel answers as he looks out the window.

"Are you sure, my voice? All I may be displaying is my boredom of your repetitive childishness," as she kisses Gabriel's face, while he mildly laughs.

She then walks to the opposite corner to sit in the awaiting chair.

"Well my knights, what brilliance has your discussion brought you?"

The two men look at one another, then, Gabriel turns back to the simplicity on the other side of the window.

"Gentlemen, you either have the scheme or the control, which is it?"

Both men begin to laugh.

"Messieurs," Angelique smiles, "you have both."

"No dear, we have only one, because both have always been the same," Scherer confesses, while holding his familiar handkerchief

"I will dress and then we will stroll away from this rut in the walkway."

"Tell her Mechant," requests Scherer.

"Carl feels a trip to London would be the best thing for us at this particular time," Gabriel says as he turns away from the window to return to the bed.

"He would be able to rest while leaving Paris to herself; she could use the rest too," Scherer jokes.

"Certainly, rest, but London? It is dismally damp at this time of the year," Angelique said distastefully.

"That may be true, lipchun, but the two of you would stay with me and perhaps our discussions there would prove to be very interesting to our mutual artistic enhancements, Monsieur Mechant," saying as he smiles at Gabriel.

"What kind of discussions?" asks Angelique.

While sitting on the edge of the bed, Gabriel answers her in a strangely unexcited way.

"A discussion on the topic of collaborating for the purpose of an opera."

"An opera!" Angelique screams while jumping to her feet with joy upon her face, "Gabriel, my voice, that would be the pinnacle of your pen. Certainly it would. You must agree to this enlightening opportunity. You must!"

"Mechant, it would be the best thing for the two of us, and the timing would be perfect."

"Carl is right, Gabriel, not only is he a wonderful composer but he is also a champion at commerce. This work would be extremely popular as well as lucrative. Gabriel, it must be written in Italian."

"Italian!" Scherer agrees.

"Italian, it will be," grins Gabriel.

Upon the stage in this theater, our opera has begun in a place where confusion is in the core of its victims' minds as well as in the core of the supposed rationality that terms itself as the outer crust. We sit here and watch, while we ourselves have been served questions that don't appear to be connected to enough details, although we are surrounded by them.

We've heard the black overture; Prelude of the Forth Coming, and within its context, the Prelude's black ballet; Insanity's Dance. However there are those amongst us that are uncertain of where the first opera may lead, and now a second opera will become the first's focal point. We have been put in a more difficult position.

It has become apparent to us that we may be becoming confused ourselves, much like those that dance behind the cages or those that die alone under their feet. And the music of this first scene has been heavily layered with a shadowed texture that never hides itself; even though it's behind doorways, under tables, or walking behind us, we are forever aware of its presence.

Perhaps, Gabriel is the only one who understands the simplicity the outside world offers. He may have lost himself beyond the boulevard of Carl's grand entrance. He may have been captivated by the golden leaves and their desires to find the handles to the skies. Gabriel is the reason for this whole arrival. He is the core in our confusion, and all that held his attention comes from outside this crust.

We will continue with our vigil for the only rational reason that is available to us, our entertainment. All that lies before us may contain splendors, emotions, carnage, and privileges. Retaining our seats in this theater with all the rest allows us to share in our mutual upheavals, enlightenments and the possible beheadings of some of our personal shallow characteristics.

Angelique summons Marta to bring in a case containing garments for Gabriel while they all leave him to dress himself. Outside the room they are joined by Dr. Mousseau.

"We are taking my husband home, Doctor."

"Certainly, Madame Beauvie," the Doctor nods.

"Could you excuse us Madame, I wish to talk to the Doctor alone," Scherer requests as he holds Mousseau's arm and leads him away.

"Of course, Herr Scherer, of course," Angelique replies.

The two men walk to an empty space down the hallway and engage in a conversation that seems to be one-sided. Scherer is doing the talking, and Mousseau, the nodding.

Angelique watches nonchalantly as Marta walks past a better groomed Gabriel after he opens the door and begins to leave his room behind him. Marta goes inside to retrieve the soiled clothes and the case.

"Angel, escort your husband out of this depression," Mechant says.

"With pleasure Gaby," Angelique agrees while holding his arm in support.

They walk toward the Doctor and Scherer, as Scherer smiles. They walk past the gentlemen who join in the procession behind the leading couple and in the rear the doting Marta aided by a nurse follows.

The group strolls past the cages, the rooms and their occupants like the incoherent do in hell, completely unaware of the cored out minds and the nests of insanities left in their place. Past all of the doors, stains and lighting bolts upon the walls, out the front doors to the stairways that lead either to the right or the left.

At the top of the stairs Mousseau is left behind after brief pleasantries, and his face instantly releases from the tension that molded it with hardness. He watches the procession choose the stairs to the right as it descends to the lighted area before the canopy of the tree-lined boulevard.

They walk right down the middle as their parade parts any oncoming footed traffic. The boots have begun the baritones as the rest of the Chorus joins in with the baton's stride. This time Angelique's foot steps begin to soar with a graceful melody by the lead Mezzo while Gabriel's add that dark feel of the competing deep bass.

They continue their advance through a flock of doves and pigeons that scatter to the branches above or to the opposite sides as the lifted golden leaflets glow in the sunlight that has begun to shine brighter through the thinning ceiling. The birds' involvement to this six part harmony uplifts the performance on stage to a feel of the triumphs and their jubilance over the frailties of the human species. The power of this group is inspirational as their faces hold no compliance to the recent past's events.

There are carriages awaiting them on the Rue du Marechal Leclerc, just past the canopy. As they enter, the birds, the leaflets and the others in the Chorus converge to the walk before them in a congregation of the supporting cast as it sends off the concurring cluster. The scene ends as the carriages sweep away their cargo of the artists of aristocracy. The coaches leave the scene as the curtain is lowered.

We in the audience seem satisfied, but defiantly prepared for the next installment. Few whisper about the wardrobes while others calmly listen to the orchestra faintly playing in the pit. Overheard is the deep effect that the first scene had on the compassionate while laughter can be heard in a box above.

The theater feels vibrant, it has come alive. There is that question that circulates from seat to seat; how would you be affected if you were put in the same situations the stage so vividly frames? The crowd uproars as a dove escapes from behind the curtain. It flies above us before settling among the lights above, that have apparently been transformed into stars. There is a gasp in the theater as a harp begins to play. All of us settle to listen as we are being entertained so superbly.

THE CRIMSON BANQUET

It falls upon the memory to bring the past to court. The little insensitivities; the words that were not uttered and the path one took from the situation. We hold our memories at bay by building barriers supported internally by a weakness of conviction. Heard appeals by solicitors who hide the conscious in order to secure the verdict of not guilty by reason of denial, leave the court room of internal justice full of mirrors incapable of reflection.

The cloud that the party resides in becomes far more important than the realities that are hidden by its shadow. Duty to self far outweighs personal involvement to the society one has been born into, unless of course, the society one has been born into is the prestigious and the preferred. This is arbitrary, however, and arbitration, while denying the facts, is the polished teeth on the face of pretension. The faked gleam of false character is the twinkle that opens the legs of the easily satisfied.

Memories must be confronted by the older judge that a well lived life instructs the intelligent to become. Memories must be treated in the way they are meant to be; with a respect for the innocence, the naivety and faults they were the products of, as well as the success of intuitiveness, awareness and sensitivity the others were the products of. Fault is a shared commodity as necessary as the air we breathe, it is hardly the result of a single involvement but if it is, life will balance the scales inevitably.

This is not a call to righteousness, it is a thought of what this witnessed opera might be. It holds potential in its weave of the finest threads that begin to construct a portrayal full of flavors. The audience is uncertain at times of our combined involvement. Are we behind the curtain or is the opera? Some have thought there really is no curtain, all it is, is a wink of the eyes, that tiny pause before the next expression. Then, there are those that remain neutral, but either way there is no seat in the theater vacant.

A soft violin begins to play a beautiful theme. Its solo hangs suspended high in the rafters moving gently in the lights as they begin to dim. The curtain is raised slowly and behind, a misty drizzle is falling on a pre-winter garden, where in the center, an enchanting pastel colored gazebo is placed that is almost fully surrounded by a coffered low hedge and rose bushes. There is a willow tree above it with naked branches that expose three empty nests. Inside this enchantment, Gabriel is playing the violin while appearing to be in a dream like trance.

From behind a larger hedge at the rear, a young lady walks and then sits on a bench under a large evergreen tree that shelters her from the droplets. She stares at the gazebo's occupant in a look of wonderment. His violin becomes more enticing as it is skillfully caressed in the hands of its lover. Gabriel with his eyes closed turns in her direction while stepping closer to the railing before her, he stops while opening his eyes as a delightful grin is presented to her in the fulfillment of her childhood dreams. All that is missing is his crown and black stallion but in her eyes his long black hair is his crown and his violin is his chariot drawn by four of the finest.

He plays the last few notes and dramatically lowers the bow and his violin to his sides while smiling intently at the red haired fair complexioned delight before him. She smiles also, before softly asking,

"Are you Gabriel Mechant?"

"My lady, who else were you expecting?" he answers.

"You are him, are you not?"

"If that is your desire then I shall not disappoint you. I am the one you came here to discover," he says charmingly while grinning that precise smile of welcome.

"Sir, it is by chance that the two of us have met. My intention was a walk in the gardens under my parasol. Your violin was overheard; it drew the path to you, not I."

"Convenient, is it not?" Gabriel inquires.

"Perhaps, Monsieur Mechant, in truthfulness my readings have been heavily supplied by your pen. I find them... how can it be put..."

"Enticing, is that an appropriate word?" Gabriel offers.

"Yes, monsieur, that particular one would explain it," she says with the slight glow of embarrassment. "Though I am sure your works have been described in countless ways," she starts while lifting herself off the bench to begin walking the circled perimeter of the gazebo. "You must be a man who tires of the continuous accolades and I am sure a conversation that does not include sentences of description as to your noticeable brilliance is a rarity to you."

"My dear, this does not sound like the dialogue of the chance meeting, either you are a master of wit and conversation or you have been well rehearsed. Tell me parasol, which is it? And, please, do not stop there; include your name and how you got into Herr Scherer's garden," Gabriel orders.

Startled by his words, she stops at the stairs and answers, "Please forgive me if I have offended you. My name is Camille and I am a neighbor to Herr Scherer. My family resides on the other end of these gardens in the house on the far hill. These gardens have a slight barrier close to the pond but I and my brother have always been welcomed on this side. In fact my brother and I are students of Herr Scherer's. Again I am sorry for the interruption and I give my word not to intrude on you any longer."

She turns to leave just as Gabriel begins to recite one of his most beloved poetic journeys, which she quickly recites with him after turning back and moving closer.

Please accept my look upon thee

My sighs for thee, and the words I plead,

Please accept my beating chest,

My heart's request and the love it sheds

Please offer the moistened tips

Of your sweetened lips, and their fragrant teases,

Please caress my gentle face

With your warm embrace and the ways it pleases.

They kiss passionately until the young lady pulls away, leaving Gabriel to watch her until she disappears behind the large hedge at the rear. He calls out to her, "Tomorrow, again at this gazebo at this time. Our second chance meeting. Oh, the ways it pleases." He begins to laugh quietly while saying to himself, "There will be delicate venison served for tea tomorrow."

That evening after supper, Carl, Angelique and Gabriel are enjoying a game of cards when Gabriel gets up to refill his glass with wine and then begins to enquire, "Carl, how long have you owned this house?"

"For close to twelve years," Scherer answers.

"But you have been in London much longer than that. At least fifteen years," Gabriel continues.

Scherer simply nods.

"Sit down Gaby, and play your hand," Angelique insists.

"Mechant, your jewel is certain her luck is changing. I think she has the diamond queen."

As he sits down at the table, he says, "How ironic, the diamond queen changes my Angel into a demon empress. Angelique is easily corrupted by power, Carl."

"Power simply outbids inhibitions. Gentlemen, Rummy! Add them up carefully, the demon empress is overseeing," laughs Angelique.

"I knew you had her," Scherer says disgustedly, while holding up the queen of diamonds.

Later in the evening the two men are in the parlor alone drinking cognac and smoking thin cigars as Gabriel has found success in his investigations about the neighbors on the hill on the other side of the pond.

"So the father is a Bavarian Count," Gabriel says.

"Yes. He is a cousin of King Willy. His wife is from France, the two have a boy named Wilhelm and his younger sister is Camille. They are both enchanting," a drunken Scherer says. "I teach both, you know, but the boy is a favorite student of mine."

"What do you teach him, Carl?" asks Gabriel while wearing a smile.

"Music, of course. And, yes, the passion for it," Herr Scherer answers as both begin to smile.

Gabriel and Angelique had been in London for ten days by then, both fully recovered from their journey. They had left Paris a week after the events in the insane asylum and Carl had made them very comfortable. It was now mid November and the couple would be joining Angelique's family in Provence for Christmas. The subject matter and direction their collaboration would take had to be finalized quickly, although no formal discussions had taken place so far.

Angelique was enjoying London, its shops, its museums, its architecture, its culture. She also enjoyed Carl's' extensive library and his books about the Renaissance. She was fascinated by the personal struggles of the artists of the time; Michelangelo, Da Vinci, and others. She found the philosophical teachings of Machiavelli highly instructive.

She was a Catholic, but found the treatment of these masters by the Church belittling and hypocritical. How could the clergy use the most gifted of God's children in these ways? She soon would begin to have discussions on this topic with the Anglican priest from a Church nearby, as well as an art dealer who was a Jewish intellectual she met by chance. Her enquiries brought her more answers than she had originally sought, as well as more intriguing questions.

Respect for the arts and their creators, was not a forged issue. It depended entirely on the conversation the viewer was capable of having with the object of attention. The language the piece spoke could be of simple understanding or of a metaphoric dialect that was not interested in clear translation. The more obscure the work, the more artistic languages the viewer had to understand.

In the case of the Renaissance Masters, they came at a time when intellectual concepts cursed the darkness of ignorance. The subject matter of their convictions asked the impossible questions that could only be answered if individual enlightenment was possible. The dark ages owned its stunted compliance to the doctrine of the Church. A doctrine that secured itself on the belief that the only worthwhile entitlement one had to secure was their place in heaven.

But the Church knew how to manipulate, and the work of these masters had extraordinary powers to convince while also having a monetary value. This is why the massive wealth the Church already accumulated increased rapidly in the Age of the Renaissance. The refinement of manipulation, built on blatant extortion. Greed was the centerpiece of Catholic absorption at the time, and Angelique understood that entirely.

The patterns of thought could hardly be centralized in the performance before us. Plots were in every vista layered with defiance or complacency and the theme was incoherent because of the unison of all the voices. All seemed to move to a disjointed tempo that somehow believed that it was moving the beats forward non-randomly.

This opera had a demanding style that moved one in a welcoming way, although, it was clear it hid a stiletto somewhere on its person. There were surely a few that already felt the edge of the blade, but was that from anticipation, artistic activism, carelessness, or a deep desire to be among those who would be sacrificed? No matter how it could be defined, it fit well with the purpose of the unfolding. Though one must not forget, the shroud that had been covering the forth coming would have to fall somewhere.

The following day the gazebo was well used by Gabriel and his newest believer. Camille recited her most favored lines from his extensive writings, while he poured his flamboyance, culture and charm. He had seduced her entirely although only a few well timed physical encounters occurred. He was subtle in his advances, be them soft glances, light kisses on the cheek or tender caresses on her neck and arms.

At the ending moments of this, their second encounter, she danced with him while they hummed a well known French tune. He predictably stopped in mid step and kissed her passionately, the manner of which was again the fulfillment of her fifteen year old desires. She did not break away; she stayed locked to his lips. The dress she wore would have fallen at that moment if that were his intention; instead he simply stopped perfectly and whispered to her, dramatically,

"Dear Camille, everything has been so rapid. You and I must secure a future together, and that can only be accomplished by harnessing our desires. Our relationship must be drawn through the skies by the pair of us in perfect balance. And that will take time. You must leave me now before we spoil this moment and our future romance."

They were the perfect words for her young heart and untested body to hear. She kissed him again, and left with a desiring glance as he called out,

"Tomorrow, at this gazebo, at this time, our third chance meeting. Oh, the ways it pleases."

After she left, Gabriel secured a mount and rode toward central London. After all, he had a pressing need that he did not please with the young neighbor. Only more mature companions would be capable of the service required. Gabriel knew that Camille was a fine gem that would be happily worn for some time to come. The precise attention must be spent on this jewel in order to find the proper setting on which it would be delicately mounted. Once that happened, it would gladly stay in place.

Once Gabriel reached his destination, he dismounted, and with a smile, he entered a tavern. As soon as he was fully exposed inside, a shout was heard,

"Mechant, you bastard, you dare enter my establishment of ill breeding and fornication," laughed a very drunk Scherer, "You have decided that your need for recuperation has passed?"

"It has passed and decayed, you sodomite," Gabriel replied quietly.

"Your shyness is lost in this cave, my dear Mechant," Scherer answers, and then with a thunderous tone to his less than distinguished words he boasts, "We are all sodomites here, with only the refined being particular! Like you Gabriel, like you. You are refined Mechant, are you not?", while he draws Gabriel closer by using his big arm wrapped around his playmate's neck.

"That, Carl, only a true voyeur like you would know," Gabriel Mechant answers as the two men laugh and begin to drink together.

The two delighted themselves to the new hours of the following day. Finally riding their horses through the cobble-stoned streets, creating echoes at the expense of the horses' trembling foot locks and their own laughter. They yelled back at the windows that their nuisance brought life with the purest forms of profanity and unfiltered flagrant filth. The two beat the sun to Herr Scherer's household and were decent enough not to awaken the entirety before they fell on their beds in deep concussion.

It was not unlike any other age, it had its form of practical behavior and decency with its reliance on a code of what was considered the product of well breeding. At the proper moments this code of conduct was required, it was restrictive in order to hide the facts and bury imperfection. The male characters of the opera we are witnessing were the refined results of vast wealth; therefore, their breeding was without question. They knew how to act or react, dependent on the situation.

They were men in their mid-forties who had experienced life from the highest levels of personal success, family privilege, political, financial and military alliances, as well as the other connections in the webs of the powerful. They were escorted at times by the soldiers of law enforcement in order to secure their good names and safety, while those left behind were gathered together to answer for the deeds that the protected had committed.

The two were companions from occasion to occasion, but they both resided on separate webs for the most part. The prey is always plentiful and the gardens are vast, there are many locations to cast a web. The seas are full of badly schooled fish and in their numbers there are always the fools, the naive and the ill positioned; this is a fact drilled into the children of the predatory class. This is a reality that is mistakenly unknown or disbelieved or denied by the tasty.

There were always those that could be served in a manner that would quench the occasion be it a sober one or one that was the result of a binge of wickedness. Scherer's London home gave easy access to both types of cuisine. Gabriel was well versed in the position of life Camille had entered. He knew she unknowingly was preparing herself in the best way to garnish and enhance the freshness of his coming meal.

Camille's chambers were her refuge from the inquiring glances, the ill timed questions, and the awkward silences that were the result of her mother's self-appointed position as sacred guard to her daughter's virtue. Inside her private cage her mind wandered through the imaginings that were helpfully supplied by writers such as Gabriel Mechant. Her mother was happy that Camille had acquired the skills of a confident member of the literate and their unmistakable talents of articulation in the practice of finery in pleasant conversation.

Her mother would never dream that among her dear child's books and essays, De Sade's works could also be found along with other writers in the unspeakable genre of the groin. Camille had been well entertained by childhood stories of fairies, magic lamps, gallant knights and heroes of every gender and description. However, the logical advance in the aging process means the material that is needed to continue the enlightenment would have to be of different sources, dependent on which part of the body was doing the awakening.

Camille was a young intellectual that found her studies of the Holy Bible a chore of futility, because of the way it was interpreted by her mother and the others in her Catholic circle for the most part. Each interpreted it in a manner that painted their deeds of fortunes and flounderings with the brushes usually supplied to the Saints themselves. In the secular writings she found an honesty in the way the characters were portrayed. She felt it was easier to identify herself alongside their deeds and misfortunes, simply for the rational reason they were not glorified, they were merely realistic.

Camille was considered of age, and she felt the feelings that were ignited by her preferred genre of reading material were normal. She welcomed them in a ritualistic manner that included the bolting of her door, the appropriate heated companion her fireplace, well placed candles along with other pleasantries she bestowed on herself during the many moments she spent inside the pages as well as the increasing time she was spending inside the covers of her bed stretched out searching for the areas on her body that were described in pleasurable detail by her choice in enhancements.

Of course the pleasures the imagination was handing her, came in vivid scenes of masculines accompanied by many different delightful and despicable circumstances. There were the gallant, the coarse, the sweet, the forceful, the quick, but her most desired was the skilled mature and well practiced lover. The graceful gentleman of fine features, of engaging eloquence, of champion charms, and of frequent prolonged favors. The lover who never overlooked a single detail when it came to the prize of satisfaction, be it found in a boudoir, in a carriage, on a picnic blanket, on a table or underneath it; or in and around a pastel colored gazebo.

Camille was aware that her mother was one of those that thought these feelings can be easily controlled by the gift of denial. She thought that when they stir, the devil was close by. Prayer will surprise these vile natures, for God gave us desires only for the purpose of multiplying. That is why she believed the young must be taught that it is the devil that seduces them, and he is a horned beast on hooves, he is not like God in his purity. The devil does not suggest that patience is truly a virtue; he believes that giving in to your desires is the appropriate deed. Why wait if the opportunity opens itself?

Camille was aware of the hypocrisy of the belief that women, however, may never attain the highest realm of virtue, for they are unlike Mary, who was the mother of God and kept her virginity intact after the birth of Jesus with aid from God, the Father. Nuns protect their purity, for they are virtuous in believing they are the Brides of Christ. Mortal women will always be tempted by the devil's bedchamber unless they pray for forgiveness for the thoughts that occur while contemplating losing their purity through the act of worldly fornication. The gravest sin mortal women commit is the fact they are not willing to wait for heaven, for heaven is the ultimate bedchamber in which to give the gift of their purity.

Camille felt this sounded very reminiscent to the act of sacrificing virgins; however, she was not aware that Gabriel was a true believer in this practice. He did not think of himself as the devil. He was a man of the world, a believer of the opened opportunity. Men like him are eventually subject to the laws of God. But a thought does need to be studied; when he is sentenced to hell, and he surely will be, will that be because he did not deny himself or will it be because he denied Jesus the gift of particular purities?

Camille knew the time may come when her parents would gladly give her chastity to the son of someone of proper position. She understood the world was the property of men and their boys, while her purity was the virgin that would be slaughtered in glory on her wedding night just like the other gifts that were laid on the beds of the sons of men and the son of God. But, why are Jesus and the other sons not held accountable for their lack of sexual purity?

At the hour of the third chance meeting, Camille was quite ready to surrender her purity, not as a gift to Gabriel but as a gift to herself. She felt her first would be better shared with an experienced man. That would be the best beginning to her sexual awakening; start the journey with someone who knows the territory, someone who would appreciate the moans and the sighs. She was well schooled by her choice of reading material. She expected all the pleasures her purity could buy. She indeed possessed a mature sense of commerce.

Before she walked from behind the hedge in the back, she made sure her shawl would not impede Gabriel's view. After she was sure she would appear obvious, she moved gracefully toward the gazebo, but it was empty. She felt that her chance for gratification was lost, but her disappointment was held back with the thought he may be late. She waited for as long as she could, but finally left with her desires placed in imaginary chastity belts, unable to understand why he did not come and rescue her by using his keys.

When she got back to her home, her mother informed her that there would be guests that evening. When Camille asked who would be arriving, her mother said, "Your musical instructor, Herr Scherer and his house guests Madam Beauvie and your favorite author, Monsieur Gabriel Mechant."

Camille squealed and ran up the stairs towards her room, while her mother yelled up the stairs after her, "Silly girl, careful or you will trip again. Dear God, when will you ever learn a lady must not appear to be in a hurry? Your girlish behavior... you must mature yourself. Control, Camille, control!" After she finished with her exercise, her mother turned and walked down the hall to make sure that the cook was preparing properly.

An interlude was begun by a pair of boy sopranos filling the air with an uplift of mood. A delightful harmony echoed through the theater defying the belief that there were only two. Soon, an oboe suspended a single note that the young voices danced around in a duet of joy that the sun had again awoken. After a glorious rein, it faded gently until a soft stillness was all that was left. We in the audience repositioned ourselves while others quietly spoke to their companions.

At that precise moment, upon the stage, a Chorus full of all the secondary characters exposed in the opera so far sang an orchestra accompanied aria of extraordinary beauty. It was devoted to its minor key that supplied the layer of melancholy so expertly. The haunting vision of the girl left to die in the cellar of the Parisian sanitarium was not easy to take for most in the theater, because she was hidden in the Chorus slightly by Dr. Mousseau. It was a well placed, though almost sadistic metaphor. The author was ordering us not to forget about her, but I wondered if anyone was really able to do so.

The Aria included a Dance of White. There were sixteen ballerinas in unison of flawless dimensions. Each wore satin white scarves of many sizes, dependent on the areas of the body they covered. The whole stage had a white glow to it only tarnished by the colors of cloths the separate characters in the Chorus were wearing. The feel was obviously a dance of purity in heaven while the rest of humanity looked on in envy.

Soon the ballerinas were joined by a male dancer dressed in scarves of crimson. After Crimson was entirely encircled by the entourage of white satin purities, one by one the separate purities entered the circle to dance with Crimson alone. After the dance was concluded, the purity just danced with, left the circle more exposed than she was before entering. Most of her scarves had fallen at the feet of the Crimson. The sacrifices of the sixteen were eventually completed, with the hardly covered ballerinas at the rim of the circle, while inside the Crimson was devouring the satin scarves of purity one by one.

While inside, the Crimson continued with his banquet, the ballerinas walked into the Chorus while the scarves they wore were turned into common garments that blended in with the supporting cast. The Crimson was left alone, but the scarves he gorged upon had turned into blood soaked skins of human flesh. The Chorus began to congregate at center stage, completely engulfing the Crimson. We in the audience were left to speculate who the Crimson was, although I am sure most of us felt it was the opera's interpretation of our mutual understanding of the starvation suffered by human desires.

Soon, the Chorus began to leave the stage, exposing the leading characters in a parlor obviously enjoying the delights of proper conversation and their accompanying activities. Scherer was at the piano with Camille and her brother Wilhelm close to him while leaning on the side of the instrument. Angelique was playing Noddy at the card table with Camille's parents, Countess Caroline and Viscount Frederick Gunner of Bavaria, while the fourth was a writer from The Times; his name was Jonathan Broadfoot.

Gabriel was playing chess with Countess Caroline's uncle Bishop Joel of Normandy. The two were enjoying their game and discussion about French politics. Camille and Wilhelm were singing delightful English, and of course French folk songs, while the maestro played an elegant accompaniment in the background when the Bishop asked his board mate,

"Monsieur Mechant, how could you be so devious?"

"Chess, as well as politics, soars in the skies of deception, Bishop Joel. Check," says Mechant, "As you can see, you can prolong this encounter by simply handing your Queen to me in sacrifice for her King's lack of perception."

"Who holds your King's eyes, Uncle Francois, is it someone in your order?" asks Frederick in a tone of stately jest while looking at his cards.

"Uncle Fran, disregard these tasteless taunts by these unmistakable bullies," Caroline laughs.

The Bishop, with the feeling there is hope without the Queen, forces her to take the lance of the black knight in the noble act of guardianship, giving her life in order to protect all that is left. Then, her assassin is killed instantly by a late arriving rook. After the bloodletting the Bishop starts to smile at Mechant with the coyness of a scholar.

"I did not... see... Bishop, you are the deceptive one. How ingenious. Angelique, I have just been served up as a plumb mutton to this Master of the board," Gabriel expresses, as Angelique smiles, "The movement of your rook exposed my king to your white bishop's check-mate. Bishop Joel, brilliantly played."

"Deception, Monsieur Mechant, is a skill all can acquire. It is like anything. All one must do is pay attention to the things that the majority ignore. God has gifted me the skills of observation, a handy little tool when it comes to chess," the Bishop confesses.

At that moment, Countess Caroline asks Gabriel to recite one of her favorite of all in the collection of Mechant's writings, a particular poetic, though tragic parable. Camille quickly agrees with the request, "Yes, Monsieur Mechant, please."

"You are more skilled as a writer than you appear to be as a chess combatant," the Viscount says with a sly taunting laugh.

"Frederick, I assure you, his abilities are considerably more than he displays with his pen; all of France is aware of his talents. Please, I too, would enjoy hearing your recitation, Monsieur Mechant," Bishop Joel compliments.

Gabriel stands in the middle of the room while Angelique sits back in her chair with a reflective look on her face as her eyes are slowly drawn to his. Camille finds a comfortable chair and gazes at him in adoration. The dinner party is still, and even the servants are silently listening from vantage points on the side walls while most of them are clustered by the doorways.

Gabriel begins to walk slowly as the wings on the words of his lament start to spread. The expressions upon his face become the images of the flock that begins to circle the stage as two young dancers make their entrance into the performance of the opera, taking position at center stage. The pair in dramatic fashion stand back to back.

Gabriel begins as the dancers start to move;

"While the snow is falling in early winter, two saddened lovers are on the same ledge, above a dangerous gorge, below an unsecured icy cliff. Both are immersed in the spray of a deafening waterfall, though on different sides of a blooming holly tree with thick underbrush, at the same defining moment. Both are deeply saddened by the outcome of a simple misunderstanding.

"Youth has betrayed them, by the use of the executioner's sword sharpened on the stone of inexperienced misunderstanding. Lack of knowledge will again have its meal, and enjoy it in the peace of the silence granted by the words unsaid, thus unheard.

"Their voices in parallel begin to sing,

I am smothered by my despair,

I have been shattered before.

Moments of darkened blindness,

I always found a door.

It seems that now the darkness

Has taken me to an open space.

All I do is wander

Without purpose, without grace.

Love has betrayed me.

I find myself mislaid,

There is no end to wander,

No place to be saved.

Left am I to chilling despair.

Cast upon coals of ice,

My heart freezes hard tonight,

Frost cuts the thinnest slice.

"On opposite sides of the bush, the two despairs believe the gorge will give them peace from lives that no longer promise hope. The pair both close in on the edge to eternity, as both cry out,

My love, where may you be, I am here a step from hell.

But that is a better fate than another breath alone.

If the winds can carry my plea, and if your ears are willing to listen, Come and save my eternal love for thee. Come save me.

"Both stand steadfast on the ledge while the tears of the waterfall blend with theirs until that moment comes. At the moment he casts himself into the flow vanishing quickly, she turns away from the ledge. She stops, because she is sure she can hear him call her name. She then runs down from the cliff believing he is waiting for her below, only to find she is still alone.

"The bush between them and its blood soaked berries obscured by the falling snow; the physical presence of the seconds they did not take to save her from a lifetime of regret and him from an eternity in hell. What was gained by not leaving their despair alone to consume itself while they found the bravery to let their hearts be heard?

"We see this tragic glance of two possible outcomes when the most passionate is not considered. Be not as foolish, allow yourselves the truth. With so many cliffs with scarring gorges and waterfalls to wipe the blood away from the jagged rocks, we must look around the bush of blood berries before we cast ourselves into the mist. Before we cast away our hopes."

Gabriel bows to the applause by all, those in the parlor, on the stage, as well as us in the audience. As the applause softens, Camille jumps to her feet and says, "Oh, the truth is the only useful way, Gabriel."

"Silly girl!" Her mother quickly says. "Her childish comment, though disrespectful can be dismissed I am sure, Monsieur Mechant, when I tell you I must agree with her. That sad air has always been amongst my favorites."

"Dear Lady, there is no need to feel that your charming daughter has offended me in any possible way. In fact I assure you, I acknowledge her choice to not make the same tragic mistake when the time comes for her opportunity to tell her future romantic passion the truth about her wishes. I am also at ease that her parents, family and home have been able to guide her morally when doing so," Gabriel says, in true decorum.

"Secular writings, I believe, can be the most convincing of temptations, Monsieur. When you write, are you conscious of tempting your readership?" asks the Bishop.

"Can I answer that question for you?" interrupts Jonathan Broadfoot. "Certainly," answers Gabriel.

"Bishop Joel, I think it is the duty of all writers to raise the questions while carefully not supplying all the answers. The purpose of the literary is to enter the conversation in order to find the consciences. Mechant's writings, along with the writings of the rest of us who fight with pen, are not to be only an observer's judgment, but most importantly another voice in the discussion, even if it was the literary that chose the topic from the outset.

"Now, you are a man of non-secular writings, however, not a single viewpoint should go unquestioned. It is possible inside consciences that a healthy wisdom survives between the opposing points of view, a newborn product of knowledge. Is that not what was alluded to by Monsieur Mechant's literary tale?"

"I believe that matter was alluded to, yes. I feel though, there are discussions that should not take place in public; this is one of those. Faith in The Holy Bible must be protected so the believers are not cast astray. This is the primary hope of the Church, to not allow the souls of the faithful to fall from the edges of heaven into the gorges of hell," Bishop Joel predictably answers.

While the fencing continues, Gabriel's smile for Camille does not go unnoticed by Scherer, Angelique, and dismissingly so by Wilhelm. Scherer starts to play the piano again softly, while Angelique stands up and goes toward Camille. Gabriel notices, while thinking he has been caught flirting once again.

"Camille, my dear, I understand that you as well as your brother are students of Herr Scherer. Tell me, what is his talent teaching you?" Angelique asks her, in a soft voice of surprisingly gentle tone.

As the women both find a davenport to continue their conversation on, Gabriel is given a whisky by a servant as he looks at the ladies casually. Soon he is caught by Scherer's stare as they both nod to one another. Scherer begins to laugh as he is engaged with Wilhelm's company. Gabriel wades in once more into the waves of the conflicting colloquy.

The night proceeds on the rails described, with all enjoying their opportunities as contributing combatants. Before the night's events are concluded, Gabriel and Camille are left on their own for a few moments by the harp in the corner.

"I found myself alone this afternoon, Monsieur Mechant. The gazebo was empty when I arrived."

"It will be occupied tomorrow, Mademoiselle. Will that be a welcome enchantment to include in your stroll through the gardens?"

"Yes, it will. Why were you absent today?"

"I knew I would be in your home this evening. I must confess to you, I felt too much of me may become tedious for you."

"I can tell you in all honesty, Gabriel, there is no threat of that developing."

"Yes, my feelings are the same about you, Camille."

The night concluded with the guests being thanked for their parts in the events of the evening's activities. All had enjoyed the occasion. The hosts were promised more visits, when the Viscount and his wife return from a few weeks in the Alps. They would be leaving the following afternoon, while their children were left in the care of the Bishop, their Grand-Uncle.

When Carl, Angelique and Gabriel returned to Scherer's house, Angelique excused herself and went to her room to prepare to sleep. Gabriel and his host shared a nightcap in the study, when Scherer enquired, "It did not take you long to notice Camille, Mechant, or did she notice you first?"

"Well, I am sure I was the first, unless of course she finds me just as beautiful as I find her."

"I found the whole evening blinding by the gleam of both of your youthful enchantments. Though, I must tell you that yours seems to be duller. Perhaps, that is because you try to shine through a thick layer of preservatives," Scherer jokes, as both laugh.

"Carl, you do shop at the same store of ointments and masks, do you not? In fact, I am very sure you were the one that told me about the establishment? And if it was not your suggestion, I have been unkind to you in not mentioning it sooner. After all, Herr Scherer, we both are aware of the fact it is the fair haired that age most quickly."

"That may be true, Mechant, but we fair haired are the first to be worn out by the many who find us the most attractive to begin with," Scherer laughs.

"That may be true, Carl, but that is not an intelligent race to put effort into winning. I prefer endurance competitions, there are far more rewards along the way than can be found in the sprints of the blonds," Gabriel observes.

After his drink, Gabriel excuses himself and walks up the stairs to the bed chambers. As he gets to Angelique's door, he knocks and then enters. He closes the door behind, then, he announces, "My dear, your husband has come to visit."

"I have a husband?" she responds from the bed. "Do you mean that old basket that has a fondness for collecting young blooms?"

"Is my weave that noticeable, Angel?"

"Only to the past blooms that you picked when their fragrance was at its freshest promise of youthful radiance."

"New blooms, Angel, are not as full of nectar as is the mature flower," he says as he pulls down the quilt covering his wife.

They spent the night together as they did on occasion. She was always welcoming and he was always the consummate lover, when the wine had not confiscated his stride. After a lengthy performance they slept and in the morning they lay in bed together while caressing each other in the way only well acquainted lovers can. They both had vast knowledge of the techniques, and an intimate understanding of how the other's body could be played with. They knew every point that would arouse, engulf and satisfy.

Their relationship consisted of her supporting the great artist while he leaned on her maturity when he misplaced his. He bedded her from time to time, most assuredly, and as described, it was mutually satisfying but his public affection for her could only be defined as casual at best. She was always by his side for performances or other such occasions as any good wife should.

Appearance was well manufactured however, in order to continue with the artist persona. No one could say for sure if the odd moments of public affection they had for one another were the result of a deep love or not. Polite society was not tolerant of flagrant displays of what was termed as private behavior or bedchamber antics, a social grace that could conveniently hide any warmth through emotional attachment.

The music in this compelling opera was of a high texture. We in the audience were moved by it considerably. I am certain that the feel we were beginning to appreciate was one of rising constantly. Was this sensation a climb to an explosive climax or to a plateau that stands in the center of surrounding horizons with breathless peaks high above the climactic reasons for their incredible summits? What possibilities lay beyond? What kind of vistas will occur as we continue with our climb?

The stage's scenery was full of colors with variations of blends and shades that assured the feel of spectacle. This opera of intriguing mystery coupled with a collection of characters and circumstances held the fixation over the audience as does the spell of a powerful wizard's incantation. Entertained is the audience when predictability vanishes. The future holds the promise of surprise when the destination is somewhere on a map that has never been drawn.

Time in London was beginning to run down, if Gabriel and Angelique still intended to be in Provence for the upcoming holidays. Gabriel and Camille met each other in the Gazebo on the third as well as a forth and the fifth occasion. Angelique continued with her enjoyments with the museums, galleries and enquiries, while Herr Scherer and his young apprentice Wilhelm were working on the collaborated opera's collection of possible themes and variations. Strangely, there had not been a single discussion of the topic of the opera or the possible libretto. The composer was beginning to become annoyed by Gabriel's avoidance of the subject.

One afternoon, Carl noticed Gabriel leaving for his afternoon walk in the gardens and decided to take the opportunity to bring the wordless opera to Gabriel's attention. It took some time for Scherer to find his prey, but when he did, he found the sought after prize buck following a fawn like doe who had her tail up in obvious invitation. Herr Scherer did not appear surprised. He held his ground and his tongue as he used his vantage point to view the mating ritual of the well antlered sire and the young hostess. There was no direct consummation, but that did not conceal the possibility the act had occurred earlier.

When the two specimens parted, the hunter waited for the appropriate amount of time to allow Gabriel to feel the coming meeting in the gardens was one of chance not one of monitoring. Gabriel noticed Carl by the first few steps on the approach to the back of Scherer's residence and called out to him.

"Herr Scherer, inspecting your steps or your ability to still scale them?"

"Mechant, what an eloquent query. I must admit, I too, have a query. Have you arrived on a topic for our venture and a description of it in, how should I say it, story form?" Scherer says in a cynical confronting manner.

"Are you referring to our opera, Carl?" Mechant answers with the same tone and intention. "We both know there is not enough time to finish an entire opera before Angelique and I must go back to France. I have been developing both the topic and its description. Though I am unsure of what to tell you, because my ideas are still unfolding at this moment, thus the value of these developments is not certain," Monsieur Mechant says with what Scherer feels is obvious avoidance.

"Mechant, I need something to score. It is impossible to put music to a topic that avoids everyone's comprehension. I am not a fool, and I do not tolerate the disrespect that comes from the act of dismissing my intelligence. You came here to rest and to begin with our collaboration. All I have noticed from you is your consistent need to indulge yourself with pleasure. How can you have possibly written anything when all you seem to do is pursue your delights and then recover from their destructive follies?"

"You have an annoying habit of rearing up on your hind legs, dear Carl, when things do not appear like you expect them to," Gabriel says with obvious anger.

"Your argument does not make sense, unless you have no topics or even ideas. Are you simply trying to avoid your work? This is the first time we have agreed to work together but not my first time at collaboration. Monsieur, you are not acting like an artist, you are acting like an actor and that is not an art. All that is, is an overblown pretence of something every mortal is capable of. I demand proof right now, right here, of your supposed attention to our venture. Can you provide any?"

"We will write the opera together Carl, but it will not happen here in England. It will be written in France in the New Year and that is the end of it. I, too, am not pleased by insults about my talents or my intelligence, Maestro. You need an instrument to prove the results of your ability and a piano is a hard thing to hide in your pocket." Gabriel exposes paper and a pencil from his pocket while continuing, "As you can see, I can bring my instrument with me everywhere I go. It makes creating a lot less demanding than it is with your art, artist." With that, Mechant sweeps by Scherer.

"I will not be going to anywhere without a topic, and more proof than your knowledge that paper is nothing without a tool to etch with!"

After the encounter both did not speak until later that evening when Carl heard a faint knock on his music room's door; when he opened it, Angelique and Gabriel were there. He invited them in and the three spent several hours in the room together, which ended with Gabriel asking Carl, "Then this arrangement will satisfy you?"

"Yes, of course it will, I do not care who I work with as long as there are words to this story. I think you are very peculiar Gabriel but I see the results. I apologize to you, but as I have confessed, I need to feel in control of my projects."

Angelique answers, "Gaby does too, Carl. So it is agreed I will work with you as Gabriel is left alone to do his writing. I have always been my husband's liaison for many different reasons. He is a master with the pen but a child at confrontation and its need for diplomacy. It would not go smoothly if he was left in a room alone with you when the two of you become aggravated."

"Then I will be in Provence in the New Year and we can start from there," Herr Scherer agrees, as he touches his mouth with his familiar handkerchief. "Gabriel, let me play for you a theme that I hope will become the main Aria."

As Scherer plays, Gabriel picks up one of the violins and in a short while he is playing along. Angelique sits back with a slight smile, happy she has brought the two together again.

"Carl, this melody is delightful," Gabriel comments. "Now that I know it, it will be simpler to work with. I will learn how to play the whole score, Carl."

"Yes," Carl says very satisfied, "Wilhelm, even at seventeen still possesses a voice reminiscent of his younger style when he was singing in the boys' choir. That will make it a joy for me when your words are synchronized with his grace. Yes, this collaboration could be a very fulfilling joy for all of us."

As Carl and Gabriel continue to play together the curtain begins to drop as the orchestra starts to mingle in with their duet. Scene Two is drawing to a close as we in the audience are left again with our perceptions of what the stage's threshold is supporting. We all understand that people in the creative fields and vineyards are run by their temperaments as are we all, but I for one, may find them enjoyable to know but childish in their reactions.

Is it reasonable to allow them their behavior for the sake of their promise of creative brilliance? Or should they be restricted like the rest of us in our lives of values, duties and practicalities? When I think about these questions, I must admit I seem to be sounding like I have become complacent to the fact that the events in my life do not parallel the spectacular. I wonder if the others in this theater are thinking about the same things.

I wish I could stop being comforted by the judgment that my playful behavior is childlike. I envy the honesty of children, their laughter to the point of straining themselves, their journeys into imagination and their art of loving just because. Perhaps, I am just confused about what allows a true artist the luxury of being childish. Could it be that the beauty of the world and beyond is not obscured to them? A disregard for formalities might be the single ingredient needed for their possible creative genius, after all, conformity confines.

PRINCESS OF UTOPIA

When twilight blinds the eyes, as the sun reverses its direction, the stars are behind a curtain that will not expose reflection. Far between the moment here and the moment there, many voices are silenced by the pattern that has lost its reputation. Character has changed its silhouettes and shadows have lost their leaders, as practical is spelled like practicing.

What was then has been humiliated by now, as now will be the failures of the future. To practice on reflections of a shadow behind a curtain, in between a blindness of a life lived like the ones that have been lived before; keep the curtain still, and what is shielded behind is nothing but numbing speculation on subjects, their suspicions and suspensions.

What will be, will not be in accordance to its parents or providers or practice. What will be, will be of a nuance in accordance to its undefined direction, all that is to be. Being is the only defining particle of a practical logic. Fools are consumed by their assumptions if they fail to realize that assumptions are what spawn the undercurrents in the river of time as it bends to life's gravity of the unquestionable fact that proves it, too, cannot be considered a reality.

When light is bent by a particle of logic, and peculiarities are the dark confessions of practicality, how can one feel firmness under their thoughts? They are moved to the description that has been altered by the performance of a soft glance or a hard stare. There is nothing that is coherent, even the hope of coherency has been sculpted by the chisel that cuts according to one's own longing. All is randomly moved between the various leaves of perception on an unfamiliar branch in the canopy above the stones of a walkway that leads someone somewhere.

All that has come proves nothing, although we are certain that it has begun. Where we are in our travel has been kindly hidden by our familiarity to our companions on the stage behind a curtain; that seems to be the cloth of a bag of building blocks that are supported by others that want to be the highest in the tower. As the curtain rises for Scene Three, the feeling in the audience is that of only one possibility, that what will continue to unfold will be built to crumble, or are we blinded again by assumption?

Scene Three begins with all the opera's characters exposed so far in the Chorus supported by the dancers and the orchestra again positioned in the pit. As we in the audience are again fitted with wings to help reestablish ourselves in the thin air of a canopy above a walkway to somewhere. We feel strange movements as the surrealism swirls through our minds in a typhoon that casts all in its path through the skies of the theater. The music intensifies as the Chorus competes with the orchestra for our undivided attention, but all we in the audience are capable of, is looking at the pieces of the puzzle.

The scene begins in the Viscount's home the evening after the ground rules for writing the Opera have been established. Wilhelm and Carl are walking into the parlor of the Viscount's home while Wilhelm is speaking.

"Maestro, this opera will bring you more into the focus of European artistic culture. I know it will supply you with the glory you deserve. I thank you for your belief in me and I promise to you I will prove your faith in me as your apprentice."

"Willy, you have always been an asset to me. Your understanding of counterpoint is spectacular. In your own compositions, your harmonies are delicately delightful. You have always been impressing."

"Thank you master," Willy smiles.

Carl sits down on the davenport as he pats the seat next to him. "You have always been an endearment Will, sit down next to me and let me see your blue eyes closely," Carl says in a strangely romantic style.

Wilhelm sits down as Carl smiles at the seventeen year old boy with reddish brown hair and delicate features. Quickly, Wilhelm moves closer to Carl allowing the two to embrace and begin kissing each other.

While they continue Wilhelm begins to loosen Carl's trousers making it easier to expose Carl. The boy's hand starts to grip with an attention to detail only possible if this sort of affection has happened many times before. Carl pushes Wilhelm's head down until it is very apparent that Carl is enjoying the effects of fellatio. The two continue in that position for some time until the voice of the Bishop interrupts them as Carl is in the beginnings of eruption.

"Herr Scherer! Wilhelm! This is abomination!"

The two stand quickly as Wilhelm wipes his mouth and Carl tightens his trousers.

"Uncle Joel, please, it is not…"

"Quiet, Wilhelm, there is no need to defend yourself, I realize you are the innocent in this matter. Herr Scherer, I must demand that you leave my niece's home and not return. Wilhelm, stay in this room, I will be back as soon as this offensive creature has been shown the way back to where he came from."

As the Bishop follows Scherer outside and into the gardens, Wilhelm begins to cry uncontrollably. He is terrified he will be subjected to a great deal of punishment and ridicule by what has been mistakenly shown to his Grand-Uncle, and he knows there is nothing that can stop the fall of his character in the eyes of his parents. This affair will not be thought of as just another in the long and established relationship he and his lover Carl Scherer have had. This affair will end it, possibly forever.

As the two outside continue their advance to the border in the gardens, Scherer asks the Bishop, who is having trouble to physically stand as high as his intentions, "What do you intend to do now that you have Wilhelm and I placed on the ledge to hell? Will you toss in two more victims? Or do you believe in mercy?"

"God will be your judge, but my intention is to make sure you no longer threaten souls with your defiance of God's will and your distaste for decent worldly normality. I hope the authorities will take my place behind you on the ledge to hell. Let the laws against such depravity push you in, my duty is to God first and to my family second."

"And, Wilhelm? What are your plans for him, old man?"

"Once his assailant has been disposed of, he in time can be taught how to not be so led astray. The Priesthood may give him the discipline that is needed to save his soul. Your soul, Herr Scherer is lost. Do not turn back and defile my family's properties any longer," Joel commands as Carl has passed the border and is now left alone at the rim of his property. The Bishop turns and walks back to his niece's home while breathing heavily. He has a chore that still needs doing. He must continue his punishment of Wilhelm for the sake of the boy's soul, no matter what joy the Bishop may receive as a result of his self-righteous behavior.

As Scherer walks toward his house he hears Gabriel's voice.

"By God, Carl, what has happened?"

"Joel found me alone with the boy."

"You were caught."

"Yes, he knows."

"You fool, in the boy's own home. It will have to be taken care of quickly. Perhaps, if I can reach Joel before he returns, there may be something that can be said or something that can be done. Were you seen by anyone?"

"No."

Gabriel starts to run toward the slow moving Bishop as Carl stands there thinking of the position he has found himself in. Homosexuals had to always be certain that they were not discovered, but this discovery was the prelude to the certainty of a death sentence. Wilhelm was a relative of King Charles, the present ruler of the British Empire. Herr Carl Scherer would be hanged without question.

On the other side of the garden as the Bishop begins to ascend the hill, he stops to catch his breath. He looks up towards the sky and notices the clouds have erased the stars. He begins again his walk to his niece's home. When he hears footsteps behind him, he turns and asks, "Who is there?" But there is no response; he turns to walk up the hill again when he hears steps and suddenly he sees a shadowed form before him.

"Who are you?" the now startled old man asks.

Quickly the shadowed form pushes Joel to the ground, and as soon as the Bishop rolls onto his back he feels the edge of a knife blade pressed against his neck, as he looks up at a scarf covered face. The shadowed form begins in a muffled voice; "You hold this knife to your neck. You hold it with zeal and comfort. You hold high your hypocrisy as you clean your hands in the tears of the souls you hold for ransom. You enslave Jesus, to serve your ideals, not his. But when you are questioned by the doubt that surrounds these ideals, you hide under God's robes and cry out; 'It is his will.' Get on your knees and out from under his robes, prepare to confront God. I am sure you hope that he has a bad memory, but I assure you, hell bound, he will remember everything."

The blade is then inserted quickly into the Bishop's throat and dragged to the other side of the neck. The assassin then removes the blade and wipes the blood off it, using the robe of the freshly slaughtered. The gold handled knife then disappears into the clothing of the shadowed form, while the form moves into the darkness, vanishing.

At that moment, Gabriel arrives and looks at the body of the Bishop. He bends down closer and sees the Bishop's throat cut from end to end. He stands up and looks around intently. After his inspection he again bends down and begins to wrap the body up in the Bishop's own robe, picks it up and walks away with it.

He gets to the lake and puts the body into the row boat that is tied to a willow tree. He then moves back into the darkness, soon returning with a small stone garden nymph. He puts the heavy stone into the boat, unties it, gets in himself and begins to row to the center. Once he is there he unties the rope from the end of the boat and uses the rope to tie around the neck of the nymph and the other end around the waist of the body. He then puts both close to the edge of the boat.

The boat is dangerously slanted as the water begins to enter. Gabriel drops the stone into the lake and pushes the body behind it. As the boat uprights itself Gabriel watches the Bishop pulled in with only a ripple. He sits down and again looks around intently while rowing back to the willow tree. Once he gets to shore he drags the boat out and turns it upside down to make sure all the water inside is drained out. He starts to walk towards Scherer's house as he notices it is beginning to chill quickly.

When he gets back to Scherer's home, he searches for Carl, finally finding him in the music room. Scherer is sitting by the piano just looking at the keys.

"Carl, we have a problem."

"We have a problem? It was me in Wilhelm's mouth, not you."

"Listen to me, damn you. The Bishop is dead!"

"Gabriel? You murdered him?"

"Who killed him is not important, I disposed of his body. Now you must take action in protecting your neck. When you left Wilhelm, were you and the Bishop seen by anyone?"

"No, I informed you earlier, it was well after half past nine, all of the Gunner servants are dismissed at a quarter past eight. There was no reason to keep a single one of them on duty."

"Then Wilhelm should be the only one still remaining in the main part of the house. Go back there and have him help you in removing some of Joel's belongings. Make it look like he was called away, but intends to return."

"The boy, what should I tell him?"

"His neck is now in your noose. Awake, Carl, this is not the first time you have had to cover your tracks. Remember, Scherer, there are only two suspects in this crime, Wilhelm and you. You are the only one who knows about me and the moving of the body. If that little morsel becomes known, you will be hanged. I have done my share to protect you, now it is the time for you and your child to protect yourselves."

Carl then leaves the room, only to come back in quickly.

"Your wife's woman was close to the door!"

"Marta?" Gabriel asks.

"Yes," Scherer whispers.

"I will take care of her Carl, go do what is needed."

Both men leave the music room at the same time. Scherer continues towards the gardens as Mechant goes toward the stairs. When Gabriel gets to the second floor landing he sees Marta going into Angelique's room. He then walks down the hall and enters his room.

The next morning, the Scherer house is still on the second floor. Gabriel goes to a window in the upstairs hallway that secures a full view of the gardens and the lake. As he looks out, a satisfied smile joins a most enjoyable vision. Snow is falling, the gardens are blanketed, the lake has a thin layer of ice on it and the snow is beginning to cover it as well. He begins to laugh as he is certain the old uncle will not have a thing to say to anyone today.

"My dear husband, you still have an appreciation for the beauty of nature," Angelique softly says as she joins him at his vantage point. He turns and kisses her ear, and then whispers to her, while holding her arms tightly.

"Your spying could ruin the opera for all of us, Angel."

"You're hurting me, Gaby. Let go."

"Do you wish your voice to be silenced? Or are you including yourself in this game of hide and seek?" he says to her while releasing her.

"I am well trained Monsieur Mechant, at the chore of cleaning up after you. You have always been sloppy. And as for this game of hide and seek, I advise you not to play a game that has not yet begun."

She then turns and walks towards the stairs and begins to descend them. He looks at her, then, decides to stop her before she reaches the bottom of the staircase. He quickly catches her halfway down and both stop on the same step of the descent.

"Be careful Mechant, you would not want to push me down the stairs, would you?"

"How much do you know?"

"Enough," she answers.

They both walk down the remaining steps arm in arm. They arrive on the main floor in perfect unison as they are met by one of Scherer's servants, holding a tray with a tea service on it.

"Where would you like to begin this morning, Madam Beauvie, Monsieur Mechant?"

"The sun room," Angelique directs.

As the pair sit down, they hear Wilhelm's voice in the corridor, "Has Herr Scherer had his morning meal yet?"

"No, my Lord, I am not even sure he has come downstairs yet."

"Willy, come join us in the sun room," Angelique calls to him as she appears at the doorway of the glassed in terrace.

Wilhelm slowly goes towards her, when she asks him, "Are you all right, you look as though you have not slept at all last night."

"Yes, it was difficult to sleep." As he moves into the terrace he seems startled to see Gabriel, but he manages to stutter, "G-g-good morning Monsieur."

"Willy, is this not a glorious morning? I love the snow, it purifies all it touches, do you agree?" Gabriel asks him with a tone of condescension.

"Why yes, Monsieur, I do find it calming."

As she pats the boy's cheek, Madam Beauvie approves, "Good for you, Wilhelm. A strong attitude is always the best way to greet a glorious day like this particular one, and remember young man, the innocent should not hang on the cross for the sins of others."

Wilhelm nods his head obediently, as he slowly sits back in his chair.

Soon the three are joined by the master of the house. The pleasant conversation along with the leisurely meal is enjoyed while the snow continues to fall on the panoramic view of the gardens, the house on the hill, and the frozen lake between.

Through the rest of the day, Carl's residence stays in the same mood of surrealism that was created in the sun room in the morning.

Nothing seems out of place, but the gazebo carries a tension to it that only the skills of a master could soften.

"I am worried Gabriel, he has gone missing."

"Camille, why must you excite yourself? He is a mature individual who could have just gone to visit anyone. Give it some time; I am sure he will return shortly. Come closer to me, you are shivering."

"Gabriel, take me to our rendezvous."

With that, the pair leaves the gazebo and walk toward a small cottage on the far side of the lake. Their 'rendezvous' is one of the small buildings on the Viscount's property. Gabriel and Camille enter as she pulls him through the door. The door shuts as the sun can be seen through the clouds. The lake is beneath the snow, as the rowboat lies still, with a shroud of white upon it.

The audience is fixed in their expressions of where the stage intends to take us next. The music and singing have been extraordinary as this third scene has moved us to this point. I find the explosion of circumstances colorful and reminiscent of a fireworks presentation; various colors fragmented against a black sky that frames the piece's apparent shallow wish of attempting to shade in the dark depth behind.

The sheer callousness of the participants at the table on the terrace, asks all of us, is it weakness or strength that allows a person to deny their position in the most horrendous of acts? Perhaps, it is nothing more than wanting the illusion to continue. Perhaps, the illusion itself is capable of anything when it comes to its own survival. Perhaps, an addiction to illusion is what was being catered to, in a terrace under the snow. Perhaps, illusion is all there is.

The lake holds the answer to a disappearance of a high symbol of the Catholic Church, although that is not all it has frozen. Time is also suspended for a period. Falsehood is disguised as irony and truth is a bendable metal that can be shaped into any conclusion the craftsman desires. Once the craftsman displays the object, its popularity will be one of perception. But will that perception be one of honesty or one that has a similar shape to the other objects on the shelves of denial? Why does it even matter when dust will collect on anything? Dust is unbiased.

Two days later, Monsieur Mechant, Angelique Beauvie and Marta leave London and return to France to visit Angelique's parents in Provence for the year end holidays. Carl remains in London to receive his coming guests for the season and to make sure the appearance of normality remains. Carl has another duty to perform, securing the permission of the Viscount and his wife to take their children with him to assist in the production of the opera, a bold undertaking, but one that continues to hold the shield.

The day after Gabriel and Angelique leave, the constabulary is notified by Wilhelm about the disappearance of Bishop Joel. The police do not find the timing of the notification odd, because only four days have passed, which seems normal when the Bishop's family felt he would most assuredly return. King Charles is told and he makes it a point that Inspector Peal of the newly established Scotland Yard is in charge of the case.

November 20th is the date of the official disappearance, the morning after Gabriel's evening boat ride. It has been snowing sporadically since, and the gardens as well as the lake are frozen and covered. The Viscount's children have been very helpful and the police are working on the theory that the Bishop left the house for some unannounced reason. Everyone is hoping for his safe return, however, Peal does not believe the old man will be fortunate enough to be granted that wish.

The children's parents had returned immediately once they were made aware of the problem that existed in London. They were informed by messenger on November 30th, and the messenger returned two days before their arrival to inform those back in the capital about their quick return on December 6th, a fortnight sooner than originally planned. Deeper into December, Pope Pius the Eighth and the establishment in France begin pressuring King Charles on the issue.

Of course, Peal in turn is feeling the urgency, even though he has told the King himself that the Bishop most likely has been murdered. The King in response has ordered Peal to find the Bishop and to keep his theory to himself. The King makes sure the Inspector is fully aware of the miring problems the King would suffer as the result of a murder in London of a French Catholic Bishop who is a relative of a relative of the King himself. The political ramifications could turn out to be nothing less than entangling mud that could last for years;

"And that would not delight the King, would it?" the King tells Peal with no attempt at subtlety. King Charles hurls at Peal these final words the moment before their well understood meeting is over,

"Find the bastard, Peal. And do not forget, the old man is still very much alive."

Through the holidays, Herr Scherer secured Wilhelm and Camille's involvement in the production of the Opera. Their parents thanked Scherer for his kindness while also feeling that it would take their children's minds off their Grand Uncle, and of course the experience would do wonders for their education. Wilhelm had been composing for years and Camille had showed promise with her excellent literary talents; it was a wonderful opportunity for both of them, an opportunity both very much wanted to experience.

Peal's investigation had always centered on the theory that the Bishop left after the snow began to fall. There were hardly any tracks in the gardens because the walkways had the snow removed from them by the servants. The ones that remained did not suggest any sort of struggle, just normal foot prints of strolls and ambles that always started from one of the walkways and returned. But at the front of the Viscount's home, there were countless tracks of carriages as well as foot prints. The front suggested the only way out without obvious return.

Gabriel and Angelique were interviewed by the French authorities, but all they could tell them about the Bishop had to do with the evening they met him. Outside of that there was nothing they could contribute. The topic of the opera came up during the interview, but only in reference that it had been established that the relatives of the Bishop would be joining Herr Scherer in Provence to begin the collaboration.

By mid January 1831 King Charles ordered that any future police investigations must not be conducted in the presence of the Viscount's children due to the stress it was causing them. The same consideration must also apply to Herr Scherer, Gabriel Mechant and Angelique Beauvie because the children would be under their guardianship during the production of the Opera. Viscount Fredrick also went so far as to commission the production and guarantee the safety of all those connected to it. Again, privilege and position had protected Gabriel, Angelique and Carl.

The massive cover up of the murder was well orchestrated by these masters of privilege and position. By late in January, Scherer and the children had joined Gabriel and Angelique in a charming cottage near Nice that was employed by the couple. The enchanting cottage enjoyed the beautiful setting on the hills overlooking the Mediterranean Sea. It was to be a stopover location for all, before continuing to the final destination where the opera would be completed, rehearsed, and performed.

Gabriel and Angelique had been at the cottage for two weeks by then, after leaving Angelique's parents in the countryside above Cannes. The travelers from London seemed very happy to be there, certainly now that the heavy distraction of the disappearance had been removed. The incident was being consistently played on in the newspapers of England by writers such as Jonathan Broadfoot. Their words had been able to swim the English Channel and surface on the shores of mainland Europe. The travelers were relieved that they had finally outrun the speculation and gossip.

The audience had been tossed and spun like toys in a nursery. All of our faculties were numbed by all of the variables. The music and words had begun to hypnotize even the most sympathetic. Deceit was at its best as its performance had been magnificent so far. Any sign of decency had been preyed upon to the point that it had become an often served delicacy. What was desired always seemed to be placed on the dessert cart, dressed to exact specifications; after all, these people were not savages.

Why must ones of such station be annoyed by the foolishness that obstructs their view on what needs to become, in the process of their entertaining lives? These people know how to get things done, and how to skillfully use the tools in the kit to construct the bridges that are built to conform to their personal directions. Hardship is for the amateurs and restrictions are for the weak. This is a game that can only be played in the one coliseum that is situated right in the middle of the true reality. All else is the dream.

Surrealism occupies every layer upon the stage. It plays in the light and sings from the shadows as it seeps deep into the crusts of the characters in this Opera of Indulgence. We in the audience are strapped onto our perches like stuffed pigeons in a historical drama about a theater sinking into the merciless fathoms of the drool that falls from the mouths of manipulators. We were the witnesses of a performance that somehow now has us playing roles in this meal of victims. We all must be careful not to adjust to a singular definition of strange, for it too, has had surrealism seep into it while it floats inside the drool with the rest of us.

Nice and its views of the Mediterranean supply enough ingredients for the purpose of artistic inspiration and romantic continuance. The strategy works instantly as the opera begins to take shape while there is time for Carl and Willy as well as time for Camille and Gabriel. Angelique seems content in her being, predisposed within her duties between sessions with Carl and Wilhelm and sessions with the librettist.

There are no eyes that need to be served views of conformity as the household has only four servants who all have homes nearby. Marta remains in service to Angelique only as she always has. All the rest are without personal attendants because views can be shared with the non-invited, though protection is always close by. Mercenaries hired by

Gabriel remain loyal to the highest bidder and they also understand their lives have blades before them as well as behind. Loyalty has more than its monetary rewards when you are in the employ of the powerful, and the connections their employer has secured have made Gabriel a very powerful individual.

"Carl, this is a topic that never has been explored with this intensity before. Gaby has painted a master's stroke with this viewpoint, we are all fortunate to be involved with what could be an operatic masterpiece."

"Yes, Herr Scherer, Madam Beauvie is entirely correct. The courts of Europe will be at your feet, while the audiences of Europe's theaters will be on theirs. I am certain my parents and their families would be thoroughly tickled by this."

"Willy, of course, she is right," Scherer agrees as he embraces Angelique, while all three are standing in a room that has been converted into a studio.

"This will surpass anything Gabriel or I have ever accomplished on our own."

As Scherer embraces Angelique she gently kisses him on his cheek, an act which is quite out of place. He lets his hand fall down her side as he slowly moves away, feeling her body without any objection. He walks toward the piano and says, "Yes, I feel the benefits. We must be sure that the whole experience is enjoyed with all it offers."

"Yes, Maestro," Willy agrees instantly.

"The whole experience, Carl," whispers the lady.

While the opera begins to take shape on the hills above the sea, there is a plentiful amount of time for Gabriel and Camille to enjoy the shops and seaside of Nice. They take walks along the water's edge that allow the gentleman to stop the chill of the vibrant Mediterranean winter winds from roosting in the bones of his rose colored enchantment. They fall into a quaint inn that has enough heat to equal the temperature inside their desires for one another. The food and wine is very satisfying on the first floor, and the on the second, there is a warm room with a feather bed that molds perfectly as their bodies move in a harmony of contortions.

Gabriel treats her with the gentleness and patience a lover would. His actions never appear to be those of a common seducer, even though she wants more and more of him, a common trait of a well devoured object. Her affection for him is, at times, too obvious for her own good, but he teaches her the proprieties of a well versed mistress and no pupil has every come to class with more openness to his lessons.

Their sessions in the feather bed are prolonged with long entanglements of petting, teasing and pleasure. He knows just when and she is learning just how. Her laughter, sighs and moans paint the finest symphonies in his ears, as it has become apparent that the man has deeply fallen in love with his conquest. She is fascinated, entranced and playful, but the love she confesses to him is young and has been seduced; therefore, the longevity of this young love she gives to him should not be thought of in terms of forever. But even the most enlightened gladly lose their eyes in order to see the splendor inside a dream.

The two are careful to return to the cottage before the other three are able to lose their attention on the opera. Of course, there are the times Gabriel spends writing in his study upstairs where his wife also works on being the appointed liaison between the words and the music. The circumstances work well with the desires of the occupants, and nothing has the ability to upset this arrangement, a celestial ring worn by all.

Carl and Wilhelm spend a great deal of time alone in the studio. At night, they take turns in the other's bed and they treat themselves to an array of fancies. Carl holds the young man in a dominant manner and Wilhelm pleases himself by granting his lover's wishes. Carl moves the young man onto his stomach and enters Willy while he lies on top of him.

The younger moans into the pillows as the older begins to gasp. When Carl is finished, he falls onto the bed next to Willy, as the younger turns onto his back and masturbates himself to the same ending. Their relationship of the risqué is truly enjoying its most unencumbered moments.

Angelique's constant smile adds contentment to the mood as all are in their glory of separate yet beautifully connected idealisms. The princesses of utopia could not feel as satisfied no matter how handsome their delusions or how many suitors of extraordinary structure waited for their next whims. These were glorious beginnings for the five and a half. After all, there is no forgetting dear Marta and her ever present nature.

The first week went by at a quickened pace and ever so often the winds off the sea held a warmth in them like the recited poems of the soon arriving spring, that always arrived like a troubadour on a white stallion. Provence and its promises responded with their gentle assurances that spring would be welcomed with the understanding of the abundant autumn harvest that would be the result of spring courting the promises of Provence. Why should there be a difference to this yearly love affair? This time there was new music in the warmth of the air.

We in the audience were released by the tensions of the past; however, most of us understood that there were still bills that remained unpaid. It is not avoidance that has captured the stage; it simply is a case of priorities being garnished in a short attention span. Priorities cleverly dressed in dreams and the pathways that fulfill them. What can one do when one needs to occupy the time somehow? These rarities could only be tasted by true preoccupation and the suspension of unfavorable memories.

One afternoon Camille and Wilhelm were walking through an olive grove that inclined to the top of a hill that offered a view of the countryside and the sea in the foreground. They had been sharing their experiences with sly reserve.

"So, sister, are you and Mechant lovers?"

"Willy, be sensible, he is as old as father. How could my virtue be given to a man of that many years? My designs are on you, but I am sure you are still hesitant because of the little negative incestuous thing?" Camille answers sarcastically while laughing.

"I am very happy Camille. This place and the past few days have been a Godsend. I am actually working on an Opera with Herr Carl Scherer and the words of Gabriel Mechant; I am in ecstasy. We have freedom for the first time in our lives, sister. There are no secrets that must be kept from Mother. She is miles away and a lifetime ago. And think of it, soon I will turn 18 and I will finally get my inheritance. When that happens, this freedom, this life will remain, and mommy cannot do a thing about it," Wilhelm expresses as the two reach the top. They both look out at the expanse and begin to scream in the wind that surely must be the blowing of a kiss from the Sahara to the south and the joys and the mysteries that will flood into their lives. Freedom is best enjoyed when it is open to the magic within.

They stay there for a while in the silence of true companionship. Nothing needs to be said, it is enough to know you are totally accepted by your friend and the rest of the moment. After long reflections they begin to walk down through the rows of olive trees as their branches are singing gently, still in their warmth of silence. After a short while;

"I will miss you, Willy, and it will be some time before I will join you in that kind of extended freedom. I could escape Father and his wife soon if I marry another in the flock of the bored. Damn, I do not want to be a bird of withering feathers in a golden cage lined with numbing propers. I want a life were my pen can sing and my legs will only have to spread when I want them to."

Wilhelm stops and holds Camille close to him as she begins to cry uncontrollably. "I promise you that I will not leave you alone with them. I will give you the opportunity you need to become what you are meant to be. Women writers are not uncommon any longer, and you know a pen name could be used. All you need is a pen that has a penis. Apparently that is all that is required. You are not lost.

"This work will take another six months or more before it will be ready for its first performance; that means this beauty could last into the summer. I will be 18 by then and things will be very different for both of us. Remember, these are only the first few moments of what will become our dreams and their lives. Camille, look; that is the Mediterranean Sea. It can float you to anywhere."

With eyes upon the Sea the two begin to walk again with Wilhelm's arm around the waist of his sister as she lays her head on his shoulder. Their hair sails in the winds of a kiss from the warm lips of the Sahara that lays stretched on the bed of North Africa. The blue before them is all that separates the two from the Bedouin in their caravans as they cross the pillows of sand that hold the imprints of European fantasies. Exotic Arabian lips that whisper in the ear tales of wisdoms that feel like the most thrilling of feather caresses, soft, slow, gentle and tantalizingly extensive. Every style of seduction and every pleasure to the seduced.

But, then, to every granted fantasy the push of endurance must be willing to climb the barrier that lies before the desire. Pleasure cannot be understood by the ones who come by them by simple request. They are treasures best tasted by the hungriest, the young who have lived in wonderment as to what lays beyond the barriers of their age. Or, by the older who once felt contented by their coos and excitements, but lost their hold because they were gentle enough not to grip so tightly that it would choke away the life within the desire.

Fulfilled desires are bestowed on the desirable, as love is given to the lovers. Lips that can kiss feel the kisses of another, as gentleness opens its arms to receive gentleness. There is no confusion in the logical, only in the typical, because the typical has blisters on its hands that claw the soft and then blame the reaction. Pain cannot be confused with gentleness, because pain is typical. The open expanse of the Sea is what opens to the open expanse of Arabian wisdom and exotics. European privilege has no European fantasies left.

All there is, is the mundane, the typical. What would Europe do without the backers of the artists and their art? But an artist must still be exalted by their hunger because that is the capacity needed to be one with the desires, the gentle kiss fired by a deep love of an affection for the thought the master desires to bring to life. It is the old master that understands desire the most, because only they have been given enough time to explore every pore of the need and every morsel that feeds its hunger. But only God understands why that should never become typical.

When the artist himself becomes the backer that could execute the hunger, unless purity in the appropriate measure holds the eyes open to new tastes and hungers. That is why there are seas and their beyonds. The paths on the other side of the clouds are the hooves of the camels that parade in the caravans on the endless Saharas of the well nurtured imagination. Flavourable fantasies that have never reached a European table because proprieties are the pubic hairs that grow on vacant testicles, while the sperm of brilliance from the living sacks below well excited pistons can be catapulted into the wombs of openness and promise.

There is no privilege in dried up reasons, as there is no practical behavior when excitement is the springtime of the embrace. There are only the sands of possibilities that can be felt between the toes as the feet are naked in their journeys. Journeys that take the hungry far away from should be's and their chiefs who never learned about herbs, spices and different tastes. Away from the kitchens with knives that can only cut in one direction and forks so the bland meals can never been felt or tasted.

I felt very moved by the performance. The idea that the panoramic views along the French Riviera were the beginnings of dreams rather than the dreams themselves again threw me into a quandary of illusionary thoughts. Possibilities of these artisans on their own was amazing enough, but to consider what their joint challenges and triumphs could be, left any type of speculative thoughts hard to chew or unkindly worn out.

The closest of my companions in the audience all seemed as emotionally prodded as I was. Whenever the familiar voices of the boys began to echo through the theater, beauty shone through the clouds of tension and bewilderment, calming all of us while allowing this storm of human frailties, deceits and hopes to be continually thrust at us from the Eden upon the stage. A garden of fractured facilities and confessing confusions, where the fruit is sweet and the colors are brilliant but the vision is vanishing behind our questions of how much of this are we capable?

None could turn away, for the obvious fact that the thoughts that have traveled through our own minds make us realize that someone in this story seems to be able to act out what most of us could only hope to do.

Each one of them was not ashamed to any degree. Each one of them enjoyed their involvement with the others. Perhaps they appeared to some as a roving gang of pillagers, or to others as rutting dogs. Say what you wish, but there seemed to be no uncertainty that they all appeared to be enjoying themselves.

The siblings held each others' hand as they walked the short steps to the cottage's doorway when they heard screaming, at the side. They ran around to notice the rest of the group trying to calm Gabriel down.

"Killing this man will prove nothing, Mechant, and could bring our efforts to a halt."

"Scherer, this is France, and I am Gabriel Mechant; the fool has made a mistake and must be taught his lesson."

"Do you really think in death he will be able to redo the test?" laughs Scherer.

"What has happened?" asks Camille.

"My dear husband, my dear Camille, has been challenged to a duel by that pretty boy over there," Angelique says facetiously while pointing down the road to a group of young men who are surrounding a very handsome young man.

"A duel? About what?" asks Wilhelm.

"Why, Willy, about your sister, of course," Angelique purrs.

"Me? Why me?" Camille confusingly inquires.

"The young man has seen the two of you by the seaside in town and also in a particular inn. He has come here to... how did he word it Angelique?" Scherer says.

"I believe his words were, 'I have come to stop the desecration of a... dream come true', was that it Gaby?" Angelique jokes as she looks at Gabriel with a smirking grin on her face, while he is not amused by the taunting.

"That was what he said? My... how charming," Camille says softly while looking directly at the creature who bows in return to his believable dream, as Gabriel witnesses the whole exchange.

At that moment, Gabriel starts to growl and with his guards, Scherer and Willy behind him, begins to run towards the group of young men who start to fan out. As the men cluster together, Gabriel and his opponent are left in the middle of an instant circle. Their swords begin to engage, but in what seems to be a blink of the eye, Gabriel's sword is in the dreamer's shoulder; that instantly forces the young man to drop his guard. Gabriel digs the point deeper then withdraws the blade, and finally, with precious precision, pierces the point back into the injured's heart, killing him while the handsome young cavalier is still on his feet. With his strings cut, the dreamer crumbles like a puppet onto the stones that were his altar a breath ago.

The stunning exhibition is more horrendous when Camille watches Gabriel turn to look at her, and on his face a disturbing smile of satisfaction begins to overpower the anger that was there previously. At that moment, Angelique nonchalantly whispers in Camille's ear as she turns and walks the shocked girl away from the sight of the male ritual of spraying your territory.

"Darling, this will teach you to remember, a lady has hypnotic powers over men, so she must always choose her words well. And dear, from now on, hide your cards better; there are always eyes upon you. Even my eyes, dear, even mine."

"Monsieur, he was beaten; there was no need for the second thrust," one of the dead man's companions says with tears in his eyes.

"Of course there was, my dear boy," Scherer offers, "Firstly, your friend would still be alive to begin this foolishness again, and more importantly, he dared to challenge Gabriel Mechant. He should have known no one has ever left one of Mechant's duels alive. You might remember the little French saying, you know, the one that goes;

'Mechant's fierceness equals two pierces'. That is the way this master signs his work. You should have known," Scherer laughs as he walks away with Willy and the champion, as their guards stand between them and what is left of the group of young companions.

"You are a champion indeed, Monsieur," Wilhelm says as he softly applauds Gabriel.

"That was not a challenge for my blade, Wilhelm, that was a crucifixion for the mortal sin of paying attention to your sister. That fool was jealous that I was feeding while he was dreaming. You and your Camille have your suitors, thus the lines must be boldly drawn," Mechant instructs as Wilhelm is stopped by the blow.

"Willy, come on then," Scherer softly says as he stops too. "He is right, is he not; you do have your suitor. That is why you are here in the first place, is it not?"

"Carl, of course, but the way he said it, did not make it sound like it is our choice."

"Willy, you made your choice the night your uncle disappeared. That night cannot be reversed. This life was what you chose, so you must not ever forget that such ugliness is the shit that brings beauty to life. And that is our reward for enduring our dark moments. It is people like us that can fly above the decaying and build the new. Most root through the refuse as they believe that to be the definition of living, while what we create becomes their new beauties. They would be lost without us."

"I understand and I agree that I made my choice, but what about Camille? She did not make the same choice."

"Do not be foolish, Wilhelm, of course she made the same choice."

"How did she do that?" Wilhelm confusedly asks.

"She welcomes her love affair with Gabriel by her bouts of heaving in the inn by the sea without complaint, Willy; that is a fact. And have you also forgotten that it was the day after Mechant and Beauvie left London before she had the authorities notified about the disappearance? Do not fool yourself, your naive sister is a true member of our band and she is getting older with every climax she is taking while learning how to give the same back to her teacher."

With that, the two begin to walk back to the cottage as the familiar January rain of Provence begins to fall on them, on the others and on the corpse down the road.

The situation of being in the undertow of one's own illusion does not supply a buoyant material to keep the dreamer afloat. Soon after the sinking begins, the water holds a mysterious grip of intensive shock that brings the drowning a sudden slap of reality. As the eyes begin to focus on the perilous situation, hope has no value when all that it will save is an ability to take action. Imagination has no place when the gasping has started and no memory of dirty air will grant a breath of it.

Strength of an individual is measured by a responsive action, not by the practicing of pretense for the others that the posing was meant to impress. Water is not the only requirement for drowning to occur, as the process can be accomplished in anything that can submerge the senses and tease the desires.

It is the quickness of focusing on the difference of a wish and a need that saves the master, for it is the master that knows that they are and always have been exactly the same thing. As the need is perused, all else is satisfied and every possible wish comes to be or comes to be left behind. Ethics are lost when need is satisfied, for when one has, one does not want. Drowning does not occur in time of mastering, for a master either knows how to swim, or simply chooses not to enter. The simplicity of satisfying a need before it hungers is the secret of all the masters.

As the curtain begins to fall, while a longing lament is played on a classical guitar, the audience sighs collectively. The third scene has rubbed our noses into the ugliness of which people are capable. I am sure we all have asked the question; how far would I go in order get what I want? Power can cover the most despicable of acts, but those of us who do not posses it, for the most part, go blindly through our lives trying to forget what another's power has done to us.

The opera we witness on the stage before us has all the extents and all their middles combined with layers of waste, horror, and the beauty that rises from it all. I, personally, find it easier to view when I search my honesty and discover there are parts of me that need far more of my own attention. The opera that forever performs in my spirit plays to an empty theater for the most part. I am learning that I must spend more attention on the wonderful layers inside myself; satisfying my need before I wish I could.

THE SIGN IN THE SEA

Softness in Gloria touches the skin of the vanquished, as the tribute is given to the fallen heart in the romantic wars of idealisms and the barbs of factual material. A swollen hand that lost its grip on a vanishing desire, reaches for the face of the hoped for, in the vain attempt to feel a sign that it is sculpted upon living marble. The fingers on the hand run along the lines that speak with an expression of disenchantment. The eyes fall towards the dust that cakes the blood of a lanced spirit. The brows are troubled by a lack of reason while the lips are full and inviting, although the invitation was long ago.

The swollen hand falls to the side of an old warrior that has seen all in the romantic wars. The eye of this fighter is surrounded by sculptures of martyred marble with the depictions of old lovers, youthful indiscretions, and other moments that are frozen like scars upon the heart. This gallery of memories brings tears to the old romantic, although they have been skillfully adapted to only fall internally. There are hunting sounds of echoed laughter that run through the chambers of this mausoleum that remind the ears of suspended delights that nested in the days of yesteryears.

As the warrior is summoned by the light of the present that streams through the exit, the sound of the fighter's steps begins to cast a muffle on the songs that were once composed and sung. As the stream of light begins to quiet the shadows that brought the internal tears, the doorway is passed and the sun of the newest opportunities warms the marbled chilled pasts away. The day is here and the wars are old but the romantic soul hopes to be found again. This old warrior mounts the war horse and gallops towards a new spring of an old redundancy.

The fourth scene has opened with a proverb. Old habits are little more than a desire to get it right for the first time, but how can that be done? Stationary lives have no need for shoes or pathways on which to explore. The music playing is a tempo that refuses to experiment with other shades, while a melody with wonderful possibilities is restrained by the duplication. Dancers at center stage suddenly appear out of the sculptures that filled the gallery of memories of the old warrior that has ridden away.

They begin to dance in place and their lack of experimentation begins to rub roughly on the exposed senses of all of us in the audience. I can hear myself pleading for more life upon the stage when I realize that I came to this theater to gain more notes for my own melody that is memorable because of its repetitive nature. This opera believes somehow that all of us in this experience have capabilities, not just to witness but to become involved. We all are warriors.

The early blooms in the gardens along the pathways are the first blushes on the landscape of Provence, as spring has begun its yearly courtship. February is on the calendar and the official arrival of the season is weeks away. However, the romance has started with soft glances, bloom scented kisses and short poetic notes that tells the comforter that comfort will soon be here.

The rain casts every new color with a fluorescent sheen that brings it all into a filtered lens focus of flavorful radiance. The birds are returning and the songs of the shrike, the lark and the oriole in chorus enchant all with a feeling of newness and an empty slate. The Mediterranean Sea is calmly whispering to be painted on by feather-like sails at the end of brushes of the masters of experiences and the wanderers with spirits full of wonderments.

The cottage also has the sheen as inside the creativity is flourishing and all are party to the new masterpiece's arrival. The music that is to be its auditory offering to the Gods of Art is beginning to have poetic descriptions embedded in every note. The story still needs more study of the time and place for its reason, as the truth is that the work still does not have the balance to walk on its own.

The labor was beginning to intensify in the most exciting of ways for the young apprentices. Wilhelm was at Scherer's side almost always as Camille had begun the chore of copying the words that were being constantly handed to her by Angelique or Gabriel. The afternoons had changed slightly due to the outcome of the duel. A new inn had been found and preying eyes were not welcome by the guards that had started to accompany the pair.

Camille was not scared off by the exhibition she had witnessed. On the contrary, she enjoyed the display of powerful prowess, and the fact that its decisions were final. After all, power is comfortable, do you not think? She was treated by her lover with the gentleness reserved for new brides. The presents he bought for her were nothing short of extravagant and she was learning how to keep the entitlements coming.

There was strangely no open disapproval by any of the others towards her, and that assured her she had taken Angelique's place in the bedroom and in Gabriel's heart. She knew, however, that she would have to be satisfied with those victories because the other territories that

Angelique occupied were heavily guarded and fortified by years of elegance to the 'king' who was still the older woman's husband.

Her brother was in his fantasies as they were beautifully coming to life. He loved his passion for music and his passion for his lover came just as easily. Their long romance had started when the boy was first being instructed by his new teacher Herr Scherer years before. When Willy was seven, Carl would kiss the boy on his lips when the young virtuoso would play his various instruments in a manner of a much more mature artist. Their affection for each other remained in the music room until the boy could be trusted to keep their rendezvous secret.

When the child was eleven, the lessons began in earnest as the prodigy was pleasured by more than his abilities with musical expression. By thirteen, the two were fully engaged in carnal as well as celestial levels. His parents never thought there were any improprieties taking place for the simple reason that they hardly thought. Why think why, when all is how it should be?

There seemed to be a hurried pace in the events after the duel and the reason for it came knocking on the door of the cottage one morning as all the characters inside were getting in place for their early day routines. The captain of the guards began to talk outside with Gabriel who was accompanied by Carl and Angelique. The four were joined by an officer of the local authorities. The conversation was plainly serious and very informative, for all of them took an active part.

The conversation was centered on Gabriel; he was questioned as he questioned in return. As it was coming to a close there were smiles on everyone's face, pleasantries along with the appropriate jesters were exchanged as the discussion ended. The captain and the officer turned and walked away from the cottage as the remaining three entered it.

"Well, that tells us that Provence again must be left behind," Angelique said.

"Mechant, from now on make sure your sword knows who it is about to kill," Scherer offered as he went directly into the studio.

"Angel, tell your Marta it is time, we will follow the coastline," Gabriel ordered.

Gabriel turned and began to walk up the staircase only to see Camille at the top smiling that smile that captivated his heart and excited his desires' taste buds.

"Gaby, my darling, is there trouble?"

As he reaches the top he turns her as they both walk slowly down the hallway arm in arm.

"Camie, there is always trouble. Now after saying that, you must be comforted by the fact that the trouble is mine not yours. As you know from your continuing experiences with me, I can make it all vanish in an instant. Say what you will my truffle, you know I am never boring," he says as he quickly has his hand inside her robe and his other on the handle on the door to her bedroom. They enter and then the door is eased shut by her body as she supports herself on it and he begins to run his tongue along her neck as she slowly enjoys his journey downwards.

After the interlude, Camille is on the floor as her body is fully exposed while her right thigh and pelvic bone support Gabriel's head as he softly touches her. Her eyes are closed and her face is satisfied. Her arms are stretched out to the sides and her breathing resembles the purring of a contented kitten.

"Are you pleased with me, Camie?"

"Oh, yes," is all she is able to whisper.

He starts to kiss her gently and blow air on her as she twitches and curls her body while remaining on her back. Her movements are calculated enough as to not disturb Gabriel or his duties, which definitely feel they are the beginnings of an encore. After all Gabriel is a consummate performer who thoroughly enjoys his moments on stage. He takes the time needed to complete every tease and skilled maneuver that makes the stage open to as many performances as possible.

While this is happening, downstairs Angelique listens as Carl plays while the gorgeous voice of Wilhelm is singing. The music and words blend together in an exquisite unison of unified beauties that fill the cottage. The imagination is swiftly transported over the water outside the cottage's windows; we are flying over the expanse when we notice an object below. We see that the outstretched wings of an angel are drying while it perches on a signpost in the middle of the Mediterranean in the warm sun above. The sign below reads 'What could have been was never to be.' As Wilhelm reaches for the highest note, upstairs Camille is climaxing as she releases with a long haaaaaaaa, as the angel on the sign in the sea joins all in the ecstasy of haaaaaaaa.

That afternoon preparations were in earnest for the journey to the final destination of the opera. Nice lost one of its finest young men of one of its finest families in the duel and the citizenry had no more patience for the preoccupied pretense of the cottage's household. With certainty, Provence is part of France, and indeed, Mechant is one of its heroes but a duel is one thing and murder is another. But in these days duels often left work for morticians no matter the circumstances. Mechant was challenged; it was not the other way around. A rule, no matter how senseless it is, is a rule nonetheless.

Messengers were sent out in opposite directions, one to secure passage and accommodation along the coastline, and the other to notify the families involved. The group would be traveling south, and that meant leaving France. All the proper authorities had to be notified as well as those that could maintain the status quo all were accustomed to. The powerful connections included not only King Charles of England, but King Charles the Tenth of France, King Ludwig the First of Bavaria, King Ferdinand the Seventh of Spain, the authorities of Genoa, and Sardinia, but of course, their largest ally was Pope Pius the Eighth.

It would take only a day and a half to allow the five to prepare to leave because of the fact there was always more than enough hands that could be pressed into service. Most of the articles would be transported by boat while two wagons, a carriage and horses would transport the group and their essential belongings. After all, anything can be purchased or persuaded along the way.

The next afternoon Carl and Angelique were alone in the study while the rest were in Nice preparing for some final details of the next morning's journey. The two sat together on the piano bench as she watched his hands on the keys before her.

"You play beautifully, Carl, my, your fingers are quick and adaptable. How long have you been playing?"

"Since I was three, Madam."

"You are a very talented man. I am finding these days with you are bringing me an exciting new impression. Up to these times I had no idea how quickly your creative mind works. I believe I am finally beginning to truly know you, and I have to say, my respect for you is growing steadily."

"You appreciate me more?"

"Yes, that is part of it."

He stops playing and looks at her with an intense expression.

"A part of it? Well, you are not a child, Angelique; tell me, what are the other parts?"

He asks as he slides his fingers on her lips. She smiles as he feels the pattern of her mouth. He then kisses her forcibly while she sits there and complies. Then, he rises from the bench and stands in front of her while he removes himself from his trousers. She begins without hesitation as he says to her,

"Your skill is also highly appreciated."

The audience ruffles as the stage holds the performance of the pair to its predictable ends. The music is melancholy as the image of the outstretched wings of the angel is shadowed on the rear wall above the piano. A soprano begins to sing a sad aria about the words on the sign in the sea. 'What could have been was not meant to be,' is heard throughout the theater. We are told about love affairs and other possibilities that were swept away by circumstance.

We are scorned for hoping that somehow our youth would reappear and the choices we made would be miraculously altered. The words to the aria speak about the outcomes of those alterations and how greatly we would have been affected. The soprano sings as her voice is projected through the ceilings of our lives and we see the heavens we passed by and their hells below them. Our choices brought us here to this moment in this opera and no amount of judgment can secure our position in our seats or the position of the pair on stage. We are all victims of our own choices. What could have been was not meant to be. That is a fact of life.

I can see how events cannot be smoothly predicted. What is happening on stage seems out of the ordinary, while it is not out of place in this opera. Conventional thinking has no bearings to a course to anywhere but here. There are no guidelines, morals, or hands to hold the weakest of those around us. We have been searching for originality, and that means it will not be constructed by our patterns of what is acceptable and what is thought to be disgusting. God invented life and life invented pleasure, there you have it, thus, there it is.

The characters in this opera are beings of pleasure. They have been reared to live lives of raptures, promiscuities and other delicacies. They believe that order must be maintained for the lower classes, for they are too naive or too ignorant to invent anything more than a fragment of themselves. After all, the fools of the lower classes hide in the intellectual thoughts of those who understood the flaws in them. The inventors of these theories have long since died or simply grown up. Even Adam knew that Eden was only an ideal, although Eve does very well by still tempting those that believe all should be forever boring. She sells the story but she has not lived there for close to forever.

The next morning was cloudy but the sun was shining through the cracks. The beams could be seen out on the sea, dotted in patterns that gave the impression that the clouds were racing to fix the holes in the ceiling they had created. One beam would be successful while another would vanish. This game played itself out until midday when the sun's stamina was too much for the condensed vapor. By that time, the party had traveled over eighteen miles and it was time to rest the horses and feed themselves.

They had traveled along the shoreline and had made it to Menton. There they were met by soldiers of Sardinia along with a contingent of guards from Genova. The French were glad to turn over the assignment to them but intended to remain with the procession until it crossed the border. After they rested for close to two hours they continued. Just past sunset they reached Ventimiglia where they stayed the night in a villa that was cleared in order to provide for them. Gabriel's private mercenaries retained command over the protection of the group, however, the others that were on hand had been ordered to their aid to secure the safe passage to Tuscany.

The roads along the coast were not the easiest on those in the wagons or the carriages so for the most part all rode horses. Once they arrived in Genova they were to stay in a villa far from disturbances. They remained there for close to two days. More work could be done on the opera, while Gabriel and Camille could spend more intimate time together.

It was mid February by then and the spring that was making overtures to Provence was also sending love letters as far north as London where the snow and ice had melted while the grounds keepers were busy with their tasks in the gardens between Scherer's home and the Viscount's. One morning in late January a worker had turned the boat upright and had noticed splatters of something inside, but there was no second thought and what was blood stains had been almost worn off by the insistent rain.

A new rope was attached to it as it was moved to the exact spot were it was always tethered to the willow tree. The missing nymph had not been discovered while all the nymphs were being removed so a small brick wall could be built to support rambling roses, which were planned as a border to one of the walkways. There were a total of seven nymphs, as each one represented a separate deadly sin. Lust coincidently, was the one that was missing. The other six were moved to a shed by an apprentice who was new to his duties, thus lust was forgotten.

The lily pads on the lake would make their return as the weather was warmed by the seasons that were approaching. The gardens would be in full bloom again with the sounds of birds, dragon flies and other simplicities that would dance with the fragrances of the roses, flowers and the other scents. The lake would stay tranquil in its stillness at one moment, and then rippled by the ducks and geese in the next. How could an old Bishop think that heaven would cover him in a more fitting manner? The murder was forgotten by the garden's normality and the minor improvements to an area that Eve must have walked in while reciting stories of the first Eden.

The villa in Genova was also surrounded by gardens that were used by the group for the days they were there. Herr Scherer and Madam Beauvie had made a point to enjoy the climate with the discovery of a secluded spot at the opening of a grotto that had an underground stream coming from beneath its rocks. They visited the location twice, and in both incidents, Angelique ended up bent over supporting herself against the wall with her hands while Scherer roughly penetrated her as her dress was conveniently lifted behind her.

Angelique enjoyed his savagery, and had no apprehension when it came to definitions about her eager availability. She strangely felt privileged to be his concubine; a duty she had no problem sharing with young Willy. Their contributions on the opera were a joy because of the ease in which the three of them worked, and the librettos that Gabriel was supplying fit perfectly, an extraordinary occurrence when he relied on his wife's interpretations. Angelique was the main cog to this mechanism, she kept everything running smoothly.

Her directions were so well crafted, that the love affair between Gabriel and Camille may have been part of her whole design. It kept the two from being underfoot and the fact that Gabriel had an immature sense of discretion did not matter. Angelique had ordered the Captain of the Guard and her faithful Marta to disguise any kind of sign of the pair's footprints along their self-indulgent pathways. That also included the freshening of their bed linens, clothes and undergarments. No stain remained noticeable, for that kind of evidence would put an instant end to the Viscount's protection and patronage.

The French authorities in Nice had been left with the task of discrediting any tales about the circumstances around the duel or Gabriel and Camille's habits in the two separate inns. Messier Mechant was protected by his status, and that assured his constant escapes from the facts. Of course, there was always gossip, but gossip is loose when it comes to details that can be lost in order to keep the topic interesting.

These days in Europe were full of talk about revolutions political, economical and intellectual. The circumstances and particulars that surrounded this group only mattered to those who had direct interest. Anyone who had indirect or casual contact could easily be persuaded to keep their memories blank and their tongues tied. Angelique was very persuasive when it came to the delicate details of decisive and direct diplomacies.

One night while still in Genova, Angelique proved her prowess when she and Gabriel were having a private discussion.

"Gaby, your antics in Nice were deplorable. You need to stop flaunting your disapproval of the common decencies…"

"I will not stop my, antics, with Camille." he defiantly answers.

"I am not suggesting you do. I have no critique when it comes to your taste, my dear. Frankly, I find her delightful in how reminiscent she appears to me when I had my turn at being seduced by you when I was her exact age over twenty years ago. No, it is only in the way you eat your meals. You must understand that napkins must be used in order to keep the crumbs off your satisfied face.

All I suggest is to learn how to eat at home; have your meals in the privacy of your own room. After all, I know from the past meals I have cooked for you that your enjoyments of them are in constant parallel to the amount of distractions there are about. The rest of us are busy with a masterpiece, I promise you, you will not be disturbed."

"My cake and the peace to enjoy it, Marie Antoinette lost her head because of the same act," Gabriel observes.

"Storytellers are not spinning these silks, my darling, we are."

"Angel, you are a personality from Shakespeare."

"Why insult me Gabriel, you know Dante would assuredly understand me better than that Englishman."

The comparison between Dante and Shakespeare was a wonderful tribute to the audience's literary knowledge. We in the theater were never taken for granted or disrespected intellectually. The opera was captivating in its mature themes and variations. The music was always in perfect alignment to the structures upon the stage. We were leaving our harbors of individual routines to sail upon an ocean that held within it currents of every description. There were other vessels that we encountered as well as migrating birds that have learned how to live their lives in the best moments of the world's various locations and various points of view.

We were being taught that the splendor in the journey was more exciting than the vision of our destination; for the journey was now and highly unpredictable, while the destination usually came with perceivable sights, reasons and outcomes. We found the waves would catapult the vessels in our armada at different times so much like the porpoises would do when they would take turns casting themselves out of the water as they traveled with us to the next stimulation.

Everyone in the audience had unfastened their safety belts that were the products of their routine behaviors and their routine patterns of thoughts. The spray from the waters in this opera was spreading itself throughout the theater and the infection was penetrating the imaginations of all of us. Where this journey would end was skillfully hidden by an abundance of possibilities and a chilling understanding of what power is capable of. We loved our views from the crow's nest of this vessel and the horizons we saw kept coming at us in kaleidoscopic visions.

On the morning when the party was to leave Genova, a messenger galloped onto the grounds of the villa. The Captain of the Guard summoned Gabriel and Carl, who met with the messenger privately. After the meeting, the messenger left as the two men joined the rest of the group, who were waiting to begin the day's journey. As the parade passed through the front gates of the villa, Angelique, who was on horseback, began her enquiries.

"Well, husband?" she softly said as the two rode side by side.

"Your curiosity is never satisfied. Tell me, when will you stop wondering about the business of others?" Gabriel barked.

"Your business is mine, Gabriel. Everything you do affects me. You are my voice, and it would not enhance my life if you were silenced. You chose this arrangement years ago without consulting me, but I intend to make sure you stay alive to fulfill your part of this ego. Tell me now, what needs to be taken care of."

"The London police seem to be concerned about some minor improvements Carl is having done in his gardens."

"What kind of improvements?"

"Herr Scherer had a brick wall built by one of his walkways."

"Which walkway?"

"The one that leads to the sloping lawn that falls into his side of the lake. I am sure you remember; the one that stops before the clump of willow trees."

"Where the rowboat is tied?"

"Yes, the rowboat." Gabriel answers while looking directly at her. With that, he rides ahead, just as Scherer rides up to take his place at her side.

"I imagine that you have been informed, Madame."

"Carl, you have made a mistake. Everything should have been left untouched."

"Angelique, work in these gardens has been done for generations. Your own parents have gardens like these, you should understand. The main garden was first constructed over two hundred years ago. They do not simply grow like this naturally. Mother Nature requires the appropriate makeup and coiffure, after all she is a tad too wild at times, you must agree. She is like any woman. Without the proper refining she is rather gamey. Not having any improvements done would be out of the ordinary. I assure you, the police know nothing, and that means they have nothing," Scherer commented while clutching his ever present handkerchief.

"Carl, men are the gamiest."

"That is what makes them so attractive, Madame, their wildness. Women, on the other hand, are at their most appealing once they have been fully domesticated. Women are nothing more than a garment that a man wears; either on his arm for show or on his protuberance for release."

"Which am I Carl, show or release?"

"It would appear odd if you were for show."

"So, I am to be worn for release only."

"Madame, you have never been a waif, you have always enjoyed the treasures bestowed on the thoroughbred in the stables of the domesticated. You have been ridden by only the most brilliant of riders and you are very aware that you remain the best in show.

But I understand you enjoy the feel of the crop on your hind quarters. We are using each other, you would not have it any other way Madame, and you know I like to make my mounts subordinate. We both are served at the same time. Perhaps, Willy would enjoy pulling my cart in tandem. What do you think, a ménage a trois?" he uncouthly asks while he laughs.

"Composer, remember your position. Is it not your garden that the King's inspectors are interested in? That can only mean that you're a suspect. I am also sure that the King's cousin would not like to hear that you have a habit of wearing Willy's ass on your... protuberance; that is how you put it, am I right?

"Never forget dear Carl, I do not require a pimp, and if I did, my clientele would never dare to whip me. Then again, all is possible if you remain aware of who really is the subordinate one. Do I make the situation clearer for you, dear Maestro?" Angelique smiles as she tears away the handkerchief from Scherer's hand and casts it into the mud and manure along the roadway.

Behind them, a carriage is following, and on the top with the driver Marta can see the whole interchange. She laughs and says to her companion, "Our Madame is schooling the children again."

"There is only room for one master," the driver says while he and Marta continue to laugh.

Madame Beauvie remained in control of the whole event by her ruthless ability to quell any type of uprising. Her status as the puppet master was again reinforced by her quick executions of the male temperament. She understood power and how it must always be decisive. She was a student of the works of Niccollo Machiavelli and his philosophy that 'The outcomes are justified by the means.' She also understood the meaning of 'Before all else, be armed.'

Her protection of Gabriel and his enormous talent was her entire motivation. She was a god when it came to tactics. She knew exactly when force or diplomacy had to be administered, and in what measures or blend. As Marta said, Angelique treated men like children who just wanted to have their own way. She understood that men react without a sense of consequence. She laughed at the fact that it was the male of the species that had developed the great wisdoms of the world, but it was the intelligent women that knew how to use them with the greatest skill.

Angelique knew how powerful knowledge was, but she also knew it must be used by the noble applier and great constrainer, reason. Emotion had no place when the juggler of situation needed to be slashed. The cold blooded always made the best killers when it applied to survival or an application of the final blow on a desired outcome. She also understood that the only boundary there was to power was a lack of imagination, and its only predator was greed.

As the journey continued with stopovers in Sestri Levante as well as Le Spezia, Angelique and Carl added Willy to the mix. He was very tentative to start, but Angelique's experience, patience and sensuality quickened his seduction. By the third evening together, the slaves and their master were thoroughly enjoying the games.

Meanwhile, Gabriel had fallen into the chasm of an intense love affair, and although Camille might have matched his physical intensity, her emotional involvement was more to do with lust. The only times they were apart was when Camille was with the other three copying the texts. At that time and in the deep nights, Gabriel was left alone to continue his compositions. He was indeed a man of great abilities and staggering paces. His appetite for physical delights was almost too much for the young girl, but she never complained and was the instigator on many occasions.

Gabriel's schedule did not seem to allow the man the proper amount of time to rest, and that is why, when the entourage entered Pisa, a ten day rest was Angelique's order before they would continue on to their final destination.

Pisa, being part of the Grand Duchy of Tuscany and under control of Leopold the Second, the Grand Duke, was a sanctuary for the whole group. Leopold was an acquaintance of Herr Scherer due to the fact that Scherer's family had business ties to the Hapsburg-Lorraine governments going back before the reign of Leopold's Great grandmother; Maria Theresa, Holy Roman Empress, Queen of Bohemia and Hungary, Archduchess of Austria and Duchess of Tuscany.

The Royal families of Europe all shared similar bloodlines. King Charles of England, King Charles of France, King Ludwig of Bavaria, Leopold of Tuscany as well as Viscount Gunner of Bavaria and Countess Caroline of Orleans and Normandy, Wilhelm and Camille's father and mother, were all related in one obscurity or fashion. These ties made the children's Great, Great, Grandfather Louis the Fourteenth, as well as distant cousins to King Charles and King Ferdinand of Spain, who were all associated with the House of Bourbon.

Angelique also had ties to royalty, as there were distant relatives associated to her well respected merchant family, who had been in business for the last three hundred years. Gabriel came from privilege also, due to merchant and political ties, but he also was a star among stars and so respected by Leopold that Pisa was virtually given to the group, symbolically.

Their lodgings in Pisa were among the finest possible. No expense was spared in the comforts availed to the party. The Tuscan army had taken full control of the protective nature to outer perimeters, while leaving Gabriel's guards in charge of the inner. Leopold gave his personal assurance that no one would interfere with their privacy while they were under his protection.

They were sealed inside an insulating cocoon that left them to do what they willed. Their promiscuities and creative beauties intermingled into the most colorful shades of grey ever witnessed. With every venture into depravity a new reach of genuine artistic possibilities was achieved. The true exercises of human nature were displayed in a symphonic style of instrumental variation of a free form explosion. They were left to discover every crevice of their spirits, talents, imaginations, and bodies, while their collaborators participated in the discoveries.

The sexual partnerships did not expand much, but everyone was aware of who the other individuals were involved with. The how's, where's, when's and why's also were understood and never interfered with. However, one small detail had begun to materialize. The fact that Gabriel and Angelique had ceased their personal intimate pleasures was also being recognized by the entire group. This was always the biggest crust when a sandwich such as this is being shared with others. Someone eventually would have to swallow it, and that meant someone else had to first chew it.

One evening during supper, the conversation took a splendid turn. The topic, of course, was the opera, when Camille suggested a different point of view about a particular event during one of the scenes.

"If you centered the dialogue on the observations of those in the crowd, it would be a fact that those observations may be obscured due to their particular positions," she started.

Angelique answered, "Of course their observations are obscured; that is why there is confusion among the voyeurs."

"Angelique is right, my dear, this is a drama, not a little girl's fairy story," Scherer arrogantly added while laughing through his handkerchief.

"Herr Scherer, I find your condescending tone and your ignorant manner toward me repulsive and sadly uncreative. You, Sir, must remember that I am a member of both the Bavarian Royal Family and the French Royal Family. Now, I understand the position my brother is in when it concerns you.

"However, I understand fully how close you neck is to the blade, and it is better for your personal safety to not forget the position you are in. Now most assuredly you are a gifted musician, but that does not mean my connections could not easily find a replacement for you, for my peace of mind as well as for the true immortal among us, Gabriel Mechant. "

"Camille!" cries Wilhelm, as both Gabriel and Angelique begin to laugh, while Carl is silenced by the threat.

While reaching over to gently touch Camille's angered face, Angelique offers, "My darling, how enjoyable it is to hear your coming of age speech." She stops to applaud as Gabriel claps his hands together simultaneously. "You are a young woman now, and with your execution of Carl's insensitivity you have taken charge of your throne. Well done, dear."

Camille smiles contently, but Angelique is not finished.

"Camille, I have a suggestion for you, and I insist that you ponder it closely before you ever again threaten any of us around this very intimate table. We five are… how should I say it to lessen the shock…?"

"Gently," Gabriel suggests.

"Barbarous," Carl arrogantly laughingly suggests, as Willy remains silent, while his sister seems utterly confused.

Just before she begins, Angelique has the room completely vacated by the service staff. Once that is accomplished, she reaches to touch Camille's face again and continues to stroke it while she talks.

"We five are interdependent, my sweet. Your Uncle was murdered, and you are very involved in the deceit. I am not sure which one of you is the murderer; you all have a vested interest, even you, Camille. Your affair with my husband and your continued escape from the hands of your parents makes you a full member of this band of semi-chaotic assassins.

"Now, correct me if I am wrong. Is it not me that has protected your precious bottom by allowing my betrothed, Monsieur Mechant, to handle the duty of its constant need of polishing? And am I not doing a similar service for your brother and his posterior? In fact, all of you are enjoying the paradise I have skillfully created. You are one of us, Camille, and your throne will only serve our purposes if you stop living the illusion and start enjoying the realities. Now from this point on, we five will cease pointing our arsenals at each other and keep them targeted on our enemies instead. Protect our necks first and that exercise will protect the opera."

Angelique raises her glass as the rest join her in this necessary pact of compliance.

"Camille, please continue with your thoughts about the crowd," Gabriel charmingly says, as it crumbles the tenseness in the room instantly.

"Yes, dear, please continue," Angelique agrees.

"Ahmm... yes... most certainly. I thought that if the dialogue included the observations from other vantage points, such as the terraces or roofs above the event, it could add a slight sense of clarity to the confusion of those on the street, which might add a delightful hint of contrast," Camille says, as she composes herself with the grace of a talented student in the arts of power and positioning. Her suggestion vaults her status in the writing of the opera to one whose opinions become sought after, and she soon starts to play the melodies on the harp while Willy continues to sing the librettos.

Also from that point, she and Angelique become true allies and friends. While they remain in Pisa, the two ladies visit the ancient sites and the art galleries that are abundant throughout the area. Their personal discussions include many issues and concerns; however, they are true companions in their love of the arts. Their passions and inquires are extraordinarily similar, as Camille glows under Angelique's tutelage.

One evening, while the males of the group are being entertained elsewhere, the two find themselves on Angelique's bed. There is no apprehension on Camille's part as Angelique treats the younger to her gifted attentions. After, the two rest in each other's arms as Angelique whispers as she caresses Camille, with her voice, lips and fingertips.

"My dear, the softness of your skin must be protected. Your breasts carry your nipples perfectly, as your slim waist and high mount of Venus are at the spring of their development. The contours of your back and the line that slides itself between them gently falls into your beautiful cheeks in the most sensuous of ways. You will be worshipped by multitudes, so choose your lovers well.

Keep your appetites slightly hungry and never gorge yourself. Remember, orgies are for amateurs, as the meals served in them are prepared for haste, not for lingering dining. One of the Ottoman Empresses once said, 'I wish I had more orifices to satisfy all my lovers.' I always enjoyed that saying until I entertained more than the idea alone. I can tell you from personal experience that being the table on which that type of banquet is served is not only exhausting but rather painful, although you are certain to experience it at least once. It's a matter of taste.

"You will grow weary of Gabriel's attention once the production finds its own momentum. At that time, London will be so bored of your uncle that all will return to normal. But you, my dear, have just started, and your newfound skills will take you to many of life's fulfillments. Until then, let us on occasion enjoy our games, their openings, middles, and climaxes."

"You are my Guardian Angel," Camille purrs as the two embrace and start anew.

The involvement that all had within the group was so incestuous that I felt any kind of moral judgment would not be able to disengage the entanglements. Who was to blame when all were being satisfied? Who was being used while all were using the others? The Bishop was slain for his moral judgment, and the young man in Nice was slain for his. But the young girl in the insane asylum was not asked her opinion, although her remains still sing in the Chorus sequences on stage in full view of us in the audience.

All of us before the stage can only see one victim in this whole circus of oddities. And it's her voice that sings the most haunting melody in this entire production. We in the audience are witnessing her villains' containments in the prisons of their needs and their insecurities. The cell has been fastened shut, and the five inside are completely unaware of how removed they are from the sweetest of life's joys. No matter how many exotic tastes and pleasures they feed on, it will never be better than the simplicity of the only true immortal, love itself.

By being removed from the Mediterranean, Pisa could only hope to hold the memories of the angel who was drying her wings on the sign in the sea. The choice to go inland meant that the gate to anywhere had been entered and a destination was in mind. 'What could have been was not meant to be,' started to be sung by the Chorus as dancers in reprisals confronted the corpses of the slain possibilities. The music was in contention while its tempo was counterbalanced as the caskets were filled with youthful hopes and other segments of the betrayed.

A shrouded procession frighteningly similar to the one we have been following from Provence was impaled by Christian crosses as they carried the corpses to the caskets. The betrayed were dropped in with disgusting thuds, as 'What could have been was not meant to be,' rang from every bell like a voice in the Chorus. A silhouette with a flame-like appearance began to cremate the filled caskets as the mourners turned into demons and gargoyles. The stage floated on a sea of blood as it was swept into the underworld, and the suffering souls kept crying, "This was not meant to be, this was not meant to be."

The caskets opened and the corpses climbed out, only to be slaughtered again in the orgies of hell. They were the freshest ones, thus becoming the brides of Lucifer. He gorged on their promiscuities and mistaken judgments as he had a taste for stale stoicisms and rancid complacency. The orgy and the orifices there were filled and punished by everything imaginable. The phallic symbols included the wands of nobility, position and pretentious arrogance. Those that wielded them in life were forced to feel the interiors of their victims no matter how degraded their orifices had become.

Lucifer's stomach stayed thin as his bowls discarded his meals instantly, while his manure was gathered by dead disciples of the self-righteous. The feces was spread on gardens that grew golden towers in the eyes of the greedy, and from the tops of these towers the manipulated were thrown into the hazes of dogmas and doctrines like sperm upon pearls in the wombs of the mothers of the gods in Hades. 'What could have been was not meant to be,' but there is no escaping what has become.

The days in Pisa ended with the procession turning east and deeper into Tuscany. They followed the Arno River as it pruned its way through a land that was the treasure case of the world's most precious art, magnificent history, and magical intellectualism; the priceless studio of Europe's, thus the Western World's enlightenment, the Renaissance. These lands were dedicated to the hierarchy of human abilities. All the philosophies of the world came here to be reconstructed into new temporal peaks and ways of seeing human existence as the beautiful graces they were always meant to be. The universe was changed here and no matter how that affected the ugly and the deficient, ignorance ceased to be an excuse.

The band we are traveling with contradicts the surroundings by their manners and actions. Defiling exquisiteness seems to be their preoccupation and their entrance into the heaven of enchanting beauties goes seemingly unnoticed by the guards at the gates. There must be something that we cannot see; a particular element that gives them access to the glories of this environment. Somewhere here they may find themselves in the valleys, mountains or countryside. They could be found in a passageway, in a painting, in a statue, in a poem or in a Cathedral. Perhaps, it is their artistic talents that may prove to be the source of their personal redemption.

There is another interesting possibility that is beginning to be expanded upon. It could be that through their lives we could find ourselves. I, for one, must admit to a lingering thought or two about what would become of me if I had the power they possessed. If I did not have to answer for my vulgarities, would they remain just below the surface or would they flow into the vineyards like an invading foreign substance? Would my sordid purity choke the roots of the vines or would the wine from these grapes have an added enchanting flavor?

I am certain that all in the audience have asked themselves what is the strongest of their possessions; their vulgarities, their denials, their truths or their beauties? And what would the wine be like if their contribution to it was more than a simple taste? The pleasures of living cannot be appreciated fully unless we are totally involved in our personal experiences. There is no true observation from the comfort of non-involvement. The audience must put their lives on the stage in order to appreciate the subtleties and the undertows of their own illusions. Never forget the wings must have been wet before the Angel on the sign in the sea spread them out to be dried.

As the procession flowed by the Arno, the curtain started to fall as the repetitive sounds found resolution in the themes of the pastoral forth comings that could be felt in the far away hills and their terraces. There were bells ringing in the distance and birds flying in the skies of March in the Grand Duchy of Tuscany, as we in the audience understood that this opera was walking towards its 'Epiphany in the New Enlightenment'.

FLOWER

The fragrant petals float from the bloom of the full moon through openings in the courtyards and alleys as the shadows are disassembled by reddish ambers that hum beneath the torched flames. The tri-toned light kisses the smoothed cobblestones of the streets and walkways that move between the beds of magnificence, elegance and splendor.

The romantic shower of the rainbow petals in their reds, yellows, blues and others sail from the skies past the steeples, towers and tiled rooftops, landing on the ground with gentle swoops. They start to dance with the soft notes in the breezes that are cast from the vibrating strings of troubadours, minstrels, and the lines that hang in the air from the high choruses.

Statues frozen in their depictions are covered with dancing petals as the fragrance embeds them by filling the cracks between the interpretations. Monumental symbolism is led by the expressions of the blooming moon as nature guides this studio of human beauty. The fullness of the pantries, the passions and the paramounts, are strokes from the same artistic instrument that speaks of the extravagance of life through the belief in the clear simplicities found in the here's and now's.

The here's and now's have our fragrances embedded in the towers and the cobblestones of our moonlit extravagance, though we feel hungry and parched from our travels in our circular journeys. We lack a fullness of artistic expression as we search for the words that could make it all understandable. We fail to see the difference between our lives and surrealism. In art, we find the reach between our desires and clarity. Art is the savior but we refuse to nourish ourselves at leisure.

Art at its finest can minimize the centuries, reassemble the years, and prolong the seconds. Art within its infinity can give you power to reach past the paradises of the heavens. Art is the knowledge of your soul, its reactions and their splendors. Art can cure your senses by teaching your eyes to see, your ears to listen, and your heart to feel. Art is the glorious moon that shines through every human condition. Art is the only true vision of reality. Art is beauty, and that can only mean that surrealism is a mere splinter of life. Life's mission is to live for beauty and when this has been understood, the Renaissance of the personal spirit has begun.

We survive in surreal paintings, operas, music, and poems. Like the petals, we see ourselves slide from one work to another. We try to understand it all as we enter another doorway that has little to do with the space before. We swim in surreal environments believing we are in control, while we are still not sure of what or who we are. We search the images of art for our personal descriptions of the roles we are playing in our very lives. We are creatures of beauty that have creative powers as we allow ourselves to float in surreal images that are the creations of others.

The unification of surrealism and beauty creates a harmony that quells the solo sigh. It creates on metaphorical canvases with pluralistic images of the harmony's children; the opera, the painting, the symphony and the dance. The accompanying images are their children's lovers; the author, the painter, the composer and the choreographer.

Simplistic harmonies are perfectly matched to again create on metaphorical canvases with pluralistic images. Art is removed from heavens and hells; for art is the mirror of the supposed opposites, and in these mirrors we see the actors, the characters, the instrumentalists, and the dancers as they live their dreams by performing in balance the solos of their hearts in perfect polyphony with others, throughout their lives.

Surrealistic beauty is an intellectual intercourse that is the result of the high inspiration. God's canvas is full of these inspirations but art creates the realities. The canvas of God has been painted over by surrealism again and again and again. So art has become the definer to those who sit and watch the performances. Surrealism is controlled if the character knows where it sits, either in the creator's box, on the stage or in the audience. Art is left on its own to be defined, though it will always remain a mirror.

Our personal artistic endeavor surrounds us in the tranquility of personal acceptance and understanding. We start to notice the forgers on God's canvas as well as the forgers on ours. We finally realize that the pure beauty in our art's reflection is the internal image of the masterpiece that is within us. We are all works of art by one of the greatest masters. We, too, can be great if we understand artistic simplicity; a great work of art simply understands itself.

We must be the creators of our canvases, our pages, or our stages. We must take our surreal lives and join them with our internal beauties. We must produce the art we were meant to. Life is for the creation of beauty. We must add our souls to existence, for existence is the artistic treasure house. Art is the reflection, thus magnifier of all that is human. We will create the new horizons as our personal Renaissance will contribute to the existence and its eternal enlightenment.

The scene has opened in the most glorious of ways, as this was the trumpet's repertoire while dancers paraded with the entourage as it passed the Palazzo Pitti. The costumes were reminiscent of a medieval fair where pole dances and minstrels and Choruses sang as children ran alongside the whole event. Down the road and onto the Ponte Vecchio, the carnival proceeded while the Arno River swam underneath. The red roofs of the familiar tiles held high the Brunelleschi architectural masterpiece, the Duomo Santa Maria del Fiore Cathedral, as the bells chimed their approval of the arrival of these jewels of art and their imaginations that rejoiced that they would be let loose on the extravagance of Florence.

They had been met earlier by representatives of the Duke as well as a member of the prestigious Corsini family, who had graciously closed the Galleria in the Palazzo Corsini so the palace could be used by the contingent for their comforts, and for the completion of the opera. An opera based on a particular event in this city that was the center of the Renaissance. The Palazzo Corsini was entered quickly, for its location was only three hundred yards from the bridge on the north side of the Arno.

The celebrations continued inside the courtyard as well as on the Lugarno Corsini, with flag tossing, drums and an array of other entertainments, as the symphony countered with a medley of Verdi,

Puccini, Rossini, and Vivaldi. The stage glowed with the joys of artistic expression and their intoxicating wines, spirits as well as their other addictive illusionary realities.

We in the audience were captured entirely by this depiction of the artistic splendor that dwelled in the interiors of the five we had been following. The contradictions were striking when compared to the lustful gluttony they had already exposed us to. The blacks and whites of these pretentious characters were so opposite that the connective tissue between these polar regions was the unclarified obscurity. How could such diversity survive in a single individual? And what were the possibilities that five of them in different stages of development could find one another?

The layers of this opera were so entangled that speculation ceased to be attempted by most because of the numbing effect it had on the mind. Wisdom and knowledge would be given only to those that continued to sample all of its variations and their resulting new anthems. The theme that spawned these variations could only be described as human expanse. That internal universe that was the biggest fear, but sadly, the last explored.

These people believed in only one god other than themselves, this god of art was calculation. Angelique was the master and the rest were her students, even Mechant and Scherer had been taught the lessons of station. The children were being schooled in the finery of what was useful and what was not. Their charms made them powerful because lust must feast and these lessons were extremely important for their futures.

The art of calculation was the product of its master, logic. Logic is reason, logistics is calculation. How to get what you want was the layman's way of describing this, without doubt a more logical way of description, for it was simplicity. The five were all students of the process after being well secured by the attainments of their desires. However, every new experience grew new teeth or made the older ones sharper.

Gabriel's blade was an example of how mastery was attained. Its skills came from the magic found in the hand that held it. This instrument had been practiced in the most intensive of ways. Exams for the hand were so extreme that failure meant death. All had to be calculated and all chance had to be sidelined. There was no room for beginner's luck, so every possibility had to be the product of the master's control. Life depended upon it, but glory meant more than life, for it was the desired trophy. Anyone that did not believe that had no hope to escape the exercise intact.

Glory at the moment it is conceived is the most addictive of the illusionary realities. It gives all to the victorious and nothing to the slain. Gabriel's blade as well as his pen drew his powers in the skies above the heaven, for it was not promised it existed. It could be felt, it could be seen, and it could be idealized. Gabriel Mechant was a walking, breathing God, and he knew his power, and he knew it was secured and protected by his wife's mastery in the art of calculation.

Angelique was so masterful that she knew Gabriel's drunken ugliness could be curtailed if he was satisfied. That was why she cultivated the relationship he had with Camille. He would be kept quiet, while inspired to write the excellence that had been exploding in the imaginations of the others in the group. Her attention towards Carl, Wilhelm and Camille was another significant calculation, as it kept them in her scope on the most revealing of levels, sexual intimacy. That tethered them to her judgments, which could be levied due her persuasive talents that were the result of her carnal craftsmanship.

She had all of them in her web as they all believed they could come and go at will. But they never left, because all of their whims were satisfied in the most gratifying of manners. The pleasures of life rained upon them as the opera advanced. Angelique was the producer, and she had her production team productively happy and joyfully fulfilled.

From the windows in their studio on the top floor of the Palazzo Corsini, the Pitti Palace and Giardino di Boboli could be seen on the other side of the Arno, as it climbed the hill to the Piazzale Michelangelo. The air was full of Tuscan radiance as the pigeons of shaded tones were scattered in the winds of the Florentine bustle that passed the windows on the street before them.

All was stately in the Corsini Palace that was built in the 16th century style, with elements of the Baroque period which included a large spiral staircase. The private art collection was funded by the Corsini family, who were related to Pope Clement the 12th. The whole environment was the secret springs of the Renaissance and its nourishing waters that excited their abundant imaginations.

The power that the five had, continued to surround them with protection and privilege, as their connections were seemingly boundless. They rested in this accustomed opulence for a few days before they continued in earnest with their project, but during those days their contentment was enriched and enhanced by the enlightenments of those that constructed this paradise of inspiration, so affectionately referred to as, the Flower.

Their families made large deposits in the banking institutions that were waiting for them and of course the children's father, the Viscount, had the funds for the opera also in place. Carl and Gabriel had assets available, but the quantity of finances the five possessed in Florence ensured the continuation of the extreme luxury that they enjoyed.

Another power was bestowed on the children. Wilhelm and Camille, who were considered a Baron and Baroness in England, were now under the recognized titles of Count and Countess in Florence. These titles granted them more powers than they had ever enjoyed and were the result of their mother's peerage; that was the reason for the change. When Wilhelm's birthday arrived within a month, the title would give him power over his father's orders, in England as well as France. Her brother's position would shield Camille from having to return to England and the stagnating life she had grown to despise. Leopold, the Grand-Duke, personally assured Camille that her titles would be acknowledged as long as she remained in Florence, even though she was only fifteen. Both were formally introduced as the Count Wilhelm and Countess Camille of

Orleans and Normandy, the House of Bourbon, Baron and Baroness of Bavaria and the United Kingdom.

Angelique and Camille enjoyed their excursions to the galleries and museums, which were missions of research for Gabriel's pen and for their personal enjoyments. Scherer and Wilhelm were busy with the orchestrations as the opera was in the final stages of writing. It was the middle of March 1831, and Angelique along with Camille still collaborated with Carl and Willy in the coupling of the music and libretto, while the artisan still entertained Carl and the young man in Carl's bedchambers. Camille was also privileged with the feel of the older woman's body and experiences, while the Contessa remained the favorite on Gabriel's menu.

He was beginning to fence competitively against the other members in the ranks of the privileged while spending more time with them entertaining himself away from the others in the Corsini Palace. His involvement in the opera was closing as he had supplied most of the required material. He was waiting for Carl, who had fallen behind. Angelique encouraged him, making sure that a tone of normality remained intact so her control was refortified.

One afternoon, Leopold escorted Angelique and Camille through the Palazzo and Galleria degli Uffizi and the Vasari Corridor that winded itself over the Ponte Vecchio to the Palazzo Pitti. Not only was the art exquisite, but the Corridor had hundreds of self-portraits of various artists including Raphael. The three were all students as well as patrons of the arts and sciences, but the Contessa's enthusiasm was not only delightful, it was contagiously charming. Leopold so thoroughly enjoyed his time with the ladies that he invited their whole group for an evening of dining and entertainment at the Palazzo Vecchio.

Camille was an anxious student, as Angelique's teaching was making the young and powerful girl a staunch ally. The two were welcomed with a high degree of respect not only because of the position of the Contessa but also the wit and charm of Madame Beauvie, who had always been considered a fine addition to the engagements of nobility throughout Europe. The two were a formidable pair, as they both possessed an enchanting joy for life and an appreciation for art that few could match.

Their conversational skills were handsomely enhanced when the two were in the company of the triumphant Gabriel Mechant. The Palazzo Vecchio and the court of the Grand Duke were thoroughly entertained by the trio and by Wilhelm's voice in tandem with the petite tunes of Herr Scherer. Scherer obviously did not shine as brilliantly when compared to the abilities of the other four, but his manner of pretentiousness held him fast to his title as the composer of the coming theatrical masterpiece all had started to anticipate.

When the five left the Palace that evening, Gabriel shared one carriage with Angelique while the other three shared another. Gabriel's tongue was feeling its familiar sharpness when he asked his wife in a nonchalant fashion, "I appreciate the fact that you have taken an interest in the body of my Camille, it has increased her stamina in the most becoming of ways."

"Hers as well as my appetites are very fulfilled in these present times, husband. I am sure that you are tranquil also?"

"Yes, thank you. How are your marathons with the Germanics? Is Scherer too rough, or have you a new appreciation for the ancient art of sex while bridled?"

"You are aware of his tastes?"

"Of course. We have been prowling together now and then for years; he likes to maintain that Bavarian attitude when it comes to the passion of power and pain. When he has consumed too much of the liquids he has a nasty habit of twisting the reigns too tightly, but Willy should be able to prevent that from happening to you."

"Gabriel, how charming, you are slyly warning me. You should be rewarded for your worry for your protector. Perhaps, a casual favor is in order."

"More tranquility? Spoil me, Angel," he accepts and she laughs while sliding her hand into his pants as she lowers her head to quicken the access. In the other carriage, the conversation is engaged in an entirely different mood.

"What an enchanting event," Camille begins.

"Sister, we are all in the same fantasy," Willy agrees, as from the other side Scherer with his handkerchief covering his mouth insists,

"This is no fantasy, children, this is the way your lives will remain. Each of you can do what you will, but I warn you not to become complacent until the opera has been brought to life. It will add a luster to your enjoyments because of your involvements. You, Willy, will begin your personal career with this triumph. We must finish the orchestrations quickly."

"Maestro, I am working as fast as I can. I promise you that they will be completed."

"Wilhelm, I had no idea that you were writing the orchestrations, I thought you were only aiding Herr Scherer."

"He is, Contessa; his work is entirely under my direction. Is that so Willy?" Scherer asks as he stares at the young Count.

"Yes… Camille… that is the way it is," Wilhelm answered in the most resigning of ways. Camille looked back and forth at the pair and then began to change the subject in the most tactful way possibly. The switch in tempo would have made both Angelique and Gabriel proud of their apprentice.

The display upon the stage echoed throughout the theater. We in the audience were becoming suspicious of the composer's abilities. Without hesitation we felt his melodies were of songs of glory, however it was apparent that his technical skills were lacking. There was assurance that the opera would be completed, yet the lingering questions remained unanswered.

The murder of the bishop was the biggest complaint for the reason that it had conveniently not entered into the strides of the continuance. The audience felt that this subject must be dealt with in a satisfying way. The undercurrent that the killer of the Grand-Uncle was among the five encouraged us to feel it was the wolf at the heels. But I personally never forgot that all of them were guilty of the cover up, and thus, all were accomplices in the murder.

I also understood that these times did not have much room for the rights of the majority. Death was common and poverty was rampant. The social structure kept most in the ranks of the unprivileged and value was placed on material things, not in the possibilities that could be found in an individual, unless of course those possibilities could be obviously noticed. Gabriel's skill with his foil was a prime example. His skill was sharpened in the hearts of the ones he had killed. His skill was far more appreciated than the lives that were sacrificed in order to gain it.

These startling comparisons with the times in which I first viewed this opera left a chill in me, for sadly, these privileges were still very much in place. Murder was on a massive scale and apathy towards the underprivileged was the sickness of the times. I suddenly felt I was witnessing an event that was taking place in the exact moment that the portrayal of this opera, placed in 1831, was. My dilemma became; had all remained the same through the ages and was time only repeating?

The intriguing details of these five ingredients blended into a mirage of colorful rainbows that jaggedly cut the darkness of their hearts and motives. The blood from these incisions tarnished every garment no matter who the fashion was covering. All were seduced by their power of nobility, artistic mastery and cascading charms. All were affected by the tempting nectar that lay a reach away from their fragrant blooms in their garden of brilliance that was the result of what was always the most adored illusionary grandeur.

The stage began to pulse as instruments of a chordophone group in a dactylic rhythmic mode began to radiate for the ballerinas starting in the fifth position. The dancers started to run in a ribbon-like wave that was joined by four more groups of dancers from behind the curtains, each with a waving ribbon of different colors. The dancers weaved the ribbons in and out of the twenty five different combinations. The five principle characters of this opera in the color of their particular ribbon in unison walked to the middle of the stage singing a 6/8 melody in perfect six part harmony.

They began to shift themselves in tandem to the color combinations of the ribbons and the dancers. The Chorus began to drone the rhythmic pattern in a haunting cluster of sounds. These sounds consisted of laughter, cries, screams, bellows, coos, pains and sighs. The conglomerate of sensual offerings was almost too much to endure, though the kaleidoscope was magnificent in its variety and its execution as the scene was in constant vibration due to the involvements within the complexities of the five.

The audience was again awoken from the deep sleep of perceived judgments based on incomplete speculations. The stage dared us to continue with the journey we had been following all along only to discover that aspects of ourselves were beginning to be understood by our interior testimonies. The blends, that these five where capable of creating, frighteningly resembled parts of ourselves that were conveniently hidden by the master stroke of apathetic denial with its blinding style. The stage had room for our shades of characters no matter how much we believed them to be of the most virginal whites. We all have deep separations between our delights and our delinquencies, but my, how both can satisfy the orifice in the middle.

As the dance ended, Camille and Angelique were left in front of Botticelli's 'Primavera;' the two were cast in the artistic spell of a true master of the Renaissance. Out of the painting, Venus appeared at center stage as her son Cupid floated above her head. Mercury was to the far left, while on the right, the metamorphosis of the nymph Chloris was being displayed. After she was raped by Zephyr, the god of the wind, she became Flora, the goddess of scattering flowers. The contradictions of the masterpiece are first thought of as a celebration of spring; however, it is much deeper than that.

The philosophical view of the scene is from an image found in classic literature. Venus plays the virgin as she gestures an invitation to the idealism of love and beauty. Mercury chases away the aspect of melancholies that were the fluttering passions of the passing winter, leaving spring to once again contend with the conflict of lust and chastity. The ladies enjoyed the power of women that so motivated men into the belief that femininity had the scalding effect of creating myths, legends and philosophies that were the basis of so many distortions.

"A woman fools herself if she believes she can love a man who can be tamed. The wild and unbridled hold more excitement than the partially gelded maidens that draw the family carriage with such unfailing consistency," Angelique whispers to Camille as the younger laughs in agreement.

"The muscular plow horse that tends the field is the biggest fool in the stable, for it has been tamed by its stoic nature that burdens it with the fixation of forever proving itself. It grunts, it beads with perspiration while it toils the soil in the field that never changes its perspective or its habits."

Again Camille laughs as Angelique continues with her observations.

"Ride the wild one, and you will feel life being pumped into yourself with such power that you will worship god for the heaven of being made a woman. Chastity can always be reinvented, but lust is one of the primal purities; a purity that will always be noticed by the instantaneous whetting of the carnal appetites."

"Angelique, do your really believe that all men are motivated by the idealism of love never ending?" Camille asks.

"Of course I do, Cherie. The poor fools forget another of the primal purities, time forever moves. That purity means that all must end; a logic that suggests that a majority of idealisms have very short life spans."

"Then how can you and your husband remain together?"

"We are not ignorant to our personal natures. He will always be wild and that still whets my appetites. We are both creatures of lust, and you are just like us, are you not?" Angelique purrs to Camille.

"Of course I am. I can hardly think of any other way of living. Life must be hell for the passionless. At this very moment Botticelli seduces me through his talent for imagery and the attention he must posses for the details of his craft. All of these abilities speak of the magnificent lust he could subject me to in his studio."

"Would you share him with me?"

"Of course I would, Angelique, I am not a barbarian."

The two again laughed as they continued through the gallery. Both enjoyed the intrigue of the stories behind the works. How the artists were motivated by the inspiration to spend so much of themselves on their expressions and views of theirs and others' lives. Through their art, a piece of themselves could be seen vividly by those sophisticated enough to see within the soul of another. They believed that art was the naked truth, honesty well worth their passions and involvements, and the ladies understood how the creative feminine would wither without the masculine inspiration; the greatest treasure, if one internally possessed both in high abundance.

The art of Florence became the demanding passion of the two ladies. Every corner had a fresco to be discovered, every alleyway led to a new artistic viewpoint that fitted into the panoramic scene in their evolving appreciations. Da Vinci and the others at the highest points of creativity constantly hummed their incredible melodies as this portion of the performance began to take a swim into the deepest parts of the surrealistic galleries of the celestial skies.

The skills were still being presented in the Florence of this time that had a hold of its Renaissance beginnings with one hand, while its outstretched arm was trying to gain the future. The present point, though balanced between the two, was continually fed from the recipes of the divine and the saints of tomorrow, who held each other at the points of the present. The older guiding the younger as its possibilities whispered youth in return. A surrealistic exercise in which all three, the past, the future and the now make love to each other infinitely.

Love, the immortal, cannot be reinvented, only rediscovered. The intercourse is merely variation, not the genesis. The young discover the feeling for the first time, but understanding the meaning is left to the old who move well past the discovery and into the binding effects. Youthful attentions fail within youthful attention spans, while the patience of the old restores the excitement with skillful expertise. The body that feels the excitement prolongs the experience with youthful stamina that was left on the floor in a past prematurity.

The opera within the womb of the five held promise of metaphoric genius, although its parents had been raped by their own selves. Rape, however, in classic literature turned Chloris into Flora; metaphorical brilliance that speaks of dirt being transformed into paradise. Dirt is dormant until it is seeded, as a human is dormant until life has turned the insides out. The seed is planted by the exterior; however, the paradise will be sterile until the interior has been raped by itself. Personal transformation is the metaphoric experience of personal salvation, the rebirth of the mortal into the god that was always within. The age of the god is eternal, while the age of mortal will always remain unspecific because of its failure to be defined by itself.

The brilliance that surrounded the five served the brilliance within, and that was the promise of the collaboration. Surrealism was the broth in the pot as art was the chief. Life was the fuel that heated both with its fire that only the masters could control. Florence was the marketplace of delicacies that could feed the hungers of the enlightened, for art in its mastery is the shop of endless conceptions and their forever contrasts. The five proved that they too understood that discipline was the herb in the foundation of anything. They came to Florence to create a paradise, and no matter what they feasted on along the way, their duty to the coming child was of the certainty that it would not be malnourished.

Perhaps, this child was their salvation, their personal Christ. It was perhaps the product of chevalier promiscuity, but that was the foundation of all that ever wandered through the jungles of life. Sin is just another metaphor and salvation is just another climax, while life heats all the possibilities in one pot of formulations and misguided righteousness. Even the pure get cold, and life's variations to some are only best served in the darkness of their denials. But indeed they eat too, while only fools believe that they were never hungry. The only impossibilities are those found in the denial of human needs and characters. It is impossible to never hunger, as it is impossible to hide from one's own denial. The five may be unlikable, but they are without doubt, human.

The opera was in its final stages of composition, and rehearsals would soon be beginning. Gabriel was beginning to hover over the proceedings with what seemed to be a new-found interest. Camille was by his side as Angelique was also closely watching, while Scherer was interviewing various artists of different disciplines until it was obvious that the task of completing the music, conducting, and the duties of overseeing the production was far too much for Scherer to attempt all at once. Gabriel and Angelique took the reins of the production and handed them to a gentleman that was well versed at the helms of administration.

A defrocked Dominican Monk named Carlo Giorgio gladly became the production manager, and soon the rehearsals were running with smoothness similar to the seductive charm of Angelique herself. Scherer began to shine with the baton in his hand, for he had always been considered a star of the conductor's podium. Wilhelm was putting the final touches to Scherer's orchestrations, while also being pushed by Carlo to sing the part of one of the main characters, a stroke of theatrical genius when you considered how glorious his voice was, along with the fact it was a rarity that a Royal performed on an operatic stage, a true marketing brilliance.

Carlo took control of every aspect of the production, from the set design to the matters of putting constraints on how the five participated. Soon Angelique had coerced her way into the position of assistant production manager and was always at Carlo's side at rehearsals. She was enhanced by the ex-monk's knowledge of house of art that went well beyond the performing wing of the subject. Camille's place at the side of Angelique in the museums and Galleries was instantaneously filled by the scholar, leaving the young Contessa in the continuous escort of Monsieur Mechant.

At rehearsals, Camille would sit next to Gabriel in the front rows of the theater, as the other three would remain on stage throughout the sessions. Carlo would move from end to end of the theater talking to various people about the long list of necessities, often consulting with his assistant who would be constantly working on the transference of the librettos to the main singers and the Chorus, making sure their lines were learned with perfection. Scherer would embrace her continually because of the expertise she was displaying in the matters of performance readiness.

Eventually Camille found herself alone in the front rows as Gabriel was beginning to aid the young female chorus members in the learning of their words, with Angelique close by making sure the proceedings would remain fixed to the intention of prolonged success. One morning in the theater, Camille sat alone in the back row crying while no one paid attention to the fallen consort of the married couple. Angelique now had Carlo, while Gabriel was working closely with the young girls in the production. Camille watched the fox in the chicken house from her empty nest and sobbed to herself, believing that she was finally graduating from the lessons she had been given by the professors of indulgence. She was uncertain, as all students are, of what to do next after the classroom doors have been shut behind them. Being prepared for life is always easier than actually living it. Theory is extremely simple when compared to the practice and its obvious exhaustions.

That particular night when Gabriel made his predictable entrance into her bedchambers, he was not greeted in the familiar submissive manner he had so skillfully nurtured. Instead, Camille's face was well dampened by her tears that were the result of her confusion.

"What is troubling you, my sweet?" Gabriel asked in obvious sincerity.

She tried to explain, but her sobs interrupted her words to the extent that they flew from her mouth with deformed wings unable to be coherent to the ears of her lover. She sat in bed like a lost child so reminiscent of the frail flower she once was before she saw Gabriel in the gazebo for the first time.

He looked at her with an astonishment that was the result of witnessing her for what she truly was; a lost child thrust into an orgy where desires are masked as needs, and fulfillments remain unsatisfying. He thought of himself with an understood disgust that he would place this innocent on a banquet table where all will eventually sample until the dish became poisonous in order to protect what little was left.

He embraced her in a way that he had never done before, and she felt a warmth in him that was also never before present. He looked at her with an adoring passion and said calmly,

"I love you, Camille, and I give you my word that I will never again disgrace you."

The two lay beside each other throughout the night. He caressed her gently and never attempted anything more than a close embrace with calming words. It was the first time he had ever made love to her with his whole being, and her response came in a form of heavily needed assurance. She whispered to him, "I love you, too." And with that, they became a truly consummated couple. They were inseparable from that night on, though while in public they maintained proper appearance in order to not jeopardize the opera or her perceived innocence.

As things were following along with ease because of Carlo Giorgio's magnified attention to the tiniest of details, the five had their mutual futures in sight when it came to what success would do for their lives. Scherer and Wilhelm were within the gates of heaven as they were left to summon the voices of the coming rapture. The singers were well experienced in performance, oratories and the subtle expressions that could captivate the audience. Every note was examined while every word became coherent; the rehearsals were being shaped into the illusion that was only understood in the minds of its creators.

The superb orchestra was also full of virtuosity with the soloists being stars of their various instruments. This was the wind that would carry the words of the story line in the most poetic of skies that would engulf any who had the opportunity to be able to witness the unfolding.

The full dress rehearsals were only two weeks away when Carlo announced to the cast that Milan's Teatro Alla Scala would be hosting the opening in the third week of July on the 22nd, exactly nine weeks away. All were overjoyed at the prospect of the glory of La Scala and the privileges that would follow the careers of all involved. The move to Milan would begin in earnest on June the 4th after the open performance and last of the dress rehearsals, in the last week of May.

Although the time was short, Carlo and Angelique were always discussing the fineries of Italian Art. She was overwhelmed by his knowledge and cultured charm, as she eased her sexual intimacies with Carl and Willy. Carlo became the sixth in their party, although he was never made fully aware of what that meant. He thoroughly enjoyed the luxury that was granted to him, and that was very apparent when the Grand Duke hosted the masked Grand Ball of Spring on May 20th. Among those in attendance would be two surprises from London, the Viscount himself and Inspector Peal of the newly formed Scotland Yard. We must not forget the Bishop, must we?

Peal and the father of the children would have been in Florence for over a week by the time of the Ball. Viscount Gunner had been convinced by the inspector that Wilhelm and Camille had information concerning the Bishop's disappearance, while also believing the children's companions were somehow responsible. Proof, however, could not be found in the otherwise learned speculation. Leopold kept their presence secret, as he was assured of a front seat at the surprise unveiling of the Viscount when he removed his mask in the presence of his children.

There was, of course, a diplomacy that needed to be followed due to the fact that Wilhelm and Camille were considered a Count and a Contessa in Tuscany, and that meant the father would be obligated to his host, the Grand Duke, to remain subordinate to the laws of Florence, and for that matter, the Hapsburgs and their Rule over the region. The King of England was concerned about any disruption to political ties the government of England was trying to maintain. He was convinced, though against his better judgment, to allow Peal to accompany his distant cousin, in order to gain evidence that would finally put the Bishop out of the focus of the Pope and the French.

Among the aristocrats of Europe, the issue of the Bishop had become the news of yesterday, even though Jonathan Broadfoot had not let the subject disappear from the pages of The London Times. In fact, the newspaper man intended to come to Florence after he received information that Peal had gone there. All this had escaped the attentions of Scherer's eyes and ears in London, so all was set for the excitement of the innuendoes.

"Carlo, do you feel the mastery of the Renaissance can still be fully appreciated today, and how about the years from now?" Angelique asks the authority one evening while the two amble alone in the Corridoio Vasariano, with the sun setting over the bridges of Florence as they span the Arno.

"Madame Beauvie, I fear the Renaissance will slowly slip into the inkwells of those that will write about the treasures, as the treasures themselves dissolve like salt in the passing streams of time. They will become third and then distant parties who will be spoken of when the appreciative find time between the courses of other meals the history of art prepares.

"The world is wide, but not becoming wiser to the past, and the wisdoms that remain perfectly noticeable to the eyes that have learned to see the sparkles in skies of the mundane times that the obscurities of every new moment define as a difference. There will be fewer and fewer that see the intellectual lessons in the piece of pottery or melody. Art will continue to need its translators, and soon the translations will become the lessons of the first intellectualism. Truth is distorted, while pure art will become only noticed in the spirits of the need to be moved in the geniuses.

The Renaissance will be replaced by future enlightenments over and over again, because every enlightenment there has ever been could never make the entirety of humanity see. Darkness to most is a sanctuary, and that will always remain the failure of even the most glorious of all the Renaissances. For within the refuge of darkness, those there will not have to ever contend with the most frightening of all their personal horrors, their own selves. The face they see in the mirror is the only face that remains nameless, and that is why possibilities seem like mortal sins to them. Enlightenment is better left to the giants who will always believe there is something that can found beyond what they have already."

"The ultimate paradox," Angelique adds.

As the two continued to discuss the difficulties faced by the results of artistic and intellectual brilliance, the corridor suddenly was crowded by all of the self-portraits that came instantly to life. The likes of Michelangelo, Beccafumi, Carracci, Salvator Rosa, Rubens, Raphael, Durer, Domenichino, Ricci, Cosimo de Medici, began to mingle with guests such as Da Vinci, Machiavelli, Dante, Caravaggio, as well as other peers from the avenues of arts and sciences in the history of Renaissance intellectualisms and masteries. The two laughed, cried and expressed all of the variations of emotions, as they relished the experience of being with the creative masters.

This corridor of magnificence vibrated in the air over the Arno with warm fragrant breezes of stunning understanding that were fashioned in the musical tones of the most brilliant of voices, in a chorus so coherent that all the magical secrets were discussed in a constant flow of glorious extravagance. The hum of excellence was heard as a soft kiss to the ears, as none felt hurried or inhibited. The words were softly spoken, while being sung by the light that cascaded through the windows.

They held each other with a perfection of understanding of the deep seeded desire that all had inside; that longing to be heard by a world so insane that sanity itself becomes a dough so flexible that it could be made into anything the believer wished. These creative gods had all been shackled in their lives by this material of compliance, as all understood the failure of humanity was its allegiance to nonsensical rules and rigidness.

They all had mourning in their souls for their metaphorical children that were either miscarried, aborted, or murdered at birth for the crimes of truth they would have committed had they lived. All of these creators found life was full of obscurity and desire, for that was the reason most of them went through their lives starving for the true nourishment of artistic freedom; just to be left alone and grow every appendage possible, instead of being pruned back by the gardeners of their times.

A quick dance step began to be played as its echo filtered through the corridor. All started to move in various forms of jigs, waltzes, and other steps, familiar or not. The air was full of joyous expression that could only exist in this purgatory between the heavens and hells that were the fictitious fixations of those that refused to live their lives in the glories of themselves. There was no one in the audience who would dare to define this magical display as a state of confusion or a peak of genius. It was and it will be forever in our visions of what mastery means; the simplicity of loving one's own's life, and the ability to live in its accepted beauty.

The stage passed vibrancy into our conceptions of what life was. There was a connection to the elements of what was being exposed in the performance. The group of five was full of contrasts in their personalities. They were corrupted by their power, though their fixations on creative outreaches held redemption in their futures. Their minds came to life in all of their creative deformities, and their sexual exploits were beginning to seem like innocent consuming at a very popular carnal bakery.

They were not passionless creatures; on the contrary, they were full of expressions that entertained more than their own wills. Their perversions seemed innocent for the times; although, I am sure there are those among us that would have hanged them long ago. But being the judge and executioner is not for the faint. It requires a certainty that the sentence passed has a shade of sanctimony in its structure, and who among us would feel righteous in the slaying of mere characters from the mind of an imaginative? How can we love the magic if we then kill the magician?

Florence grew rich in the Tuscan garden. A place where the food, wine, and laughter had the garnish of intellectualism in its art, song and romances. A place that rarely cowered before the sword of ignorant repression and unbreathable beliefs. We all were moved by the highlights of humanity that were displayed so graciously on the stage before us. All had purpose, all held inspiration, and all were glad to grow into magnificence. Every member of the audience felt a lightness that was due to the metaphoric shedding of the outer layer of skin that was hardened by our misconception of ourselves.

This vibration that was being mutually felt suddenly exploded as 'The Symphony of Spring' could be heard, along with the full chorus in unison. Soon, the harmonies held fluorescent colors to them as the whole theater became an ever changing scene in a kaleidoscope of senses. Our ears were caressed with words that stood tall on music of disbelief, as fragrances from the Giardino di Boboli paraded through our noses. The tastes of living in its many courses filled our palates past the rims and overflowed into our souls. The warmth of the moment brought a new awareness to the innocent but stale virginity of the feelings our body had fooled us with until this moment. And our eyes were softened by the sights of the heavens that grow abundant on the trees in the groves of paradise.

As the curtain fell, all in this audience had been shocked into acknowledging the occurrence of the seeing parts of themselves in the performance. I felt that I had been dissected from my opinions that had been forged in the stubborn granite of my youth, as those opinions started melding with circumstances that came long after that first mold. Was growth possible in a seat of an imaginary theater? Or is all imaginary in those that surround me in this opera I call my life?

I can no longer shield myself with my tattered understandings and their constant hallucinations of my purities or my sins. They all try to hold me in a definition of myself that cannot change, due to its crippled intention to hold onto its canes and crutches found in their lies of who I truly am. I have learned that my deathbed will introduce me to the being I will finally become, and that means that all I travel through until that moment will be only the pasts that I have chosen to remember or forget. Tomorrow will pass, so my will is to experience it to the fullest, for it may grant my powers the understanding they need in order to drink the nectars from the heavens that grow on the trees in the groves of paradise.

MASK

The curtain rose as the silence was broken by the soul of the dead girl in the cellar of the insane asylum, as she began to speak in a darkness shadowed by a window up above.

"A window opened to the kindness outside as the winter in here blows gales of emotion through the tattered sails on my flesh. I see the horizon clearly in what appears to resemble a pore on the face of my often used expression. The one that remained fastened to my hatred of all of my dreams that floated in my heart that I have bolted shut with the rust of my failures. My pains cling to me as I am their savior from the gales that try to blow out their flames that burn away my strength. All I do is squint to see the light in a pore that begins to fill with dirt in an oily substance. Soon the pore is a reservoir of generated pus from another boil of an old favorite fear. The fear of losing an expression and understanding of all the failures I will not ever make if I remain here in the dark.

"There will be no more failures, for I will no longer attempt to find the doors in my denial that will lead to some distant spring. I will not grow, thus, I refuse to be judged by those that lack the fear to remain conservatively in place. I have no waking dreams, for I never sleep on this bed for rest, I only lie here to pass the time and dwindle in the stale mists of my breath's vapor. My breath is shallow and hollow of taste. It is the excuse I use for living, as living is an excuse I use for mistrusting all without and all within.

"There are seconds when the ins and outs combine and I am served with an eviction notice from this sanctuary. I run from wall to wall holding them steady, but I cannot remain in one place because another area of my self cries as the excitement is far too much to bear. I scream to be left alone in my world of noninvolvement, though I know these walls hold a door, but I blind my eyes for I fear it may be unlocked. Here I do my best in what little that may be. Here there is no confrontation by choices or growth. I can stay pure in my stagnation and clean in my own filth.

"The gales of emotion shake my fortress from the basements to the buttresses. Dust moves through this air only noticed in the light that sneaks through the cracks in my molding tears. If these walls fall I will be naked, as my fears will run from the sunlight and leave me there with someone I have never met before. A face that may scorn me and laugh at my scars. Eyes that will penetrate my heart and sweep away the rust, freeing my dreams so they can fly away while leaving me behind.

"Please, do not tear down these walls, for outside that face awaits. It wears a happy grin as it holds compassion for someone I was meant to be. Hold old walls; be determined to keep me pale and un-colored by life and all of its falsehoods; love, sympathy, passion and the other descriptions of unrealistic involvements. Keep the mask on, my lover, keep these walls between us. And never suggest that mine is the face I fear. Leave me here in hell, for I have committed the despicable sin of having once owned a fresh body."

As the girl is shadowed away from the stage, a lone dancer emerges from what appears to be a dream left behind. The ballerina circles an altar that is in the center of the stage. In a flash from above, the altar receives the lifeless body of the girl, who lies stretched upon it. The dancer is quickly joined by a male counterpart as the two begin to entwine themselves in a continuous circle around the altar. The rest of the stage now has a resemblance to the interior of the Duomo Santa Maria del Fiore in Florence.

The body on the altar begins to drip blood on the floor below as the dancers start to move sensuously through the Cathedral. They weave through the pillars below the frescos on the tombs, crypts and other mausoleums that are displayed throughout the structure. The girl on the altar comes alive and begins to dance. Her wrists and feet have similar wounds to those of the crucified, and from these wounds blood is trickling.

The Chorus is magnificently singing Sublime Chants of the Catholic Masses in a haunting offering to god. Missa de Angelis, Missa Simplex, Pange Lingua, Adoro te Devote, Ave Verum Corpus, O Filii et Filiae, Salve Regina, are followed by the Litany of the Saints, as the entombed rise from their deaths to join in the sensual moving in this Dance of Stigmata. All have blood trickling from wounds of crucifixion as they move in their passion filled sorrows.

Michelangelo and Machiavelli serve as altar boys to Pope Eugene the IVth, who raises his hands toward the congregation that includes our five among them. Galileo, Brunelleschi, Lorenzo di Giovanni, Da Vinci, David, and the other sacrifices stop their dance and kneel in the pews as the Pope, resurrected, recites the Mass of Crucifixion. All clutch their hands together as the blood of life trickles from their personal sacrifices to the laws, precedents, and warnings, over their various lives.

Gloria fills the vacant spaces that rise in the domes to the light that rushes through the ceiling as the girl in the cell is turned into a wafer that is placed into the mouths of those that take the Mass. Her blood is drunk as the wounds on the devoted miraculously vanish. The two dancers disappear in a vapor symbolic of the passion of life that is being denied by those that will soon return to their cells beneath the marbled floor. All begin to walk to their memorials like the meek who are devoted to their masters.

Again it is displayed how the masters of glory somehow fall at the feet of the powerful. Glory remains a rented commodity to the souls that are hollow. The Duomo is hollow, but somehow it is filled by those that grant it glory, for the structure would be made of dust if it were not for those that hold it above themselves. Was the Duomo built to the glory of God or was the Duomo built to the glory of persuasion?

The stage remains in resemblance to the interior of the Cathedral. The only occupants are Carlo and Angelique as they walk through the structure while he explains the enormous artistic motivations found there. We watch them move from monument to monument when all of a sudden Angelique begins to cry. The visual stirs through the audience as this breakdown is so alarmingly uncharacteristic. We watch her fall to the floor like a crumbling empire into the dust and sand below her. Carlo holds the grieving woman closely as he is lost for the proper words to console her.

They sit side by side on the marble floor as the painting of Dante by Domenico di Michelino has come to life. Virgil, who then appears in the form of an apparition off the painting, sits down next to Angelique as she has an expression of horror on her face. Dante, who stands in front of the three, begins to read from his Divine Comedy as Virgil smiles at him. Only Virgil and Angelique appear to hear Dante, although we in the audience are also blessed by her delusion. She listens intently to his voice as it soars through the air with words that describe the similarities between the seventh of the nine circles of hell and the seventh of the seven terraces of purgatory.

"These words are my artistic descriptions of what the ones before me cast into the minds of the simpletons and the ignorant. You sit there unaware that the Seventh Circle and the Seventh Terrace await your arrival. The three rings could hold you in their grasp, but are you a blasphemer, usurer, sodomite, or are you a nurturer of suicide?

"The Terrace defines you as a lustful sexual sinner, who seduces any that may excite you through your own deviant temptations. You are your own satanic demonic and you cast your spell in seclusion and in company. I myself await you on this terrace, as does Virgil the pagan, who sits beside you."

Dante's eloquence is valuably welcomed within the theater; he adds a tone of righteous preaching to his words, but he is smiling calmly as he seems to understand that his conclusions are merely artistic interpretations of the blessings and sorrows of the pure and the stained. His worldly manner offers his poetic beauties with a compelling excellence.

"Your deeds in life have left you with a choice between a terrace beneath the enlightenments and an inner circle within the labyrinths of Lucifer. See yourself as you will be in the act of payment for your earthly motives. Are you satisfied with their outcomes when you consider their shortsightedness? How skillful were you when you understood that your every pleasure would turn to agony if it never reached its finality?

"Your wings have stretched in a similar expanse to a vulture as it comes to rest on the carrion of those whose life you have suckled on like a babe in search of a breast that never drains. Your lie mistreats all those in your vicinity; no matter how sheltered they consider themselves. Your venom is constricting so you can feed at your leisure. And now you begin to feel your own paralysis as your now present dementia begins to feed on you."

Angelique stands up and runs from the building in hysterics with Carlo following her. At the exact moment Dante returns to his position in the painting, Virgil stands and begins to speak to those who remain in this graveyard.

"O, move thee from this tomb, why must you remain captive in your deaths, did you not pay the price for your greatnesses in life? Reclaim your bones from the grave robbers of Christ. Release your souls from the cells beneath this floor. Jump from the infinities in the painting upon these walls. Leave the simpletons and the ignorant that still come to worship your tormenters. Run from this Labyrinth of Christ as did the woman before you. Copy her need for freedom from the serpent in her mind. I demand that you awake from this pandemonium."

There is no response to the pleas of Virgil. The Cathedral remains still in its silence, as if God in Its Trinity dismisses the vain attempt. But Virgil is not through.

"King David, look upon your depictions. You were the King of the Jews, but here in these lies your foreskin has grown back. In your death they have made you a follower of their words. Dear Jesus, even you have been used, as they stand on your corpse and pronounce themselves saved. But who has saved you from these descriptions? Awake, and leave this place. I implore you, I implore all of you to awake and see life in the pure light, free from any predeterminations."

197

But again the emptiness remains unstirred until Virgil bows his head and begins to cry. The sound of his tears echoes through the cavern, reminiscent to the sound of raindrops on the hardened ground. Virgil raises his eyes towards the roof, where a large black cloud now resides, absorbing any exterior light from entering. Lighting flashes as the eyes in the painting and on the statues come to life just as the thunder clashes next. The crypts in the floor begin to open as a deluge of blood rains down, blinding the eyes and flooding the crypts below.

Virgil screams as the storm lashes wind that blows the words and letters from their resting places in Bibles, upon the floor, on the works of art, as well as the other surfaces within the catacomb. The letters are intermingled into a funnel that becomes a fountain above the altar. In an instant, all is silent again as Virgil walks towards the flowing water in order to drink of its purity, but his every step begins to fade both him and the fountain until the pair has completely disappeared.

The Cathedral again has light streaming in from its windows and doors as more followers are ushered in. The men wear solemn expressions and the women wear veils while the young begin to play on the steps and chase each other through the pews. There is nothing out of the ordinary, or so it seems to us in the audience. The explosion that has been the opening

198

of the sixth scene has been captivating for us, although we are left unclear as to what was illusion and what was reality.

Surrealism has again reinforced its position in the opera. The music has been visual in nature, adding to the apparent delusions of Angelique, and indeed, the rest of us. We are perplexed by the suspicion that other events that have occurred thus far in the performance may also have been a part of our heroine's, if you wish to call her that, fantasies. The edges of the seats in the audience have been well used during the last few euphoric events. We all realize that the shoreline is a vast distance away, as we remain on this liner in the seas of creative realisms. Passage from before to where does not rely on a compass, map, or sky chart as it tips in the turbulence of what may be.

There can only be the feelings and their hoped for similarities to events experienced before. However, around the corner, mysteries can be entertaining if you do not forget they are supposed to be make-believe. Though as I look at the others on board this theater, I must say I am skeptical that all of the passengers remain seat-belted to that particular conception. I am beginning to understand that what is real can turn out to be the obscured, and thus, the delusion can enjoy its worshipers.

The stage before us has presented conclusions based on nonfactual material. We have watched and heard the participants live their lives in the paradises of hell, or should they be described alternatively as the hells of paradise. When you word it in these manners you are confronted with how both hell and paradise are just obscurities in a long stream of concepts that have never been defined in the same way by two true individuals. What is personal paradise if another would think it was a personal hell if they had to totally agree? All is subjective, perhaps, another simplicity?

We may philosophize as we are rocked in these waters of creative realisms, though that may aid in losing our grip on the railing of this vessel. The time will come to actively acknowledge the deliveries this performance has been making on our perceptions. But, I for one, remain quite assured that this opera has moved my foundations on what are the rights and wrongs in what I now humbly term as my life. Although I must confess, I am no longer sure that the expression, 'my life' is a point of fact, as even now I give myself to this opera that I have no control over. I must tell you, though, that I have promised myself to not become too entwined in the similarities to what I know about myself, even if part of this description continues to sound hauntingly reminiscent.

As the events inside the Duomo were taking place, outside the Cathedral, Gabriel and Carl were lunching beneath an awning in the Piazza del Duomo.

"I find it very interesting, Mechant, that you have not yet taken a sample of the local female gentry, or the other cats of the lower classes that you have found before in the streets and in the allies. Am I right in thinking that you have misplaced your heart somewhere in Camille's boudoir?" Scherer inquires, while holding his ever present handkerchief.

"Carl, I find it interesting how you have still failed to discover that your cutting directness makes you appear to be a pompous bully. Certainly, you are aware your size intimidates. Why have you not learned that it itself is enough of a requirement to announce your presence?

"Camille, if your curiosity needs satisfying, does have a grip on my heart, and at this time I find her more appealing than those felines that amble in the streets or those cats that hold their tails high in the allies, although I know they will always be there if I need a quick bite or a long heavy meal.

"Tell me what you think of those pampered kitties that are given gentle strokes on the lap of another man's wife. Is it true that the only hazard is the odd occasion when the poor puss gets its claws caught in the bed linen? Meow, Scherer, meow!"

"I can tell you about one pampered cat that has lost his privileges of being welcomed on a well known lap and in a fondly remembered bed, dear Gabriel. But perhaps that is a familiar story to all short tails, after they have been cut off.

"Although at this time I think it would be better to turn your attention nonchalantly to the subject of those two gentlemen," Scherer points casually to the Viscount and Inspector Peal as the two ride by in a carriage with the shades only drawn slightly. Both Carl and Gabriel are successful in expertly staying anonymous.

"Damn! Damn! Carl, our parade will encounter a gully soon."

"I wish your country's Bonaparte was still with us. He most assuredly would have started some trouble somewhere in Europe, and that would have certainly taken minds off of the Bishop," Carl says as Gabriel nods, while both men have a look of concern drawn upon their brows. "The masked ball tomorrow evening may hold more than a few surprises, do you not agree Mechant?"

"Well, at least we know that a fox and a falcon will be present. That little fact has just been made apparent to us, but I wonder if that was an intended mistake. I hardly think that they have just arrived. We must see what we can learn before the falcon strikes and the fox begins to chew."

The two linger for a short while until a scream is heard near the Cathedral. The men both stand to see what caused the commotion when they notice Marta run to an ailing Angelique, as she appears from the Duomo. Carlo is close behind her as the three rush towards the waiting carriage. Angelique gets inside, Marta follows, and Carlo climbs on top as the horses are persuaded to quickly trot away.

The men have looks of concern and extreme surprise, as the sight of Angelique in such distress is highly out of place from the usual cemented calmness and consistent composure that the lady normally displays. Gabriel drops coins on the table in a callous way as his attention is now on what appears to be the end game of the five.

"Gabriel, come… this way," Scherer says as he punches people out of his way, making an instant pathway to an available carriage.

"The Palazzo Corsini," Scherer tells the driver as the pair is only moments behind the distressed Madame Beauvie.

"Do you think the Monk is the reason for her hysterics?" Mechant asks Scherer, while both hold on as the driver maneuvers through the crowds.

"He would have to do a great deal more than any romantic advance or sexual overture. She was afraid. The Monk has no power that I am aware of that could frighten her to that extreme. She did not look as though she had experienced any kind of physical injury."

The two men look at each other in a mutual concern for her and what is an apparent emotional distress. Scherer bends his head out of the window and demands the driver go faster. They both clutch the straps as Gabriel starts to punch at the wall above the door.

"Gabriel…," Scherer starts to say as he reaches his hand out and lays it upon his companion's shoulder.

The carriage arrives, but before it can stop, Gabriel has jumped out the door and has run through the gates. The driver stops at the entrance as Scherer's door is opened for him. He then tells his waiting attendant to pay the driver. He walks slowly toward the front door like a man who is about to hear the verdict for his undefended crimes; resigned, melancholic and unresisting.

As Scherer enters, he sees Carlo and promptly asks the man what has happened just as Gabriel reaches both of them.

"Gabriel, how is she?" Scherer asks.

"She is fine. She speaks of the occurrence as nothing more than a stumble followed by a faint episode. She wants to rest; Marta is with her."

"Monsieur Mechant, I do not wish to alarm you, but what I witnessed does not correlate with that explanation. She was frantic, and I am certain that she saw an illusion of some kind that had the apparent ability to hold her in its power," Carlo explained.

"What kind of illusion?" asks Scherer.

"I would only speculate that the Cathedral is full of images that most pray to, whereas others find multitudes of passions while being in the presence of the Masters entombed there. Perhaps, Madame Beauvie was overtaken by her artistic imagination, though I am again certain that it was all so real to her. Although, it could have a great deal of accordance to the subjects she has been discussing with me."

"What subjects?" Gabriel inquires.

"She seems transfixed on the relationship of the Church to the artists it manipulated during the Enlightenment, but I thought that could be explained by the drama of the coming performance."

"An outside observer may suggest that she is feeling remorse due to some irritating guilt," offers Scherer, as he looks directly at Mechant.

"Catholic guilt is the hardest to shed, gentlemen. It is not a mere sore; it is an infestation that infects all around it. I, for one, was breeder of the infestation on the innocent, and that fact still leaves a stain on my heart, though my past brethren still look upon that occupation as a just weapon, a necessary evil in the saving of souls," Giorgio admits.

"Insanity!" cries Gabriel.

"I hope our dear Angelique was running from it and not running toward it," Scherer says quaintly.

That night, Gabriel remained ever diligent of his wife's condition. When the summoned physician left her bedchambers, Gabriel and Carl were in the hallway awaiting his report.

"She will be fine. She had a spell, that is all," the Doctor begins.

"How does that explain her hysterics, doctor?" Mechant demands.

"She was merely overwhelmed by the whole experience. She is coherent and laughing about the event. There is no sign of what could become a long term effect. I assure you, this is normal behavior for a woman like her. After all, we all have minor frailties, do we not, Monsieur?"

"Thank you, Doctor," Gabriel says as he and Scherer watch the man go down the stairs.

"You know that Angelique does not become… overwhelmed!" Scherer whispers, as he then glides down the stairs himself.

Gabriel watches him and then turns toward Angelique's door. He opens it, and as soon as he appears Marta quickly leaves the two of them alone.

"Gaby, how kind you are to be worried about me, or are you worried about what I may say should madness become my close consort?"

"Your jesting is distasteful and insulting, my dear," her husband responds.

"Tell me then, what about this situation is not distasteful? I find it not only frightening, but this particular moment is not suited for an intellectual weakness."

"There is no appropriate moment for intellectual weakness."

"That is right, my husband, after all, you are the authority when it comes to public displays of madness. That is a matter of truism," she says sharply.

"The drink brings on my madness. I have the knowledge that the same excuses can not be used by you. Is your madness pure, Angel?" is Gabriel's cruel response.

With those words, she begins to cry softly, as her head falls slowly onto the waiting pillow.

"Gaby, how long has it been since you have lost your love for me? Have we gone so far, that there is no hope of returning?"

He lies on her bed beside her. As he holds his wife close to him, he says, "I still love you. You know I do. But we have allowed many to join us in our beds. The result of our indulgences must add a negative strain on our resolve for one another. We are affected by our personal decisions as well as by our mutual ones. Mistakes have been made by the both of us. But we are still together."

"That togetherness may be a result of the need for one another in the practice. Can you tell me truthfully, that need is not the only reason for our relationship?"

Gabriel puts his hand under the bed linen and begins to feel her. "Our love making has always been mutual, Angel."

She moves herself away, quickly reaching her feet to the floor and as she walks around the bed, she begins to lecture Gabriel, "You find mutual desire in many females. Why should your advances be motivated by your love with me if anyone is appealing when you have an erection to attend to? You have always been a dog, and any kennel will satisfy you, be it the ones of high breeding or the brothels of the flea sharing mutts who dig through the garbage piles at the ends of your wanderings.

"You will never again bring your filth into my bed. You are not entitled to shove that rancid excuse for manhood into me. I may have become mad, but then again I may have finally found my reason. Do not worry, I will perform as before. I promise you, this will be the end of my hysterics. Now get your disgusting hide out of my room, and remember, from here on you are no longer welcome in my bed or in me."

Gabriel looks at her and begins to grin. He says as he starts to leave, "The masked ball tomorrow evening will be attended by two surprises, the children's father and the ever inquisitive Inspector Peal. Your promise will be tested quickly. Good night, Angel; most assuredly I will return soon for a taste of my property, but tonight you need your rest," he arrogantly says as he passes through her doorway, shutting the door behind him.

As soon as the door shuts, Angelique begins to cry; she then lies upon the bed in the fetal position. Within a minute, Marta returns, and as she slowly walks toward the bed, she says in a strange tone just before she sits next to her duty, "My sweetheart, my soft Angel, is life distressing you again? You have always and will always control these circumstances. You are fretting more these days than usual. All is proceeding as planned, is it not? Your opera will be glorious, and heaven will always be aware of you."

Angelique moves to lay her head on Marta's lap, while she softly replies, as her tears stop falling, "Mama, you are my only reliance. You are closer to me than I am to myself, and I love you without exception."

Marta strokes her duty on the forehead with a gentleness that so far in the performance has not shown itself. "My child, you stir yourself far too much. There is nothing that can harm you if you remember to wear your face in the appropriate manner. This event will prove itself to be immaterial, as it will be forgotten and never again will be spoken of."

"But mother, my face is becoming too heavy to wear. I find it harder to gather the strength required to keep it in place."

"Daughter, do not be foolish. Your face wears itself. Remember the fact that it has been in place for close to thirty years. Everyone is aware of your strengths. You will maintain your control because you have surrounded yourself with puppets. Puppets that need you to think for them.

You have trained them so well that they will hold the strings for you until you desire movement from them. And now that you are requiring chastity, the effort needed will diminish a great deal. When you have sexually seduced all those that needed that push into compliance, just the thought that you may again entertain them is enough to maintain your dominance."

Again the audience is twisted as the relationship between Angelique and Marta is revealed, after the whole opera has suddenly been cast in a different direction. My personal interpretations have been dragged in and out of coherence. I am lost in this performance, as I no longer seem to be able to intellectually control the information I am served. The music that entwines with the visual images rarely parallels the story; that has the effect of breathlessness as I am forced to run against the turbulence of the hurricane on the stage.

I think to myself, although I feel I am being overheard, that the pen that wrote this entanglement must be either the wand of a very powerful magician or the cutting edge of a confused mind. Even my explanations seem somehow to be in compliance with the will of the director. Again, the stage has somehow transferred its surrealism into my awareness. I am beginning to feel that even I am a figment of imagination. If that is so, then the rest of those in this audience must be, too. Or, perhaps they have been placed here to add to the confusion I am experiencing.

As all this is running through my mind, the stage has been instantly transformed into a vast ballroom that is nothing less than the Salone dei Cinquecento in the Palazzo Vecchio. The music that is filling this extraordinary opulence is a stunning Sonata by Baldassare Galuppi who is fondly referred to as "padre del l'opera buffa" because of his reputation for comic opera. But the Sonata playing is a gracious work of romantic beauty that again has transported my attention far away from my idealistic questions.

The vast room is littered with artistic examples of magnificent elegance as the ceiling has thirty-nine divided panels richly graced with scenes and allegories of Florentine history and one of the Medici family. The walls caress two of the most famous paintings, "Soldiers Bathing," by Michelangelo and "Battle of Anghiari" by Leonardo. On the left, the Audience Room has statues by Bandinelli, de'Rossi, and Caccini. However, on the far wall, elegantly placed is Michelangelo's "Genius of Victory," a work so superior that one may feel the whole structure was built in order to be its elaborate frame.

The dancers take to the floor as a Suite by Domenico Zipoli starts the excitement. A sentimental favorite of Leopold assures that he can be seen amongst the group, luckily with Angelique as his partner. The two, even though masked, are unmistakably recognizable. His frame is obvious, while she is wearing a gold-encrusted red gown that accents her auburn hair. A necklace full of diamonds and emeralds with one large ruby that lays in the center is the appropriate announcer of her breathtaking enhancements. The mask, that cannot hope to cover her beauty, is mostly black, with the exception of a gold sequence of outlines and slight golden flecked feathers at the sides. She has the appearance of a flame flickering as it moves upon its heavenly candlestick, while Leopold has little else but his title that allows him to be seen with her.

Her smile sparkles with a brilliant radiance and through her mask her eyes have that familiar glow so perfectly placed. She is in her element, with her powers of hypnotic persuasion casting instant spells on all that gaze at her. She leaves the dance floor burning behind her, with coals so hot that beads of perspiration begin to appear on the foreheads of all the men unable to do more than choke on their desire for her. The room is seduced by her, as no master work present has the ability to move as she does in her animation.

Her laughter glides through the air, softly kissing every lobe. Her style of conversation with its wit, depth, and humor gathers even the harshest critic into her web of appreciation. She, again, can feed at her leisure as she continues to fortify her walls of defense with the most powerful in attendance.

Carl and Gabriel are close to the doorway that leads to the Studiolo di Francesco I de' Medici, where they are watching with great interest the grand performance of Madame Beauvie. Scherer lowers his glass of wine and while wiping his mouth with his handkerchief he says, "She is indeed in her glory this evening. Her every step is superbly timed. She is back to normal Mechant, do you agree?"

"Yes I do Carl. It certainly appears our decisive weapon is back in working condition, and as lethal as always. I hope, for our sakes, it stays in its present position."

"Present position? What are you referring to?" Scherer asks tentatively.

"Why, pointed at any direction other than ours of course."

"I was not aware that we were under a direct threat other than the one that became evident yesterday."

"Perhaps you are not in her target unless you stand too close to my beliefs. It seems my wife has forbidden me to entertain any semblance of what could be considered a romantic step toward her boudoir."

"Are you telling me that the Grand Master has been cast from paradise?" laughs Scherer. "Have you become one of the cropped winged cupids that send Angelique nothing more than their hardly hidden disappointments? Poor boy. Do not fret. Remember, as you have said, large meals and light bites are everywhere, in the streets, in the alleyways. You, my fellow Tom, will never be without a purr to peck.

"The only person that I know who can match your wife's skill at seduction is you. Every female in this room would gladly lift her skirts and bend over for you at any time you wished. And of course you still have the sweet Camille, unless her fat father has come to rescue her from being your penis warmer", Scherer offers in his style-less crudeness.

"Your bloated underbelly is dragging on the floor again. Tell me, Herr Scherer, is there nothing in your verbal repertoire that can stop you from being an ass? You laid a crop on my wife's behind. I saw the marks. You allowed your boy to exercise himself on her back as well as in her mouth. Do not forget that I did not kill the both of you for your mutual desecration of what is considered to be my territory. Laughing at me at this particular moment tells me of the certainty of your disregard toward my feelings. Never forget Scherer, my blade is always sharp and never misses." With those words left behind him, Gabriel Mechant walks slowly away from the shocked conductor.

Bernardo Pasquini's 'Toccata' fills the room, as again the dance floor is flooded with the energetic. Gabriel has partnered with the very popular Maria Alessandro, a woman of northern fairness. He smiles, while he looks towards the slightly wounded Scherer, as the bloodied returns the glance with the lifting of his glass in a tribute to the winner of the just past engagement.

On the other side of the room, it is very apparent that the Count and Contessa have been surprised by their father. Both seem rather happy that the Viscount is in Florence, and the surprise is really not much of a jolt when one considers the opera is almost ready and the gentleman was the one who financed it. Peal has not yet been noticed; however, there are many masks and many in attendance. Blending in would not be considered a difficulty, and the police do possess the nasty habit of waiting in the most inconvenient location within an unwelcome moment.

The knowledge that the two would be in attendance has been shared with the children, as Gabriel's life has instructed him excellently.

He is aware that the knowledge of an unwelcome surprise is like an unabated hook; its lack of taste is obvious and its edge is a declaration of the predator's presence. Prey served with these foreshadowings survives because the attack has nothing left to do but follow the choreography.

As the night lingered in a welcomed illusionary slow motion, the guests were well treated with the finest that Tuscany had to offer. The Grand Duke and his wife were not only gracious hosts, but were the type that enjoyed occasions such as these because the frivolity was always served with the eventual ganders, backhanded remarks and the off-color amusements that added that sauciness and playfulness people of their station normally were not treated to. After all, it is well known that political diplomacy and stately administration can be agonizingly sterile and painfully unhurried.

There were the cat and mouse chases as the young found quick moments of privacy behind curtains or in unattended corners of slight seclusion. Of course, there were the eventual scoldings by mother once the mice were found in the mouths of the cats, but what would become of a Masked Ball if half hidden heathenism was not invited? Being civilized means that the treatment of these social misdemeanors should allow for the spice of liberalism. After all, the young need to experiment in the kitchen in order to feed themselves in the future.

All that was meant to happen happened. But of course, there were the surprises that came in the well performed subtleties by the older and more experienced when it came to the game of masquerade. Eventually Peal surfaced, but Gabriel was quite aware of his fin in the ocean-like crowd, even though Peal was well trained at adaptation. The encounter came as Gabriel was at the banquet table having a plate prepared.

"Monsieur Mechant, or am I mistaken?" Peal began as he appeared behind his prey while also having a plate prepared.

"That depends. You do not seem to be sure, Senore. That can only mean that you have not been formally introduced to this Mechant you are trying to find," Gabriel replied.

"Well, I must concede to your skillful observation. Perhaps if I introduce myself first then you might be willing to tell me if I am indeed mistaken or not," Peal says as he tries again.

"I have to be honest with you, there is an obstacle between me and the answering of your question. I came to this function only when I was promised that I was not required to climb more than a few stairs," Gabriel replies as he starts to eat some pâté.

"Mechant's stubbornness is well documented. That character trait also describes you as the person I think you are," Peal presses, as Gabriel is becoming angry.

"Are you normally annoying? Or are you just ill-bred? Please, do not bother answering. It is simply obvious that your demeanor, Senore, is obtuse, unoriginal, obnoxious and speaks unkindly of your inadequacies. Good-bye!"

With that, Gabriel walks away, but Peal is not through.

"Mechant, my name is Inspector Peal and my concern is the disappearance of Bishop Joel. You are familiar with him, are you not?"

Gabriel turns around and angrily says, "You must be napping Peal, look around, you may notice, things are out of place. You, my poor man, are the most out of place ornament here. This is Florence, Inspector, not London."

Gabriel then walks right up to Peal and continues, "This Mechant fellow is very deadly with a sword, I have heard. If I were him, I would be very happy that it was Florence. You could be killed for your insistence, and all that would be said after your demise would be, 'Peal was a fool'."

With that, Gabriel leaves as the Inspector understands he has very little protection in Tuscany. He also has gained an insight as to what is understood as the normal response of Monsieur Mechant when he is angered. Peal's perception has been proven; Gabriel can turn quickly into a killer who is cold and calculating, a well known talent the writer adds to his other abilities.

A while later, Benedetto Marcello's "Toccata" welcomes to the dance floor the young and the enthusiastic. Camille and Gabriel are among the vibrancies that lighten all those that are there for the enjoyment. However,

Peal and the Viscount are not there for that healthy offering. They watch the festivities that are occupying the majority for a while and then go to sit and talk in the Sala del Dugento.

"Viscount, Mechant is a killer, there is no mistaking, however he is a womanizer, and the only motive he may have had may have something to do with his present dance partner."

"That has crossed my mind. They both look comfortable together; that could be the result of the time the group of them have been sharing, though."

"It could be. Mechant's wife is a very intelligent woman and I am certain that she would be aware of the affair if it had been ongoing," agreed Peal.

"You will be leaving before the performance Peal, what else do you hope to find?"

"I would like to discuss this matter with Madame Beauvie herself, but she is constantly engaged this evening and I am sure there will be no opportunity to get her alone. Her husband has threatened me directly, but his attitude was the result of my insistence. The both of them are covered by the defenses that Tuscany and for that matter mainland Europe spends on them."

"What about the composer? I am certain he buggers my son at will. Even as I spoke to him tonight, he hardly could talk without knowing where his teacher was. I must admit to you that his mother has never suspected that her son's feminine manners are not due to his artistic pursuits."

"That, Viscount, is the motive. But your suspicions are not enough to pursue that possibility. Your son is effeminate, but that is hardly out of place in upper classes of the British Empire. We must have proof, and I can tell you from experience that truth when it comes to those matters is never handed over unless the purpose for the unveiling is to murder the sodomite without killing him."

"Then you will fill your last few days here with the intention of solidifying that motive?"

"Yes, as we and the King have determined. This group is somehow connected to more than the opera and themselves. Letting your children believe it was to keep them from the prying eyes of Broadfoot and the newspapers that fostered your belief they would be better off in the company of Scherer, Beauvie and Mechant, was excellently handled by yourself. I am sorry, however, that the result of this charade may turn out badly."

"Yes, Peal, I am too, but I refuse to protect even my own children if they did participate in the end result of their Grand Uncle," the Viscount says sadly.

The rest of the evening was not only entertaining for almost all in attendance, but it helped to refocus on the nasty annoyance of the Bishop and his whereabouts. The admission that the children were sent to Provence to help in the investigation seems notoriously repugnant, when it is remembered all that has transpired since. There was a prevailing feeling that there would be more difficulties to endure until what seemed to be destined to become a verse from a Greek Tragedy. All those in the audience were sure to stay in their seats and witness all that would pass before the outcome.

But the Ball was still in progress upon the stage, and there were still masks perfectly in place. Another Toccata started those who still had the energy to enjoy 'A song of a Cuckoo' by Pasquini. The light musical treat had the most boisterous on their feet, a group of dancers that included Scherer with one partner and Wilhelm with another. There was no mistaking; the two were definitely dancing with each other. The women acted as mere deflections from the performance. Mechant and Angelique rushed onto the floor with the intention of masking the pair from displaying themselves so blatantly. They rescued the lovers from exposing themselves for the homosexuals they were. This was not the appropriate event to announce the fact to the noble classes of Europe.

The Viscount did not witness the display, and for that matter hardly anyone did. We in the audience seemed to be the only ones besides Angelique and Gabriel who noticed a thud of pretence was about to splatter on the royal floor. It was skillfully handled by the pair as they camouflaged it well, and we in the theater felt instantly like accomplices to the crime of the well placed avoidance. The thought that one's sexuality could create so much distress held my head under the waters of intolerance, hatred and stupidity.

Again, I must chastise the author for his blatant attempt to make me question my own prejudices. I find this is a common occurrence in this opera. Is it entertaining when one must comfort themselves and their particular beliefs? Why must artists feel it is their duty to ask the most difficult of questions? This creator must be blaming someone for these portrayed discomforts, or perhaps the creator needs to rid these hatreds from himself. I hope this theatrical study also encounters his frailties in the shadows of his own indulgences. That would satisfy me fully, but I will continue with my vigil, for I have come too far to find my way back. And if I could, I would not recognize the person that started this journey under that canopy of trees.

I find myself running my fingers on my face in a vain attempt to gain more insight into the occurrence upon the stage. They dance without a conceivable care, although they bump into one another due to their magically never empty glasses. The glasses are refilled or exchanged by a troop of servers who are always close in this performance. They never talk, but there is a sign language that they communicate with that is never misunderstood. I start to notice that the servers are starting to mingle with the dancers. Soon they are the only ones on the dance floor as the masked served have taken their places behind trays, tables and dirty porcelain.

The 'Ballet of Servants' begins in earnest with the entirety of the refined looking service staff well polished and positioned formally at center stage. The Chorus and Masks begin a rhythmic repetitive chant wonderfully reminiscent of a grand Waltz. They start by snapping their fingers in a ¾ time while casually sneering, whispering, motioning, and gesturing while singing;

No, you fool, come with me,

Far too cool, tea for three.

The servants in unison start to go in circles at a dizzying pace until they stop, fall to the floor, and do tricks much like dogs would do. They then stand and begin again. This goes on repeatedly until the whole sequence has taken place six times. After the sixth, the stage is emptied and flooded with instant darkness except for one light that is cast down upon a lone scrub woman on her hands and knees while she cleans the various scuff marks off the floor of the Salone dei Cinquecento.

She begins to sing a beautiful Aria about her sore back, bruised knees and pain-ridden hands. She sings about her life and how many scuff marks she has polished off. She sings about the fumes from solvents and other liquids she has used in order to keep from going hungry. She sings of how her child died from disease and how her husband left her long ago. She sings about the time she wasted dreaming of a different life. And she sings about the disappointment she may have in death when the promise of heaven is nothing more than an endless Ballroom with endless scuff marks.

I watch as her beautiful voice brings tears to my eyes. I am certain the rest of the audience has been moved as I have. I have nothing to give the woman, I have nothing to offer. I begin to find my emotions exhausting me. I feel a rage inside me. An anger that I can not explain because I am being shaken yet again. I see this old woman with her life beating down on her, and I am ashamed by my thoughts of how dare she expose me to her plight, how dare she complain, and how dare she remove her Mask.

THE FAILURES OF VENUS

Eden in the mouth of a serpent hung helpless as it was carried up the tree of knowledge. With every slither and with drops from the fangs, closer to the top of the canopy the heaven was brought. Once the peak was captured, the cold blooded coiled as it placed Eden in the nest of Venus. As it began to hiss, the viper was laid upon skies in the form of a whirling star gallery of pulsating colors found in the crown of tranquility. The glow of every gem threw rays of dust upon the wide expanse that formed the galaxies that play up above in the midnight.

Under the crown of tranquility Eden shivered in the nest of Venus as the garden was left unattended. There it stayed in the midnight while Venus held the heart of the Sun. All in the skies were lit by their reflections of what they were before transformation through the weave of metamorphoses. The Sun had lost the will to shine, as its ideal had fastened its heart on a string from the spool of the fine thread of blind passion. Venus swung the object through the midnight, while those not of the skies understood the motions as the shooting stars in their paths searched for answers.

Eden's shivering came to an end when the talons of a dragon clutched it close to its warm underbelly. The two flew through the reflections, past the crown of tranquility, and finally came to rest on the swinging thread of blind passion. The combined weight of the heart of the Sun and the dragon with Eden tattered blind passion as the Sun began to shine on the dragon and its theft of Eden. The dragon in its embarrassment dropped Eden. The garden grew in the eyes of those not of the skies, as its promise of the first season was sung beautifully to those below as they longed to have wings.

Venus in her anger entered Eden and solemnly swore to entice the Sun for eternity. The garden took root in the minds of those without wings and soon the Sun warmed Venus as she grew more and more beautiful. The Sun called her spring and the first eternal season bloomed under the Crown of Tranquility. Eden became abundant and promising as the second season came to be. The Sun called the pregnant Venus summer as he lovingly cast upon her every warmth and affection his obsession could bear. Venus was receptive to the gifts and care of the Sun as her beauty continued to grow.

Soon the attentions of the Sun became brief as its shine needed more rest between its diligences. The third season came to be as Venus understood the need to return the favors of the sun. She called the moment autumn and she returned to the dimming Sun more hopes for future enticements and their hard earned rewards. The Sun felt fooled by Venus and left her to experience the fourth season she sadly called winter.

Through the darkness of midnight the serpent of the star gallery entered her in the forms of what was the first fear, loneliness, a hard experience for Venus to endure. The Crown of Tranquility took the shape of the tattered thread of blind passion. The two ends appeared like horns in the skies of midnight and Venus became terrified of this first perception of Lucifer, the tormenter for those that committed the sin of never satisfying the promise. Lucifer brought hell into existence and from that moment on, hell grew in the minds of those without wings, for they too, feared loneliness under the cold skies of midnight in winter. They had fooled themselves by their ignorance, for what they thought was Lucifer was only the Dragon that would forever long to repossess Eden.

Venus again blamed these false perceptions on the Sun, and those without wings unknowingly supplied her with more enticements as they created from their perceptions wonderful illusions of art until the spring appeared again and the eternal cycle was then destined to forever turn. The Sun became infatuated once more, for there was more promise in the Garden of Eden than there was before. Venus had learned that Sun could be fooled, so that is why she started to wear the ornaments the ones without wings weaved in acknowledgement of her eternal love affair.

The dragon became more patient as the cycle was repeated again and again. It knew, with every new spring, the truth would be harder to see through the oceans of beliefs that every drop from a new spring would become. Fears had also grown in the fertile soil of Eden. The paradise produced many separate visions in the cold skies of winter midnights. Venus and the Sun played their foolish game of love as love itself became nothing more than another fear to the ones without wings.

The stage was full of master perceptions as dancers, acrobats, and others acted out the wondrous story-like libretto the Chorus sang in this mystical beginning of the Seventh Scene. The strings vibrated with dreams as they seemed to be moved by a magical hand of classic portraits that had cast spells on ancient perceptions and modern ideals. I felt rejuvenated as it was quite apparent how illusion can infiltrate. I was sure this new frame of reference would add more excitement, spins and curls to this opera. All of us in the audience seemed prepared to advance.

I could see the correlation this opening had to what had come to pass in the performance so far. I was also encouraged by what the correlation would be as it moved in its unorthodox tunnel. I must call it a tunnel because it seems to bore through my subconscious leavening little fragments behind as it ate away at my sterile conservatisms. I would like to consider myself to be an open individual, however, there are many perceptions I have attached myself to. This opera does have a nagging way of forcing me to let go of them.

The next morning, Camille was not feeling well. She was complaining of a headache and nausea, and she was experiencing difficulty breathing. The Doctor was summoned and after he examined her, he spoke to Wilhelm and Angelique privately, as the others in the household had left before the discovery.

"She has skin irritations and other symptoms of the pox."

"The pox?" Wilhelm frantically asks.

"Steady, Willy," Angelique calmly says before she asked the Doctor, "How far has it advanced?"

Before the doctor can answer, Wilhelm excuses himself and enters Camille's room.

"I must insist that she be institutionalized, and begin mercury treatments immediately. I cannot be certain, though it appears to have advanced to a stage that may be well beyond any hope."

"Yes doctor, of course you're right. I am sure you understand that a high degree of discretion is in order," Angelique says as she hands the man a small satchel of gold coins, which in turn he deposits in his bag quickly and without notice.

"This girl is a Contessa and only fifteen years of age. Her Grand –Uncle was the same Bishop Joel of Normandy that went missing in London last fall. It is imperative that you understand that the ability to not entertain memory of this event is important to you in order to maintain the clientele that affords you the luxury in life I am aware that you enjoy."

"Madame Beauvie, I do understand that these matters are better attended to in the appropriate manner. Would you like for me to arrange transport for the young lady?"

"No doctor, that will not be necessary; the child's father is in Florence, I will notify him. I am sure he will handle this issue with the utmost taste and respect for all those involved," Angelique assures the doctor as he bows and then sits in a chair close to Camille's door, like just another servant.

Angelique prepares a message for the Viscount and has a rider deliver it; she then enters the girl's room. Inside, a worried Wilhelm is holding his sister as he sits on the bed close to her; Camille is sobbing.

"You two must not worry about this. Camille, you will be well cared for and soon your health will return. Wilhelm, this ailment has been caught in time, this fuss is not required if your sister is sure to recover."

"Is that what the Doctor told you?" Wilhelm asks with hope.

"Yes dear, of course. You father has been summoned, and no expense will be spared in the war for the defense of your life, sweet Camille," Angelique says as she sits close to the pair on the bed. Camille's tears stop falling as Wilhelm's face is released from the strain upon his heart.

"Angelique, you have always brought me comfort. I thank you in all sincerity and I want you to know how much you mean to me and how much I will always love you," Camille whispers.

"My sister's words were said in unison with the words my soul was saying. I, too, love you, Madame Beauvie," Wilhelm agrees.

Angelique kisses both their cheeks and then says before she leaves the pair, "You are the children that I never had, but our intimacies have brought us closer than is possible in a normal mother and child relationship. In the future there will be time to reacquaint ourselves with those special moments. Now I must prepare for your father. I will send in your maid to help you. Your father should arrive soon."

In less than an hour, the Viscount comes through the front gates of the Palazzo Corsini, and before the morning is through, Camille has begun the long trip to Paris with a small entourage that includes her father and the doctor, who would go along with her for a short while. The Viscount promises to be with her soon, as his intentions are to see the performance of the dress rehearsal first. Wilhelm is duty bound to do the same.

After all has been done, Angelique has a few things to say to the distraught brother. The two are in the courtyard as she takes him through the gate to walk in the sun by the Arno. "She will be well cared for, Willy. I am sure the ailment was discovered early. Paris is the right place for her to be. She will be close to your mother, your family and the best medical facilities Europe has. Do not allow this setback to affect you negatively. You know me in passion as well as in stability and you know you can trust me to do what is right.

"Concern yourself with the opera. You need to go to the rehearsals quickly, before my husband returns from his morning rituals. I alone must tell him of all that has happened so far today. Now go and tell the conductor and the production administrator nothing. I will also take that burden myself."

"Thank you Angelique. As usual you are the strongest one." He then hurries across the street and through the gate. Angelique looks toward the confusion on the Ponte Vecchio and the Piazzale Michelangelo above it, as she whispers to herself, "My dear Gabriel, will this be the end of our new beginning before it has even begun?"

A harpsichord starts to blend with the tension with which the stage is filling the theater. Its sound is pungently poignant as it plays the haunting Sonata in C minor by the brilliant Domenico Scarlatti. I feel I am witnessing the lightning cracks beginning to appear behind the calming outwards appearance of this panoramic vision of the splendor of Florence, and the astounding beauty that created such a paradigm paradise. The portraits on the walls of Chatham start to twirl through my memories of the first scene in this opera, so fond of the distortions found in the minds of the troubled, the deceitful and the manipulative. Those warnings found in the Prelude of the 'Forth Coming' that was so well placed in the strides of an earlier Herr Scherer, have been acted out in such detail.

I feel I am among those in that cage who watched the perceived sane walk by as they were reminded by us of how far the drop is from the heights of acceptance in the grinding normality found in the colorless worlds of compliance and apathy. Sanity was one of the virtues of those that were well schooled in the dullness of what was perceived to be acceptable. Staleness is the stench that the finest perfumes attempt to cover, as originality is better bought than fostered.

I cannot be certain that those around me are as affected as I am, but by the looks upon their faces it is clear that their minds have been batted back and forth by the enormous amount of detail they are being asked to consume. Surely, there are those among us inside this cage of confusion that feel they are being force-fed undesirable intellectual cuisines that withhold any description as to what this dish is made of. Surprises are mostly welcome, although this stage serves more than food for simple entertainment. The menu here has filling dilemmas with rich sauces that come with heavy mixtures of human frailties, human glories and human disregard. Being in a cage with others that have lost touch seems to be the safest place to be.

Gabriel was greeted in the courtyard upon his arrival by Angelique, as he returned from his morning at the fencing club. He was ecstatic due to his personal brilliance and he was pleasantly entwined in his personal arrogance.

"Ah, my wife awaits her conquering enchantment. Yes, I will allow you to adore me, and because of my status with the foil, you can touch my person," he says with an extension of his frivolity. Angelique smiles as she quaintly applauds obedient strokes. While still laughing, he continues, "You serve my glory with a small portion of respect, but I know you Angel, I can see through your apparent approval. There is something on your tongue that you require me to hear. What is it?"

She takes his arm and guides him inside. His smile has disappeared as there is no mistaking that his posture defines that he has prepared himself to receive a blow. She kisses him gently as they enter the first private room available. Once the door has been shut, he says, "There is a silent atmosphere under this roof, why?"

"Gaby, Camille was examined by the doctor this morning, and he believes the poor girl has an advanced case of pox."

"Pox? Where is she?" he demands.

"Her father has taken her to Paris, as the doctor feels she needs the best care available. I have told her and Willy that it has been detected early and there is a certainty that she will regain her health. Their father agrees that the truth at this time would not be kind to them."

Gabriel is lost for words and seems to be as helpless as he was in the asylum in the first scene of this performance. He looks not only distraught but teetering on the edge of destruction. He finds the closest availability and sits himself down.

"I am so sorry, Gabriel. I truly did not know that you had gone far beyond a lust for this child," she says as she sits next to the obviously distraught man, as he begins to quietly weep. Angelique's face becomes compassionless as she sits upright and looks at the distress of her husband. She is angered by his love for Camille, and any sympathy that may have been surfacing has disappeared in the most violent of quiet manners. She kisses him on his forehead as she rises and walks out of the room with only the sound of her steps being heard. Left alone to console himself, Gabriel begins to speak, "My sweet Camille, do you know how much I love and adore you? You are familiar with the way my soul dances when my eyes are blessed with your vision. Will my need to bestow on you magical feelings to every curve, nerve and pore serve you with passionate memories? Have I not proved my sincerity? Have I not proved my dedication? Have I not proved my conviction?

"You, God, have again found a victim in your game against humanity. You inspire our passions with the most tastefully desired purities and then lay your sicknesses and scars on all those who appreciate the masterpiece. I hear your laughter, God; what can I offer to you when you purposely sacrifice the love I have been learning about? How can you send me my redeemer and then sweep her away with all the other dust of the past? You warn me about the cruelty found in Hades, which I cannot be sure of. But your cruelty I am aware of and I am certain that a heaven that brings me closer to you would be the hell you tormented me with. Again this paradox speaks well of your intentional savagery.

"I will no longer entertain thoughts of what has been described to me as civilized behavior. There is nothing factual in the floating meanings of proprieties, principals, or other distortions the fools that follow you believe as they call themselves civilized. Liars, hypocrites, betrayers all. I know how they all align themselves with your teaching as they abuse all within their path. I know because I am just like you, God. I, too, create my worlds in order for myself to be served and satisfied. I, too, can be sinned against and I, too, have a hell I can throw my disbelievers into. I am just like you, and that is why I am better than you. For I am the truly honest one, I am the one that is not afraid of what is factual.

"You can do with me what you want, but I will no longer entertain any hope of redemption. I will roll myself in my distastefulness. I will cast from my soul any guilt that needs refuge from the deaths that they cheated. Take your guilts, God, take your savagery, God, and take your heaven, God and dig yourself a hole to bugger yourself with. You are the only one that truly deserves to be condemned to the underworld. Stay away from me, bastard."

Gabriel then balances himself before he leaves the room and enters what will become his new world. Later that day, Angelique tells Scherer and Carlo the sad news of Camille falling into illness. Madame Beauvie spares the opera administrator the details, however when those sad details are transferred to Scherer he seems unsurprised and even casually remarks, "It was a certainty that the child would eventually be affected, she mistakenly chose a whoremaster as her guide into those particular studies."

Angelique simply smiles at him without any other form of expression.

That night, Gabriel did not return to the household, but by dawn the following morning, he staggered through the front gates and into the courtyard as drunk as a man could be. Herr Scherer walked out the front door to witness Mechant's agony. The composer then told the guards to take him into the Palace and lay him on his bed, have one of the maids clean him and make sure he rests. "Watch him closely, never leave his side and inform his wife that he has 'returned in the familiar condition.'"

After Scherer had taken care of this nasty business, he left for rehearsals for the open performance that was just six days away. These events were not welcome at this date, as Angelique's control over the entirety had lost the reins. She was also feeling the effects in an emotional way that had never before been displayed. Her face had begun to show the strain of her interior feeling, an occurrence that was stunningly out of place for the normally controlled woman.

All the service staff in the Palazzo Corsini were shocked by the echoes of her screams that circulated through the halls and rooms when she was told of Gabriel's condition. The sound was so uncharacteristic that everyone was affected. Only Marta was able to calm the woman, while no one else would attempt the task. The rest of the day rested in what was thought to be normality, although the staff believed their masters were all crazed. Gossip had found new pastures to run rampant in and the embellishments would soon make the fictions more desirable than the facts, another simple normality.

When Gabriel surfaced from his illness, the evening meal was being served to Angelique, Carl, Wilhelm and Carlo while they were discussing a few points about the coming performance that they were certain was going to be a triumph in the world of operatic expression.

Gabriel had overheard a part of their conversation and when he walked through the doorway he promptly offered his opinion as he poured wine into a glass.

"I suggest we tell the whole audience that they not be seated for the performance unless they are all completely naked."

Carlo was confused by the remark of the well-respected writer while the others sitting at the table kept eating without a trace of confusion. Gabriel proceeded. "Now I do not want any of you to think I have lost my taste, of course the fat and the other undesirables must stay fully clothed throughout the performance. Now let us decide together who we would all like to see in the buff," Gabriel directs while he sits himself at the table. Faint laughter can be heard coming from the service staff; Angelique turns to see who finds these words amusing as the snickering ceases instantly. Carl comments, "I think this topic is on the edges of the disgusting, Mechant."

As Gabriel grabs the maid that has been serving him, he drops her into his lap and starts to kiss her neck while he fondles her clothed breasts, "Disgusting, Carl? Is this disgusting, Carl? Tell me Carl, tell all of us what you think is disgusting."

Gabriel then releases the woman and continues, "Who at this table without hypocrisy is able to judge what is or is not disgusting? I find the total lack of remorse for our dear Camille the most…"

"Mechant, how dare you accuse me of a lack of remorse for my sister? I am not a brainless brat that only cares about his toys. I love Camille with all my heart, for she to me is more than a sister. She is my companion and my dearest friend, and I failed her when I refused to rescue her from you, you old ugly, filthy man," Wilhelm screams as he walks from his chair, as the staff leaves quickly.

"Wilhelm, you are entirely mistaken, I love your sister and she returned the same in kind."

"Are you certain, my husband, that the Contessa loved you? Could it be that her motive was to seduce you for the purpose of being entertained? I find it rather funny that you of all people could be fooled by your own tricks," Angelique drools from her venomous fangs. "There are occasions when the truth must be understood, Gaby. This is one of them. Join us in reality. You may find it less strenuous than your ventures into incoherence."

All in the room watch in silence as Monsieur Mechant drops his glass of wine on the table, as he is unable to support it and the added weight of the blow his wife has just administered. No one comes to aid him as he bleeds openly onto the table where the spilled wine blends perfectly with his flowing wound. Carl and Angelique remain seated as they enjoy their meals, while Wilhelm stares at the broken man. Carlo is fixed in stunned disbelief.

The next morning, a warm sun cast its eye upon Florence, not unlike the glance of one lover on the other. While the one slowly opened her eyes, a gentle smile wiped away the sleep so the dream could come true in the full appreciation of all that belonged to clarity. Florence smiled back at the sun with a love for all the fullness their mutual intimacy had created. Those that shared the moment between the pair were able to feel the expression in their beautiful embrace. All of those that had their desire close were inspired to feel the lips of the other in the glory of a mutual worship for love eternal.

Gabriel was in the shadows by the Arno, under the arches of the Uffizi, leaning on the wall that bordered the river. He was sober, but drunken with grief, as he watched the morning chase away the sleep from Florence. He crossed over until he walked down the stairs into the long courtyard that eventually met the busy Piazza della Signoria. He watched the crowds with an observer's perfection as he noticed the subtle; the smile, the brooch, the hug, the pointing finger, all of the simple gestures that defined the various individuals.

His melancholies had entered the kingdom of non-compliance. The world where all you have taken for granted begins to be the only thing worthy of your full attention. That garden where humanity buds, flowers and blooms so fragrantly and abundantly in its traits of tranquilities only found if your spirit is all that needs to be nourished. He could see all the similarities in all those that lived in that precise moment shared with one another. He could feel a faint hope being restored within the spirit that he faintly called his own. He slowly understood that he was his redeemer and no other was responsible for his failures as a man.

He thought of his Camille and how her journey to Paris was an unnecessary ordeal. He realized decorum must at all costs be maintained, and how his obsession's illness would leave a nasty scar on all those connected to her and those she had come to know. But the ugliness of the whole procedure was nothing more than finding another Jesus to nail to the cross of sacrifice for the sins of the others. The pain and suffering of the sacrificed may be documented, but that is as far away from the agony as one can get, unless they are gifted with the strength of the uncaring in the lands of perfect denial.

He thought how easy it was for his wife to sweep away the undesirable. He thought how her hardness was becoming visible to those that would have never believed her to be capable of such anger, resentment, and vengeance. His mood changed to one of fury; the same fury that was so evident on the hillside that overlooked the Mediterranean Sea in Provence, where he killed a minor opponent in an execution that had been disguised as a duel.

That night Carl found Gabriel drinking in a street level bistro. The composer sat across from the writer at the same table and had two bottles of the best wine brought over. Monsieur Mechant was not alone; he had in his lap a voluptuous woman practiced at the art of accommodation as her guest was well nestled between her ample cushions.

"I see, Mechant, that you have found comfort from your strains."

"Carl! Dear Carl. Tell me, how is life treating you, with respect I hope. How dare anything take you away from your favorite delight."

"What do you consider my favorite delight is?" asked Scherer.

"Why, your pompousness of course, my large dear peacock. I am sure you can remember your words to me last night. That is right, I remember this time. How dare you use your hypocrisy vainly for the purposes of discrediting me?"

"These types of descriptions you have heard many times before. Why now do you choose to listen to them? Have you felt a healing of sorts from the hands of Camille?" Carl asks with unmistakable sincerity. Gabriel waves the woman away until there is no one at the table but the two collaborators. Herr Scherer then adds, "Your work on our opera is a magnificent feat of creative imagination. You have proven your genius. Soon the world of art and every world beyond will use your name in reverence. They will include you with all of the classic greats. But still you fall from those graces into places like this, where you treat yourself to the privileges of the easiest found filth. No, Mechant, you are no genius, for you are too foolish to hold yourself up in reverence."

"Are you trying to save me for my well being or yours?"

"Again you are a fool. If you start to care for yourself, after this opera you would be able to collaborate with others like you. It is true that other geniuses would seek you out and beg you to find the most dignified words to dress their wondrous music with. I know that you have always understood that my talents have reached their limit. That I will surrender to you. This work will be my greatest triumph, because I will never be able to duplicate it.

"You, though, cannot even comprehend how glorious is your gift. You have no limits, unless you continue to limit yourself. I am arrogant and all of those other peculiarities that make one unlikable. I have never been humble, for there is nothing other than my teaching ability to be humble for. This will be my masterpiece as well as yours. This will give me respect and the opportunity to be humble and perhaps even loved."

Carl then rises to leave but before he does, he has a few more words to add. "Gabriel, I do care for you. You are the only friend I have ever had. In all honesty, I would be willing to lose your loyalty if it was the result of you coming to your senses."

Before the man reaches the door, Gabriel stands and yells to him, "The world will be fooled again, noble. The world will be fooled again. I am a fraud, I am nothing but a well trained monkey. Ow, ow, ow."

As Scherer turns in confusion to look at the drunkard he is treated to the sad sight of the artistic genius, laughing as he dances like a monkey on the same table that had been the platform for Carl's eloquent pronouncement. That night Gabriel did not return.

The next day, Carlo and Angelique were off to see an exhibition of the paintings of Caravaggio. Most of his finest works were on display in the Sala di Marte at the Palazzo Pitti. The Room of Mars' ceiling was painted in the theme of war by the wonderful Pietro da Cortona. Caravaggio's work was intermingled with Rubens' "The Consequences of War," in which Venus is trying in vain to keep entertaining Mars so he will not to go to war. Tintoretto's portrait of Alvise Cornaro, Rubens' self portrait as well as his "Four Philosophers," Murillo's "Madonna with the Rosary," Titian's portrait of Cardinal Ippolito de' Medici and others also were upon the walls.

Caravaggio's "Medusa" and his disturbing "David with the Head of Goliath" were among the collection of his works that were present. The story behind the disturbance is a troubling one indeed. It seems that the Pope had wanted the head of Caravaggio himself to be delivered without its normal attachments. This degree was the result of the artist's ability to get drunk, become argumentative, fight and kill; an irony in its obvious coincidence.

Carlo was in a guarded stance because of his last experience with Angelique alone. Her outburst two evenings past did not quell his position. Of course this type of behavior was not of a foreign variety to him. He had been of the opinion that Madame Beauvie was not only gracious in manner but in speech as well. Her cries in the Cathedral and the words she had bludgeoned her husband with, were far from the descriptions of those that had known her before, and more disturbingly, than the comfort in her elegance he had come to know and to expect.

The outing began at the Corsini where both the lady and the administrator entered the carriage that would handsomely take them to the Pitti in accustomed comfort. The sun was again lovingly caressing Florence and the jewels on the Ponte Vecchio tempted the lady so invitingly that she had the carriage stop so she could do some marketing. After a while the carriage was re-entered by the pair who were laughing about the venture into the shops of trinkets. She found them long on value but short on quality and taste. An opinion the craftsmen inside the establishments did not share, but conveniently did not convey.

As the carriage proceeded up the hill towards the Pitti, Carlo was telling Angelique about the interesting life of Caravaggio; his mastery over art and life's mastery over him. The parallels to Gabriel were most astonishing, but it seemed to be a necessity when it came to the extraordinary. Most of the hierarchy of gods in the universe of art all had wounds inflicted by their continuous rub against the mediocrity of what was tormentingly described as normality.

Genius is misunderstood because of the simplicity that there are few geniuses. People like Caravaggio, Gabriel, and the others of astounding abilities are understood only in the splinters of themselves and their works, while the being that creates the masterpieces remains in the shadows of their accomplishments because of their personal peculiarities and eccentricities. Rare are those of immortal lives that live for fame, almost all prefer the privacy in their studios and in their homes. Psychologically speaking, the ones that run to the footlights are usually the most insecure; the mature master looks at the footlights with reticent compliance to the marketplace that even genius has to accept in order to supply the needs of the studio and the home.

Then there are those that have a physical need to battle with normality, rather than hand the fight to their celestial abilities. Artists like Gabriel and Caravaggio had no patience and a smaller amount of respect for the people and other elements that got in the way of their expressions, and no tolerance for interruptions of their performances. They fought back but because of their emotional insecurities and physical abilities, these fights would end up spilling the substance that inspires metaphoric blood. The results of these encounters were usually left on the floor of the stages they occurred on, although at times they turned deadly.

The life blood of these encounters is the liquid of distilleries, fermentation and brewing or other forms of incoherence. When intolerance of any kind is mixed with uncontrollability, force is the choice when rationality loses its footing. The genius that also possesses physical prowess is an unrelenting opponent. The characteristic that makes them obsess on a work they are creating is the same ingredient that they use in a disagreement. The passion that supplies the emotion at times overstimulates the necessity to make the point. Caravaggio and Gabriel were related when it came to their drive of motivations.

Angelique listened to Carlo's explanations of the beasts of art with an interest that had the same intensity as the one that Carlo was describing with. As they turned into the driveway of the Pitti, Angelique asked a very interesting question, "How does a female artistic genius act in these circumstances?"

The enquiry seemed to puzzle Carlo, as he did not offer his usual quick response. Perhaps the reason for that was women were simply not considered to have the necessary components to attain what was considered as artistic genius. Or, could the reason be that they were hardly ever taken seriously? Even in art, men blanket their contempt for the full membership of women in the club of humanity by blinding themselves with their romantic idealisms.

Venus's emancipation will only come when she starts to refuse to mount the pedestal. But when she does, how long will it take for her to realize that more effort is required off the throne than on it? Perhaps Venus is just lazy, while her sisters are not. Some of her sisters, though, are thankful that when in need the pedestal is close by. This skill however is not a basic requirement in a stable relationship, be it romantic or a passionate love affair with one's own art. The true artist suffers, for only messiahs are capable of being crucified for the souls of their metaphoric children, their separate works of art. Venus prefers to be the prize for redemption; she only hangs on the cross for herself or for profit.

When Angelique and Carlo entered the Palazzo Pitti, the first galleria they encountered was the Sala deli Iliade where they spent time being fascinated by the décor that had been completed six years earlier. Homer's Iliade in the lunettes supplied the inspiration for the ceiling where scenes depicting Olympus were painted by Luigi Sabatelli. Other marvelous works adorned the splendid space.

The second galleria was the Sala di Saturno, the Saturn Room, with portraits by Raphael of Tommaso Inghirami, and Agnolo Doni, along with "Vision of Ezekiel" and "Madonna with Baldachin". Of course, there were other paintings by his contemporaries Andrea del Santo, Perugino and others. Carlo spent time in front of the "Vision of Ezekiel" telling Angelique about Raphael's belief in the Catholic faith and how it inspired him to put images to the stories the Church was based on.

The third galleria was the Sala di Giove, the Jupiter Room, where Pietro da Cortona had also painted the ceiling. Inside this jewel "The Three Ages of Man" by Giorgione, Andrea del Santo's "John the Baptist", "Madonna with the Little Swallow" by Guercino, "Descent from the Cross" by Fra Bartolomeo and the great work by Raphael "La Formarina" or "La Velata", The Veiled Woman, perhaps the finest of his female portraits.

As they entered the Sala di Marte, Caravaggio's passion could be felt instantaneously. Angelique was overwhelmed by the difference his paintings displayed in comparison to the brighter side of Catholic teachings through its finalization of redemption. Caravaggio's style was darker with the feel of what was truly the result of human engagement, its pains, its conflicts and its violence. He spared no one from the actualities of the encounters that were the results of conflict in its unbalance. His art had a more human approach in its textures.

Within his images, layers of lines on the faces of his characters told countless stories of experiences as they were involved passionately with the conceptual subject of the painting. Angelique was mesmerized by Medusa as she tried to understand the horror it portrayed. Later, Carlo was at the woman's side when Angelique encountered Caravaggio's self-portrait "David with the Head of Goliath". Of course she had already been told of the emotional story behind the work, but it hardly prepared her for what she saw in it.

She stared at it with hardly any apparent movement for what seemed to be a prolonged period. Carlo was concerned and asked in a diplomatic way, "It is of a difference, do you agree Madame Beauvie?"

But still she stared without movement and with no apparent acknowledgement of the question she had been asked. Again Carlo inquired diplomatically, "Perhaps you can see something in it that you could share with me?"

This time there was a response from the entranced. "Why is David carrying my head? Am I Goliath?"

A confused Carlo delicately paused before continuing. Not knowing how to respond, and also anxious to not repeat the incident at the Cathedral, he asked her, "David is carrying your head? But you are not

Goliath. You are Madame Beauvie, the enchanting wife of Gabriel Mechant, of course you remember. Do you remember, my lady?"

Angelique turned ever so quietly, and with a blank look on her face she seemed to look through her companion until he asked her, "Are you feeling ill, Angelique?"

She then focused on him with a sad, confused expression. "Carlo, you called me Angelique. You sweet, gentle man. I think I have had enough today. Please take me to the carriage Carlo, I think I need some fresh air."

Carlo held her arm as he guided her out of the Pitti to their waiting transport. Once inside, the driver was told to go into the countryside to find a place of seclusion so the lady could walk and regain herself. As they sat alone in the carriage Angelique seemed troubled and exhausted.

"Are you sure that a walk is what you require at this moment? Perhaps a rest in your own bedchambers is what you need."

"Carlo, do you feel it is appropriate to mention my bedchambers? Do you feel it is time that we should become more familiar with each other?"

"Madame, no! You are mistaken!" Carlo says in embarrassment, but before he can move to the opposite side of the carriage, Angelique holds his hand, keeping him close to her.

"Carlo, you are kind to me and I value your friendship. I need your confidence at this time. Please tell me that I can confide in you," she pleads.

"Angelique, I am trustworthy, but you have been displaced today, much like you were at the Cathedral. I will remain loyal to your confidence, though you must try to understand my worry about your visions."

"Carlo, David did hold me by the hair as he carried my head. He had a solemn look on his face because he was sad he had to perform the duty. His consensus feels my sins while his heart is heavy with remorse by my passing. I have the talent it takes to stop the pain in others. I can do the same for you. I promise to never stop pleasuring you, if you return my head to where it came from.

"I can give you money and position and my heart and my loyalty and my chastity. I promise you that no other will be able to handle my body the way you can. Steal my head back from the boy; place it on its trunk. Let me live again, Carlo, and you will posses me until you have no use for me ever again."

Carlo stayed still as the head of the lady was placed on his shoulder. He patted her hand as he tried to comprehend all that had just transpired.

He had the driver turn back toward Angelique's residence, and once they were there he convinced her to rest. He then left the Corsini on foot toward the theater where rehearsals were still taking place. The poor man did not know what was the right way to deal with the woman's apparent madness. All was beginning to crumble.

Around midnight that evening, a drunken Gabriel danced through the front gates at the Corsini Palace. Scherer and Wilhelm, who were still in the parlor, were asked to come to the courtyard by one of the guards posted there. When the composer and the Count appeared in the fresh night air, Gabriel was urinating on one of the statues in the walkway. A moment later, Marta came through the doorway, also witnessing what happened next.

"Where is my wife? She should be here to see what I think of stone hardened women," Gabriel laughed, as he finished his aim at the face of the maiden depicted on the statue.

"Mechant, so good to see you in such high spirits, is there anything else you would like to piss on?" Carl asked.

"Ahh… Carl, always the gracious host. Anything for your guests. Ah… but I reside here, do I not? That can only mean I am home from my crusade of follies. Bring me wine, slaughter a young lamb, and tell my wife to warm her bed, for there will be two under the covers when all my other needs have vanished."

Marta ran back through the steps and up the stairs as Scherer and Wilhelm escorted Gabriel inside.

"You will be happy to learn that all is ready for the performance. Two nights from now, Florence will be notifying the world that an opera of a true Nova Supremacy has been born in their city," Wilhelm offered.

"Yes, Gabriel, in spite of yourself and your crusades, this major work of ours will be offered to those that can afford to be enlightened. I am sure you will be happy in the morning when you will be able to understand fully, that your taste for excess will continue to have enough gold coins to get you into your troubles with more than enough to again get you out."

"You mean I will be able to drink myself to death, Carl. Your generosity has always been slower than your opinions. That slight fact has always been the most painful throne on your vine of un-bloomed flowers. You will never lose that charm of yours, Scherer," Gabriel says as he pats Scherer's face.

"You, Gabriel, are the most brilliant of us all," is Scherer's sarcastic response as he brushes his face with his handkerchief.

The three sat in the dining room together as Gabriel fed himself and drank more wine, until the author excused himself. Gabriel then went to his room, dragged a wash cloth over his face and other locations on his body. He changed into some night wear and then left his room. As he walked toward his wife's room, Marta approached him in the hallway, blocking him from continuing his amble to Angelique's door.

"Monsieur Mechant, my lady is not well, and although it may not be my place, I must offer you the suggestion that she be left to rest."

"Marta, you are the sorriest liar that I have ever known. Woman, how many times in the past have you attempted to deflect me from my duties to my bride? Her body is long overdue for one of my visits, and Marta, you know I will not be stopped. Now move yourself away," he angrily snaps.

But the woman stood fixed to her position, still not allowing the man to complete his intention.

"Old lady, I have long hoped for an excuse, I warn you to not to make it a simple decision."

At that moment, Scherer and a guard appeared and promptly placed themselves between the two combatants. Marta was held by the guard as Mechant smiled at her and proceeded down the hall.

"Please leave my girl alone," Marta wept, as Carl only had this to offer her,

"Angelique is his wife, Marta. There is nothing but death that can put an end to that. Your lady is his property."

As Gabriel walked through the door to Angelique's boudoir, the others watched him go inside. The guard released Marta as she sat down in the closest chair and began to cry softly.

"Stay here and make sure the old woman does not interfere with the man and his wife," Herr Scherer orders the guard before he leaves.

Once inside, Gabriel walks towards Angelique's bed; she is lying on her bed silently watching his movements towards her as a lone pair of candles flicker on the bed stand. She begins to speak with a tone of compliance. "David, is it time to do your duty? May I offer you myself before your sword is raised? Please, let me show you my gentleness as I supply you with my favors."

"You can call me anything you like, my whore, but be certain that your husband is back to reclaim you wayward ass."

Angelique screams in horror, as Gabriel stops wide-eyed while he looks at her in amazement.

"No, you demon, my chastity is promised to my deliverer. David will not want to taste my flesh if its purity has been stolen by you!"

"Clever, Angel, but you have no purity left. I am not here for your cleanliness, I have come for your filth."

"Your intention is to take what is not offered to you. How can there be satisfaction in the rape of a headless body?"

"Well, headless body, rape is the oldest form of conception, is it not? A fine invention by God himself as he most assuredly used the technique on the once-virgin Mary. This is not rape however; it is nothing but a husband getting ready to plow his land. Wet your gardens or you may find this painful."

Angelique screams as her husband forces himself on her. After a short while the screams have subsided, as Angelique stares at the ceiling while he labors on top of her to maintain his erection. After he has spilled what little there has been, he stands and walks out of her room as she lies still without a sound. When Gabriel enters the hallway, a sobbing Marta brushes past him and into the room. The guard looks at the triumphant warrior as he walks by, leaving the hallway almost empty. The guard then lowers himself on the chair, holds his head in his hands and tries to release the incredible strain, but the rugged man cannot hold back his own tears.

I am so sorry for Angelique that I have to feel tears in my eyes as I remain seated on this comfortable chair in this refined audience, surrounded by the elegance of this beautiful old opera house. The voices of the performers have been astonishing as they move elegantly through the brilliant score and its compelling libretto. The story being performed upon the stage before us has all the necessities to move our emotions throughout our entireties. The empiric powers the five once used in a high degree of subtlety have become arrogant, lazy, and uninspired.

Their apparent downfalls are as separate in definition as are their characters, but the motives are similar in this well named extravaganza. Indulgence has hardly any character wrapped in the most precious of pretence. The types of pretence that make the victims feel worthy enough, the accomplices feel clean enough and the witnesses feel paid enough. When all can be explained away by the petite line, 'so is life'; then all can be tolerated as it is known it can also be forgotten. I wonder how long it will take before I have finally forgotten.

As these thoughts run through me, the stage has again appeared as the curtain is being raised. Before us, a second theater and a second audience is beginning to sit in front of a second stage. In this audience, all the main players of our opera are there. Angelique, Gabriel, Wilhelm and Carlo can be seen in a box to the right of the stage. On the opposite side, the Grand Duke is also in attendance with a small entourage. The children's father, the Viscount is present, and in his company, Inspector Peal is also seated. Herr Scherer stands on the podium as the second audience applauds enthusiastically. The curtain begins to open as the conductor raises his baton, while both audiences seem fixed to their separate positions.

I feel the surrealism thickening as I am unsure of what is about to take place. I am lost in the question of which reality I am in. The one about to begin, the one I have been watching, or the one that brought me here in one of those past beginnings? I am lost in my position, unsure if I am a player or the entertained. I will not trouble those around me, for I can see they, too, are trying to discover what the vision is and whose eyes they are looking through. This is the first time I have noticed that I am in the gaze of your eyes. Whose gaze are you in?

THE PRECURSOR

The Date is September 22nd, 1496, in Florence.

The opening Prelude begins as the stage is dark and foreboding. Dancers are barely visible while covered with hooded black robes as they dance in an awkward choreography. The Musical eloquence modulates between relative majors and minors before it settles in a dark Dorian that perfectly supports the images on stage. The strengthened warning so frighteningly portrays the instant doubt that is cast upon the entirety of both audiences. The Chorus soon joins in with the highly intimidating recitative.

A legion of fully robed shadows surrounded a tiny flame that cast the only light in the darkness that was their home. They chanted as they attempted to blow away the light, but the flicker would only dance. The legion swelled as more robed envies added to the winds while the chant grew deafening. Soon an Aria began from a lone child, as in the distance of the darkness a boy walked from the Cross of Crucifixion. The legion of the robed moved in creation of the pathway to the flame as the boy sang so movingly. His words echoed through the theater as their meaning was hauntingly apparent.

'What is this power? A small flame that refuses to be extinguished. You bring contradiction in your flicker, while you ignore the presence of my examiners. They poured the fluid of the belief upon you while you danced through the torrent. You defy my explanation by your will of noncompliance. Look back and behold the cross I bore and the punishments I endured in order to solidify the darkness you now try to burn away. What is the fuel you use, what powers your resolve?'

The boy circled the tiny light as the Legion encircled the boy. Soon the flame became fuller as the boy circled counter to the Legion's encirclement. A word was thrown at the flame from a single voice in the Legion, as the rest of the robed began to chant the word; Blasphemy, Blasphemy, Blasphemy.

The Legion became uncontrolled as it rushed the flame with its judgment. Soon the boy was trampled by the rhetoric of the examiners until the child could no longer be seen. The Cross of Crucifixion now was full with a man upon it, as the flame grew in its defiance toward the Legion of the Robed. The Legion covered their eyes as the flame's light push them back into the shadows. They then turned to see Christ on the Cross as they found power in the wine of the eternal crucifixion of the boy their feet had crushed in their righteousness.

They turned back to the flame while still covered by the robes of their beliefs as Christ bled and suffered behind them. They sang in a distorted harmony as they tried to blame the flame.

'Look how he suffers, how can you allow this to happen? Repent your sin of Enlightenment. There is no wisdom other than your total belief in the Legion. See how we serve the Son of God as you in your defiance nail him to the cross with your sin. You are a heretic, a treasonous blasphemer. You are the incarnate of the Anti-Christ. The devourer of the word, of the belief. We demand that you extinguish your sin against God. Kneel before us, surrender your inaccurate definitions.'

The flame started to move between the robed as a few caught fire and ran past the Cross of Crucifixion. The flame then spoke to the Legion as it cowered in any space that was filled with Darkness.

'You fear the exposing of your lies.'

The flame then was tiny again, as the Legion in futility chanted and tried to blow out the light.

In the small studio of Roberto Gale di Anti, a mature woman sits still by an open window. She is partly covered in a faint pink open blouse that hangs off her shoulders exposing her breasts and her torso while her hands are placed upon her lap leaving only a small part of the area visual.

There are flowers in a blue jar and a plate of cheese, bread and sausage with a glass of red wine on the table next to her. The arched window frames the scene of a bountiful garden with ripe tomatoes and grapes on their separate vines. She is a sensual woman of raven beauty as her long black hair and dark eyes have that look of invitation. Her mouth is partly opened by her full moist lips that add to the powerful image of ampleness.

The artist is quickly trying to complete the complexity of the expression the woman has created. She has been patient but her limit has finally been reached. She begins to talk to the painter while trying to fasten the expression still. A recitative starts in a beautiful Bel Canto style:

"Robbie, I have to pee."

"Another moment," he pleads.

Still without her mouth moving she says, "I can hear you but my pee refuses to listen."

"Fine, fine, go piss to your delight," the old man allows as he keeps mumbling to himself, as she gets up and kisses him on his cheek as she runs out of the room.

Her voice can be heard coming from elsewhere in the flat as she asks, "Am I beautiful Robbie?"

"Even while you pee?" he asks.

"No, on the canvas. Stop playing. Take me seriously. One day I will stop modeling for you, and you will never see my body again," she finishes saying as she then walks back into the room still only wearing the open blouse.

He smiles at her before saying, "You, my sweet, were born to be naked, that is why you hardly clothe yourself as it is. I see you now and that is why I will see it forever. I have a good memory. Now get back to work."

She smiles as she replaces herself back in the identical pose, as he too, replaces himself in the proper position to keep painting.

All through the studio there are magnificent paintings leaning on the walls and on themselves. There must be at least a hundred of the same high excellence with the signature of Roberto Gale di Anti in the lower left corner. There are a fine number with the same model in various poses and different expressions. There are a few self-portraits in mostly a contemplative style. The colors are bright and the backgrounds are often comfortable with only a few sad distractions. Mostly joy radiates from the superb collection. The vast amount of this work appears strangely out of place when the quality has been considered.

Soon a knock can be heard as a call from the door echoes, "Gale di Anti, are you busy or are you just painting?"

"If that is Sandro, find your way to the studio without ratting through my pantry this time," laughs the old man, as his model loses her expression to the interchange.

"Stop playing Marianna, hold yourself," he says as he smiles.

As the guest walks into the studio he moves immediately over to the canvas that Gale di Anti is working on and as he looks intently at the painting the artist says, "Marianna, have you seen this boy before?"

"Yes I have Robbie, was he the one that drank all your wine a few afternoons past?" The woman again spoke through her still expression.

"My dear lady, you are exaggerating. I know I poured you at least two glasses as this old man never seemed to stop his sipping. Robbie, you make her look more beautiful than she is. How do you do it?"

"Simple, I know how beautiful she is inside."

"Forever charming," the man says as he then begins to look at the canvases on the floor.

"I can have all this removed for you and in its place not only will you gain more space but you will also gain financially as you gain fame and acceptance. Dear teacher, you deserve all your talent can give you."

"Botticelli, do you accept me?"

"Yes, of course I do. But master, you are again avoiding the point. You are the inventor of this style. There are few that can create such glory from an every day occurrence. You take the expression in the moment and give it a glory that an addition of a halo cannot.

"Look at your treasure. Each one is a rose, a jewel, a pearl of delicate simplicity that can only be found in the extravagance of the mere mortal. You paint life, you paint reality. I paint about the dreams of others. You paint what is real."

"Robbie, listen to him. If he says that he can make your more stable, he must be listened to," Marianna shouts at the old man as she stands before the pair of masters.

"The pose, the pose!" Gale di Anti screams.

"Old man, what good is the pose if all it will do is dry with the rest of your failures? You are a perfectionist who will never get good enough until you give these children of yours to the hands of those who will appreciate them," Sandro Botticelli demands.

The old man lays his brush on the easel as he then sits in the same chair that Marianna had posed in. The lady, who now has a dressing gown on, kneels in front of him as Botticelli pours the man a glass of wine.

"Robbie, you have gotten old. There is only a little time left, you must reward yourself for all you have done," she says softly as she smiles at him.

"Please Robbie, listen to her. You are known by the ones who will buy. The attitude that binds you is not young anymore. Your bitterness needs to die before you do. It is time, my mentor."

"It is time," Gale di Anti agrees softly.

The music then switches to a pianissimo as the next scene has a rich Verismo texture.

A Dominican Father with a sharp facial structure looks upon the faces of his followers. He lifts his arm up and points to the sky as he begins to speak in the Piazzo della Signoria.

"God, the Father, looks down from heaven and in his sadness he tells me, the last days are coming. The purge of Armageddon is running through these decadent streets carried by fornicators that are scarred with the scorches of the French Pox. Listen to them as they speak about their tiny fixations they find in the short time that they call their lives. They laugh at the words and warnings as their insanity infects the youngest among us.

"They wish to make all bend as they sodomize whomever they wish. They serve the weakest of us fortified wine as they infect the minds of the inferiors of intellect and of reason. They lay man next to man, woman next to woman and adult next to child. They even rape the animals in the fields as there is no control that can stop their tastes for depravity.

"Surely they worship Lucifer as they are the warriors in the cause of stealing souls from the Trinity. The saints say to me that this stench that surrounds us is the new plague. Only ridding it in its nests, in the distorted minds that incubate this disease, is the Holy way to stop it from exterminating all that is glorious and worthy of forgiveness through our personal redemptions.

"There in the minds of the so-called artists, authors and craftsman, this evil of an open sore pusses itself on the canvases with their naked images, on papers with their deliberate abominations and the other trinkets that are worn by the vile as they adorn themselves in these vulgar conceits.

"God's heaven has no place for these egotistical symbols that have risen from the depths of Hades, as the souls of these sorted burn alive while they run from the virtue of the cleansing healing of our penance through worldly pain, that is the rightful and moralistic payment required for eternal life. Look at them with their finery, blasphemous philosophies, and their musical instruments that they use in their secular masses of the satanic rituals that include feasting, orgies, and other self-indulgencies only designed to mock our Savior as he hangs on the Cross in pain and agony for the very souls they choose to hand to Lucifer.

"We must be the saviors of Christ. It is our calling to clean these streets as we rid the decay that these serpents of Hades have dropped like they drop their feces. It is our duty; we are the ones who must rid the heretics, their beliefs, their images and their conceits. We are the righteous, God himself has told me. If Armageddon is only steps away, then we must stand and encounter these soldiers of the Anti-Christ and retake this bastion of God. May our vengeance be swift, be exacting and be uncompromising."

The scene that follows is in a plain room lighted by candles that litter the walls with shadows reminiscent of the domain of the Legion of the Robed. Father Girolamo Savonarola and Sandro Botticelli are in a consultation that does not have room for separate opinions. The Chorus speaks faintly in a vocal harmony that leaves the impression that the walls and the shadows on them are speaking quietly.

"This is no longer the Florence of the de Medicis, Botticelli. The Dominicans are now in charge. Talent from now on will be noticed only if it is used in the glorification of the Church. Secular art, no matter how it is expressed, is not considered worthy enough for the minds and souls we have been chosen to care for," Girolamo Savonarola says as Sandro Botticelli listens without one interruption.

"You are a master. You have the ability to be used by God as a conveyor of his word. Through you, God can reach the minds of the lost souls that are the easy prey of the pleasures Lucifer uses to seduce the vile and un-repentant. I understand you to be a man of reason while I also understand you to be a devout follower of God and his Church. We and others like us are the saviors of more than the simple minds and souls in these streets below us. We are more importantly the saviors of the Catholic Church itself.

"The Pope's corruption is well known by thinkers such as us. The Vatican itself is built on the same conceits that we see while walking among the condemned. You have an opportunity to secure your position with this new and justified rule of Tuscany and the movement it is akin to.

"The inquisitors are slowly flushing the bowels of decadence, and through this procedure the excrement of our society is being flushed out and justly purified. The heretics that are hooked, hung, and burned, serve the same notice on the minds of the easily compromised as your art does.

Your work is less painful, I must admit, but while one is taking place in the public squares, the other persuasion will without doubt seem like the intelligent choice.

"Sandro, as a true follower of the word of our Lord God, you have only one path to walk, and that path is the same path I and the other righteous will travel with you. Walk with us as we serve the true meanings of the words of our Father. You will be continually blessed in this life and in the eternity of the next life you will share with us and with Jesus.

"If you stay still and not choose to walk by our sides then it is out of my hands, and I will not be able to secure your passage through the cleansing currents that are rescuing the broken minds and tattered souls of those you would be aligning yourself with. Be intelligent, Botticelli, the walk down our united pathway will most assuredly ensure that your hands will not be severed or more tragically stricken with paralysis, leaving you forced to endure a lifetime of failures as you try to make them work again. Is this example of sadness more to your liking?"

"No, Father Savonarola, neither this sadness nor another example would be to my liking. But this is not my motivation when I say from my deepest conviction that I agree that something must be done. Could you guide me in how I can better serve the purpose?"

"As I have said, Sandro, your talent will forever be recognized as you skillfully paint the appropriate images. Paint scenes that speak of the plenty found in the righteous teachings of the Church. I will give you words that will inspire you to create the proper stimulus for the imaginations of those souls we are entrusted with. Walk on this path with us and soon you will feel the same lightness that we feel. It is the lightness that God's glory bestows on our journey. Our shoulders no longer bear the weight of mortal lives. God's strength moves through our veins, making us certain as we move on this pathway of righteousness."

"I thank you, father, for making me see that my abilities will allow God to speak through me. I walk with you as we walk with the others, in reverence, in redemption and in the glory of righteousness."

"My dear Sandro, I knew from the outset that you did not require much more than a refocusing on the persuasions."

The opening Prelude begins again, however, a crescendo is echoed through the cavern.

In the darkness, the Legion of the Robed surrounds the flicker and again chants 'Blasphemy, Blasphemy, Blasphemy.' The flame heats as its warmth makes the steam from their mouths turn into a swarm of blood sucking insects that burn as they try to penetrate the flame. The darkness begins to disappear as the light from the burning creatures allows the Legion's region to be recognized for what it is. A cave with pillars that rise to the ceilings where paintings full of illusions can be seen.

The Legion stops its verbal attack on the flame, and in a few moments, the last of the creatures burns itself out, allowing the darkness to retain its throne against the small flame of enlightenment. The eyes of the individuals in the Legion can be seen in the shadows once again as they continue to glare at the flame as it flickers while piercing the darkness.

The chant is recovered, but only as a whisper. The two remain diligent of one another as both are kept in their place. One is in the open, unafraid of itself as it continues to learn about its surroundings and the darkness that remains un-persuaded to reveal its knowledge. As the other glares from its sanctuary of unmovable arrogance where it remains steadfast in the far past teachings that have lost their value in a conservatism that has no place in this time of a new dawning.

In Gale di Anti's studio a young boy is having difficulty with his lesson. He and his instructor begin to sing the libretto in a moving Aria of the glories of human involvement.

"Teacher, I at times feel nothing at the easel. You have taught that the internal emotion moves the brush so the canvas can then sway the one behind the eyes. How can you always feel while you paint?" the boy begins in high triumph of the melodic soprano.

The mature voice of the baritone calmly counters with a tone of marvelous sophistication, "For me feelings never endure. They have their conceptions and their deaths. The lives they live in the betweens are shared and mingled with the other emotional feelings that are living lives at the same moment. For me, the easel allows one to come into focus while the others are held at bay by my preoccupation. This feeling and the emotion that gave it life become my lovers as I paint a reflection of our intercourse. My brush strokes caress the paint with my hope for it to stay still on the imagination that comes to play in the reality of the image. The struggle I internally am trying to cope with releases me from its embrace, as I give it life.

"I try to run from the turmoils inside me, but I am weak in conviction. I give these turmoils eternal lives, so they can then enter the ones behind the eyes. That is what an artist is, a transferor of an emotion that is nothing but an image. We are the communicators, linguists of languages that are universal. We speak in smiles, tears, failures, passions, and all the rest of the human commonalities.

"I am also experienced in the tactile realm. I have loved a living beauty, while I have heard her whisper for more. I have felt my tears fall so painfully that the horrendous fear entranced me to plead for the downfall to cease. I have thought of selling my soul for one kind word, and I have thought of taking my life when I realized my soul was not enough for even one letter.

"My life has taught these feeling to seep from my pores, blanketing me in my own embrace. Although I washed that embrace away more quickly than it appeared, it came again and again until one night I forgave myself for the sin of being mortal. That is the sin that many others cannot forgive me, and that is why my easel is my most trusted confidant.

"It is through my paintings that I try to convince the ones who judge me that it is they that deny their mortality. They keep their eyes on others because they cannot bear the sight of themselves. I do not judge them; my only disagreement with them is in the confusion of who owns my life and who must live my life. How can they own my life when the feeling I have inside, I alone must contend with?

"My easel supports my definitions. You will learn to feel when you begin to accept the fact that you are alive. I promise you, my boy, that life will most assuredly make you a believer."

"Teacher, you sparkled as you answered me. You can feel my confusion. I thank you for not chastising me."

"I am sorry to tell you that the experience of life may not be as understanding as this old man is. Believe in your easel, boy, it will always support your definitions."

The scene ends as the two sit with their backs towards the audience as the pair look at the easel.

In early January, with the dampness and cold driving all indoors, a knock is heard at the front door of Gale di Anti's home.

"Are you busy, or are you just painting?"

"Boy, I am in studio, try to leave my pantry to the thieves that are already there."

Botticelli walks into the studio while eating a piece of bread.

"I am concerned about you, Sandro, you are constantly ravenous. Do you think that one day you will be able to feed that gullet of yours without having to eat the stale morsels that even the mice cannot digest?"

"By the look at the space here I am sure you can afford to satisfy my appetites. You have sold most of it, Robbie, I am happy for you."

"I have been told that you have become a follower of the Dominican Father, is it true?"

"I have become a persuaded follower. He has a way of offering his believers a tiny benefit."

"What kind of benefit?"

"Shall I say, my occupation. He is very friendly after you have compromised yourself. Robbie, they have started to notice your work as well."

"The ones who buy or the ones that are among the Dominican?"

"The Dominican's bunch. I came to warn you that they may come to see you. I hope, my mentor, that I can convince you to take what you can and travel to Rome where you will be safe from these inquisitors. The Pope is not a supporter of Savonarola, you will be safe there."

"What can they do to me, I am an old man. I am not a threat to them."

"Your work is the threat, you paint what they see as the conceits of man. Marianna's life is also in danger, because it is her and her body that you have painted, on more than a quarter of your paintings. She must go with you, and soon."

"She has three children to care for, it would not be an easy accomplishment. I am not going to leave at this late date in my life.

Florence has always been my home and I have promised her my decaying body to feed upon."

"Robbie, artistic romanticism has its place, but not in the faculties of the idiots that presently have the power in their hands. These people have a low degree of tolerance to any idea that runs contrary to their views of godly dominion over our lives. They are inflicted with sanctimonious single mindedness and they will stop at nothing in order to rid what they see as a sickness.

"I will help Marianna leave, I have the tools to accomplish the task. But you must understand that my hands could be lost if I am found to be her benefactor. Please Robbie, swallow your bravery and rest your romantic ideals. Pope Alexander is not a person that enjoys to be called the corrupted of the corrupted clergy.

"Savonarola is a man of absolutes. In his beliefs there are no grey areas, only the whites of purity and the blacks of evil defiance. I am sure he is internally what he portrays himself to be; colorless and bland but emotionally convicted."

"When they come for me I shall be prepared. I will give them my servitude in the same illusion that they believe in. God is a life giver, not a shallow emptiness. God does not destroy, God creates. It is the narrow, the ignorant and the frightened that destroy.

"Knowledge, imagination and discussion fuel the brilliance they are calling the Enlightenment. I will smile at these zealots as I hide the torch of wisdom in my soul. And when the time has come, these fools of fear will be forced to burn in the fires of intelligence. God rest their ignorance in the decay of the dust of all the other past lunacies."

The stunning Arioso completes itself as the two masters of artistic intellectualisms hold one another in the apparent eye of the turbulence that surrounds them.

A Coloratura starts its whirlwind of extravagant ornamentation as dancers of incredible balance and precision move in a unison of controlled yet incredible confusion. Every contradiction spins in the turmoil as Sandro Botticelli and Roberto Gale di Anti sing along with the Coloratura. The sound painting is the description of the power found in secular reasoning, where imagination has become the only worthwhile belief.

"Politics and religion make sorry companions, Fra Silvestro. The two should always be kept separate."

"Senore de Medici, you and your family had ruled Tuscany for a very long time. Father Savonarola now has the task and the will to oversee the resurgence of morality that your rule neglected while substituting it with commerce and art. Glorification of human sin is not what the Holy Bible teaches. God comes before the Church, and even the Church adorns itself with vain trinkets; that is seen in their processions and masses. In Rome the Pope spends the Church's richness on more and more secular abominations.

"Look at your walls, de Medici. You have images of naked harlots that pose only for the purpose of temptation. Look how the art you display relies on the beliefs of pagans, their rituals, their praise to more than one god and their unrepentant destruction of humility, modesty and servitude. These paintings, the literature and philosophies are what must be eradicated, burned, and torn out of the minds that have these insanities deeply embedded."

"Fra Silvestro, these are not pornographic toys. These are the highest forms of sophistication in art that there is. This is the work of one God, our God. These incredible masters feel God run through them as they create these joys. These servants of the great gifts of our Lord, live lives as humans as their creator intended. These are not weapons designed for the purpose of tempting the uneducated. These are the imaginings that come from the minds of geniuses. These artists are the superiors among us. They observe the rest of us and then ask us to contemplate a different view. They add to the discussion. They do not try to destroy it like you do."

"That is your failure, Senore de Medici; you actually believe that God's will can be discussed. There is no discussion. God's intentions are easily understood through his Holy words in his Holy Text. We did not write the words of God as your geniuses try to do. No, we only enforce them by doing his will. God invented Paradise, Lucifer invented argument. You are showing me how lost you are. The educated love to discuss, but this is the true ignorance. The supposed ignorant choose not to discuss because they have intelligently decided what life is meant for. Life was granted to learn the awareness of God, all else is futile, and only meant to exalt frail humans above God, the Father."

"You are an intelligent man, Fra Silvestro. I hope that observation is not taken as an insult to the Holy Father. Though there is the paradox that can be seen when the Holy Bible is now beginning to be interpreted in many different ways. This will distort your beliefs as it will distort contrary definitions. How can your answer continue to be burning, torture, destruction and the other beauties of your inquisition? Are you making followers or are you making enemies?"

"You, de Medici, are sounding like you are no longer a supporter of my associate Savonarola. Ah, I see you have been adding to your collection of secular vanities. Roberto Gale di Anti? Is he that old man that once taught Botticelli? I think he is; an interesting style. Has the old man been hoarding? Good day Lorenzo, I am late for a meeting with Fra Domenico da Pescia, I thank you for a wonderfully educating discussion. I hope there will be enough time for another. Good day."

The Cross of Crucifixion is all that can be seen on stage. Its occupant is a lone child signifying innocence as he wears a halo crown. The boy falls from the cross, and then struggles to right himself as he starts to express the innermost thoughts of purity. The orchestra accompanies him in the most electrifying of Arias with the haunting texture of the complexities found in the depths of a melancholy emotion.

"I of no destiny, I have not been taught enough material to allow my imagination to think between oppositions. I of no opposition, I have not been taught that my imagination is not meant to be sacrificed to a delusion. I of no delusion, I have not been taught the feel of an unbiased opinion. I of no opinion, I have not been taught to silence those who attempt to blind me. I of no me, I have not been taught to search for freedom. I of no freedom, I have not been taught to question the answer. I of no answer, I have not been taught to know my destiny.

"My ignorance is kind to me. There is nothing that can penetrate my purity. All will remain white, as all has no purpose. My ignorance protects me from experience. My white purity will not ever fade from unnecessary worldly involvements. There is no need for maturity, for innocence is the only need, and that need has been satisfied within my purity. There is no need for worldly involvement, how can that delusion hold any significance. My ignorance is kind to me. My ignorance is my savior.

"See life for what it is not. Life is without innocence, all are sacrificed to the laws of involvements. Purity is not a third cousin of sophistication, or a great grand nephew of worldly. Purity is the sensual lover of bigotry, of fear, and of violence. Purity is what hangs on the cross. Purity is savagely crucified by its supposed followers. Purity in its only possible eloquence is mind numbing boredom that is forever used as a persuasion to keep the whip in one hand and the scars on the backs of all the rest. Purity is a lie and the only sin there is. All else must be eradicated to bring purity eternal life, and that truth is not what purity is supposed to be.

"I of no destiny, I have not been taught enough material to allow my imagination to think between oppositions. I of no opposition, I have not been taught that my imagination is not meant to be sacrificed to a delusion. I of no delusion, I have not been taught the feel of an unbiased opinion. I of no opinion, I have not been taught to silence those who attempt to blind me. I of no me, I have not been taught to search for freedom. I of no freedom, I have not been taught to question the answer. I of no answer, I have not been taught to know my destiny."

As the child finishes, he then turns to retake his place on the Cross of Crucifixion. In the same instant, he changes into the adult Christ, bleeding for the purities the illusion needs in order to survive, while the Legion of the Robed are in their familiar positions ever diligent of the flame of enlightenment. The Chorus then echoes through the theater, 'How can Christ be pure and mature?' The orchestra fades as it symbolizes its tongue's refusal to answer the Question. But a single voice can be heard: 'I of no destiny.'

The time of Shrove Tuesday is only a few days away when Father Savonarola is again speaking to a large crowd that has assembled in the Piazza della Signoria.

"The fires have been burning as purity has again found a precious breath. God and the Saints are happy with us; they speak to me in the silences of the nights. They tell me that all the pagan symbols must be found and burned in this Piazza on Shrove Tuesday. Boys will knock on doors and collect all the vanities that are stored inside. These households will begin to feel the cleansing touch of God as they cast their worldly frailties into the gutters. Feel the glory of God as he blesses us with renewed lives of the heavenly purities that await our souls once we have finished our worldly work of servitude to our one God in his trinity.

"Pope Alexander the VIth witnesses our revival of the Holy Word. He dresses himself as an Emperor as he is held aloft like a Caesar. His Cardinals and Bishops adorn themselves in the same vanities our righteousness is eradicating. The corruption in Rome will watch our purifying flames burn away the same decadence that they themselves employ in their ravages of all that is sacred, decent and pure. Watch the 'Bonfire of the Vanities,' Alexander. See it for what it is. Purification over the sickness of the same corruptions of all that is meant to be an unstained virtue in the service of our Lord. We are the soldiers that have been empowered by the Word, and we will carry on with our duties that are justified kindnesses in the saving of the world's eternal souls. God continues to bless us. Amen."

"Are you working or are you just painting?"

"I am in the pantry."

"Ah, you do stop now and then."

"Botticelli, they are gathering my paintings for the main event on Tuesday. How could you betray me?"

"Robbie, I did not betray you. I, too, will lose some of my babies. You must understand that this is the only way through the insanity that the Dominicans are forcing us to be part of."

"Sandro, you knew what they were doing, your argument about my studio exposed me."

"Have they come to see you? Have they threatened you?"

"Do not be a naive fool. Their power threatens everyone. You are twenty two years younger than me; you will recover from the loss of a few of your paintings. I will not have time to recover. I only have a few in my possession, all the rest I have let go."

"Robbie, that is the price you have to pay for what little time you will have left. I am with you and I will never allow them to harm you. All of my peers are beholden to you. You are not alone Gale di Anti, and you will never be."

The whole ensemble begins to harmonize in incredible polyphony of the intermingling layers of emotions, beliefs and convictions. They sing to the audience as they sing to their oppositions. Their unified motives showcase the complexities involved in this human drama played out in the High Renaissance. The defiance of the Dominicans in the face of the Sciences and of the Arts seems as immaterial as the lives of the others that are symbolically crushed in this tournament of jousting.

The dancers move between the calamity in a way reminiscent of how the beautiful simplicities of life can be so easily discarded and forgotten, even though they dance seductively right before your eyes. Every voice has words within them worthy of an uninterrupted moment, but none are coherent as every one of them sings louder until the ears of the bystanders are covered by their protective hands.

Out of the confusion the boy appears again, this time with a very distraught expression upon his idyllic face. All are silenced while the Ensemble is joined by the hooded Legion of the Robed. The boy holds out his hand, and in his palms the tiny flame of Enlightenment flickers as he starts to repeat his song.

"I of no destiny, I have not been taught enough material to allow my imagination to think between oppositions. I of no opposition, I have not been taught that my imagination is not meant to be sacrificed to a delusion. I of no delusion, I have not been taught the feel of an unbiased opinion. I of no opinion, I have not been taught to silence those who attempt to blind me. I of no me, I have not been taught to search for freedom. I of no freedom, I have not been taught to question the answer. I of no answer, I have not been taught to know my destiny.

"I am the purity of every generation. How long must I fight against the tides of God's gift of Life? How can I swim in the seas of life but still be dry? How can I thank God for the gift of life while I stay secure in a craft built from the forests of denial? I refuse to float on a cross any longer. I refuse to hold this flicker of hope in the palms of my hands. The time has come for the seas of life to fuel the flames of enlightenment."

At that moment, the boy threw the flame in the air as the rest of those present watched in enlightenment as books, painting, music scores, fine tapestries, silks, and all of the other human creations could be seen in the glowing fire. All watched as they fell to their knees in reverence to all these dreams that have gained their maturity in the proof of reality.

The boy then said, "I am the only object that has not gained my maturity through the proof of reality."

With that, the boy and the Cross of Crucifixion crumbled into dust that was blown away by a swift wind while all the objects fell to the ground as the flame of enlightenment was blown out. The whole Ensemble started to stand and began to silently walk away, except for the three Dominicans and the Legion of the Robed, who remained and began chanting at the fallen objects and those who had no more attention to give them, "Blasphemy, Blasphemy, Blasphemy."

On the morning of Shrove Tuesday, boys were building a pile of vanities in the Piazza della Signoria. Within the soon to be scorched, there were books of various Sciences, Philosophies, Arts, Craftsmanships, Music, lutes, violins, flutes, hair brushes, dresses, mirrors, ribbons, wedding bands, portraits, painting, and many more treasures of human creativity.

There were masterworks built from the imaginations of past civilizations. Priceless artifacts that could never be replaced, as the insanity was about to do what could never be undone; steal from humanity in order to fill the bare cupboards of intellectualisms with improvable truths based on the fears of the immature and the ignorant. God in his glory was blamed for this rape, as the Dominicans held distorted fairytales and half truths collected in an entirety they called the Holy Bible. This is God's Will, they cried, but God was not ever proven to be one of the torch bearers, while the Dominicans have only ever confessed to being innocent accomplices.

As the fire began, Gale di Anti and Botticelli stood shoulder to shoulder as the flames started to caress Marianna's body. The old man began to sob as he witnessed painting after painting being destroyed. Botticelli held the weakening man as he too, saw three of his works burn amongst the rest. The sheer number of the old man's paintings that were lost in the Bonfire of the Vanities was staggering. The estimates were close to 70 per cent of his total output, and the devastation of his life's work crushed his spirit so openly that many of the tears that fell that day, fell for the loss felt by the once proud Roberto Gale di Anti.

As the fire raged, six more works by the old man were cast on the torrent. He began to scream as he rushed into the fire in a vain attempt to rescue them. The guards as well as Botticelli could not hold him back. His clothes caught fire as he was burned quite severely before he could be dragged back and the flames upon him smothered out. Robbie, through his blackened face could only be heard to say, "My six, my dearest," before he died in the arms of Marianna, who appeared out of the crowd.

She wept as she attempted to brush away the soot and ashes that once were her dear friend's clothes, as Botticelli through tears watched the last of the six begin to be reached by the fires as the incredible masterpiece could be seen by all as it stood on top of the pile in a defiant pose that seemed to warn the inquisitors that wisdom can never be destroyed. Marianna raised her head and as she saw the marvel, sang out,

"Gallant Gale di Anti, I see you upon the flames, you are alive in your masterpiece. You are the Magician."

THE CREATOR

Imagination has the scent of sweet rose petals as it smolders in the fires of a manufactured hell. All the beauties that are the offspring of mastery, brilliance, inspiration and life-induced experience run towards heaven as they try to save themselves from sanctimony. They are regarded as the evils of the flesh in the judgment of fools who have no basic understanding of what they themselves are made of. Imagination is the power behind the intellect and the puppet master of knowledge. Imagination spurs the individual from the moments of want to the supernatural fields of abundance. Imagination is what God possesses and what that entity so handsomely shares.

As the flames drew closer to the painting at the top of the vanities, the imaginations within it ran towards heaven but its creator, its god, lay at the side of the manufactured hell blackened by the fire that was lit by zealous lunatics. Its sacrificed lord, who was torched for the crime of attempting to save the souls of its creations, ceased the imaginations' advance to Paradise. The imaginations sprang to life above the hysterical storm beneath, and lit the sky with not what will be, but what once was.

All the minds within the grounded turbulence witnessed the true meaning of Blasphemy.

The painting depicted a tragic scene of the wonders of distant wisdoms being eradicated from the face of humanity for the crime of not conforming to the appropriate expression. This face had the audacity to smile while dreaming of what can only be described as Magic, that substance that lies just beneath the flesh of every human. It is the substance, that when allowed to seep through the pores, congregates into languages, art, philosophy, and unity. It is simply understood as communication. A web that ties all to all, no matter how the imagination behind it built its version.

It serves as the explainer or the teacher of the ingredient it adds to the table of wonders. It has its songs, its stories, its glories, its tragedies. It warms you with its expressive spirit and will only coil up and hiss in defense of itself. It stays open to openness and has no fear of those who greet it with acceptance, joy and a large space in their heart perfectly designed for the heaven found in mutual giving. It has no formal obligation to follow in accordance to law or ritual designed to make one have prestige over another. They may have their kings, their priests, their administrators, their critics but this is because there are those that have these kinds of abilities, and it is their right to express them, even though some may think of them as underachievers.

The painting was Gale di Anti's greatest triumph. It depicted the kingdoms of splendor burning in the distance as five characters on five white Arabians galloped in the sky, barely escaping the blinding smoke of the fires that raged on the Paradise that once was. The five were; the Fool who had discarded all worldly ties and enjoyed the bliss of no constraint. He was the pure essence of imagination allowed to flow beyond any barrier, discipline or border. The Emperor was also upon an Arabian. He bore the opposite of the Fool, for he was responsible, courageous, determined and the natural leader of the Empire born of the two ultimates, imagination and reality.

The Empress on her white charger was the supreme nurturer. She brought the comforts of life together in calming securities that were the fertile home that was the womb of creativity. Next to her on an identical horse rode The High Priestess. She was the foreseer; she was the seductress of the sixth power, the power of inspiration.

But in front rode the Magician, a man of great power, skill, cunning, and adaptability. A believer in non-judgment, whose open mind and intelligence searched for knowledge not only in the glories of final climaxes of the extraordinary, but also in mistakes that had the material to be rearranged into another success. He was a believer in the inspiration, the nourishment, the playfulness and the discipline in the process of creating the wonders of the infinite expanses.

The five rode as the worlds in their minds could be seen before them. The same beauties that burned behind them, in the flames of ignorant defiance of the power their god had created. The painting portrayed how the facts of God and the gifts bestowed were being distorted by those that longed for the powers of the five. Jealousy, envy, and unfulfilled vanities were the reasons for their destruction of what they themselves were not able to duplicate. The real reason behind their childish complication was the simple fact that they were too lazy to build upon what they detested inside themselves.

They wanted all of humanity to feel the same smothering that killed their own personal identities, so they burned all that was not sterile, vacuous, and deafeningly darkened. The sun shed light upon them, but they could not be seen as they covered themselves in their insanities, as they continually destroyed the brilliances of the Five on the Five Arabians.

The Five rode beyond frailties as they built all the human beauties with their eternal will for unified creation. The High Priestess and her lover, the Magician, lived close to the palace of the Emperor and the Empress, who made the structure the symbol of a resilient soil capable of growing any delight. The Fool entertained all with games sheared from the daydreams that roamed fat in fields of tall grasses and songbirds. The Paradise of growth had roads that entered, but none used those roads to leave unless they believed they could return with an added enlightenment.

There was only room for ignorance if it itself longed for inspiration. But ignorance can only destroy, for it has nothing that it is able to communicate. It withers in a drought of inspiration as it feeds on the dust of ideas long ago spread like ashes on the ground, so hardened by hunger that all it is capable of doing is turning into barrenness.

The Five of mythical expression were the substance of extreme resilience, capable of all that was progressively positive and punctual. They advanced their individual skills, for they too, spent years in apprenticeship. The Fool had a youth full of erratic behaviors, impulsiveness, directionless, and paths taken that proved to be regrettable. One day when confronted by his ability to cause pain, he found his maturity by learning the lessons taught by the Magician. The Fool made amends to those he had wronged, forgave himself, and began his life anew in the service of stimulating the growth of imagination.

The Emperor in his youth was a privileged child of immaturity, insensitivity, and was highly overbearing. He feared the position he was born into and constantly ran from responsibility. His rite of passage from boyhood to manhood came by the ancient manner of having to face his fear, a test administered by his teacher, the Magician. The Empress had to overcome her wasting habits when it came to her personal abilities. She experienced physiological trauma due to her urge to overextend herself. Again, the Magician gave her the understanding of how her nature must abide to the need of self-fulfillment. She, too, must be served; she learned how to recuperate.

The High Priestess was the temptress. She lured the earthly with her sexual seductions, while sadly losing the love she had been given. She met her match in the Magician, when she herself for the first time felt seduced by his sensual powers as they became lovers. The Magician had to overcome his youthful obsession with materialism. He was a young master in the art of deceit. He was an unscrupulous salesman, a trickster, a charlatan. He learned from his personal epiphany the ability to love another when he first set eyes upon the High Priestess.

The Five are the pillars of growth and harmony, thus creativity. They are the mysteries the individual must find within themselves in order to build the empire that lays dormant there. The Five were hunted by the powers that be and the freedom from the terrain of false perceptions, fragmented fears, and the imbalance created by the enslavers of the imagination. The creations of the Five were searched out and destroyed, but not before the wealth of power sustainability was thoroughly inspected by the wiser puppet masters of the dark deceits.

The Five could not be destroyed by conventional means, so the dark deceits used the same tricks the Magician had used in his youth, only with more sophistication that was the result of many centuries in pursuit of the dark perfections. Philosophies that spoke of graces while they burned any alternate perception, an obvious hypocrisy that relied on the skill of spreading ignorance, a direct conflict to the idealisms of The Five, who believed in the expanse of expressionism.

Before The Five were the images of what will come; a world of art and the necessary freedom allowed the artist that resides in the spirits of all. But even that future will be hunted down by the makers of ignorance and prevaricators of the guilts that eat away any desire to flee the circumstance. The shells of those that stayed and watched the fires that burn the glories of the gift of life remain in the ashes like the desecrated, but they can walk, so they are fooled into believing that they are still alive.

Shallowness is all that there is when one is a shell. Burrowed throughout, and all that remains is a vacant hollowness. A facade incapable of retention, incapable of a genuine emotion, for these are the privileges of those who believe there is something inside worth saving. The ones who ran took with them the only Holy Grail there could be. The ones who stayed and fought the oppression became forgotten martyrs. These martyrs are the heroes that opposed the oppression. But they become forgotten as more shells were created. Hollowness becomes the prize when all else is drained away.

The Five have in their possession the truth. The Holy Grail is only an imaginary material object that symbolizes the wisdom The Five build futures with. The truth is the metaphoric substance that dwells in the power of the individuals of The Five. The Fool is Imagination. The Emperor is Protection. The Empress is Fertility. The High Priestess is Inspiration. And of course, the Magician is the Creator. This is the secret behind creationism. Without The Five fully intact, one will forever walk in hollowness.

Those that search for the Holy Grail are the incapable. Warriors who fight the exteriors in order to fill the emptiness that dwells inside themselves; hardened mercenaries who run from the needs of their own souls as they continue to sacrifice their spirits to a God that will never be able to fill their crack-ridden shells. They are romanticized by those who again are in the procession of hollowed beings that hope for others to fill the empty spaces.

These emptinesses fight for the legions of the robed that darken the skies with the soot of the fires they set while certain of their righteousness. Another layer in the decay of the incapables, who use the ignorant to carry out their perversions. The mercenaries rape the beautiful and pillage the treasures of wisdom for momentary pleasures that are left to burn in fires of non sustainability. The empires they create are not from the ashes, and that is why they turn incestuous and rot from within, for there was never a truth that the territory was built upon, only a shallow pretence for the use of the pretentiously shallow.

The Five's escape is yet another advance as the gifted also adapt in order to defend from the new yet familiar enemy. Isolationism is not what The Five seek but how they must defend the enlightenments. Growth is their purpose, so they convince ones of substance to drink from the pools of discussion and creativity while the new sacreds add freshness to the ancient beliefs of entitlements. All are masters in their lives, for only a master is capable of listening.

When The Five reach their new horizon, they will quickly begin to build the new paradise. The Emperor will set out the parameters he will defend as his wife secures the interiors with the enriched environments of education, so wisdoms are free to grow into new enchanting forests. The Fool would play amongst the forests spreading his imaginations throughout all that will grow there as the High Priestess roams the expanse in the mists and twinkles of seductive inspirations. The Magician will search for solitude in the new horizon of the wealth and begin to create anew in honor of all that caresses him.

From the strengths of The Five a new enlightenment will fill all those of substance with an evolved pattern of personal expression. And from the population, growth will be magnified by thousands upon thousands, as the Empire remains free to blossom in its beauty. The Five will rest as others take their positions. A New Five with the same skilled motives will continue the unstoppable. The New Five will be willing to preserve the wisdom when the inevitable fires begin to burn again.

Ignorance has no sense of satisfaction as it must be forever served from the menu of the tasteless. Its bland diets consist of the quick and the ineffectual. Ignorance is easily hypnotized because it is vacant and unable to concentrate. Ignorance finds warmth close to the fires that burn wisdom, for wisdom is a fuel so concentrated that it can give off heat for far longer than an ignorant's attention span.

Before the fires can begin, the dark irrationalities study the wisdoms before the torches are set. They fill themselves with the enlightenments but isolate the knowledge. They do not do so for future education, they keep the wisdoms close in order to grow more of the ignorant. Their fatal mistake: they worship the Magic while they try to kill the Magician. The true creator is murdered so a substitute can take the throne. A puppet master's dream is a drone that cares more for the costume than the powers it represents.

The painting on top released the enlightenment of how The Five will forever prevail. It left the smoke in order to cast on all those present the vision of how a single person could find freedom from the oppression of ignorance. Imagination, Protection, Fertility, and Inspiration are the powers of the Magician, although all these powers were taught how to strengthen themselves by the intelligence of the Magician in the first place. For it was the belief of the individual that all that was needed was already present; the Magician's Magic was how to serve the magic he already possessed. He was merely patient, with himself, and with his talents.

Every advanced civilization furthered the wisdoms, a repetitive technique that goes back to the creator that perfected the procedure. There have always been those that feel it is easier to take the treasures of others than to build their own. Of course, the mistake these thieves make is that they find no value in what easily has been acquired, so they commit the sin of squandering. Once it is gone they require to be fed again, as those without fertility must search for fertile fields. They then repeat the destructive process.

Predators of all species over time develop a genetic makeup that makes them prone to conquer and kill, so it is essential that those who pursue wisdom learn how to defend themselves. Enlightenment is the key. The Five are the key, and Gale di Anti had captured that enlightenment with an astounding elegance of certainty. The painting played itself out over the ravenous crowd in the piazza that day.

The Five were riding to the future enlightenments as the smoke of the past could be seen behind them. But below the smoke, one could see the Pyramids of Egypt, the Pillars of Greece, and the Great Wall of China, among other symbols of wisdoms destroyed by the ignorant, and the smoke in the painting came from the fires that had been set in the Moorish kingdoms of the Iberian Peninsula. Again another step backward for the ignorant while the wisdoms there stood fixed in the prints they left behind. A testament to the consistent lesson that sadly repeats itself until more and more enlightened individuals begin to defend the creators inside themselves.

The image hung in the air as the smoke from The Bonfire of the Vanities burned pure art and the incredible wisdoms inside them. All felt the pain of a part of themselves being ripped away in a barbaric surgery where nothing but promised redemption was used as an anesthetic. The Five above on White Arabians were dearly welcomed by those who had not been completely hollowed out in the piazza. The words of the Dominicans began to be silenced, for even the air refused to hold their defiance any longer. A slow trickle of singular individuals turned away from the rampage of the manufactured hell to witness The Five start a new civilization in the empty spirits of those that believed Paradise could be built inside of themselves.

The Bonfire of the Vanities could be seen for what it was, an ignorant exposure of how insane dogma can become. Frenzied expression has little to do with rationality, as it is nothing more than the passing of the putrid gas of a rotting intellect. To congregate for the purpose of distortion of what is beautiful in every human being is little more than mass hysteria.

Ugliness can only surface through behaviors, and the fires of supposed purity are the ugliest of all.

What truly is being witnessed is the mass suicide of individuality. All the followers of the supposed purifiers hate all that is inside of themselves, but they are too weak to pay a service to sanity by physically destroying themselves before they dissect the innocent. They linger before they die and as they do, they try to infect all around them with their un-provable beliefs and their stifling inactions. The dark ages are the wisdoms that dogmatic beliefs create; a nothingness that can only sustain itself if every being wears away the fertile soil inside themselves by serving their repetitive duty, with the belief that their reward will be handed to them after they die. This can only work if alternatives are continually kept out of reach.

Stagnation was simple in the dark ages, as sickness trimmed down the population. Age was rarely reached, so the questions of the experienced were rarely asked. It is the old that create wisdom, and if one never repeated the mistake enough to adapt, then how could the individual learn adaptation? Gale di Anti was an old man who through his paintings was able to reach and inspire others. The Dominicans made a mistake by throwing the painting of The Five on top of the pile. All could see the glory of the creator inside themselves, not inside the words of a lunatic.

After the cremation of The Five, an interlude dramatically changed the mood. The burning of the secrets of wisdom was framed by the soiled flames of ignorance. The whole extravagance of the wisdoms being burned because they dared to compete with God was so plainly insane. The beauties of the librettos, the coloraturas, the ballet, and recitative all for the purpose of the rich depth inside the magnificent Verismo, brought the frightening surrealism of the event to the shocking attention of all that had the privilege to witness the recreation of this whirlwind of insanity.

The Dominican Father began an Arioso supported by a melody of impaling tension written in the dark shade of C minor. The orchestra crept behind his words as though every syllable had the power to turn all nonbelievers into ash.

"Look how these abominations have no power against these sanitizing flames. See how God has no desire to save these evils of earthly indulgence. This Bonfire of the Vanities should be remembered as a warning to those who in private pursue these Ungodly pastimes, for this will be the result of a life spent in glorifying earthly vanities, for all will perish and all will inevitably burn in the fires of the eternal Hades. Do not look away, turn and see your very souls in these flames. Cleanse yourselves in the hands of forgiveness. We are here to save your souls from this inevitability. Come and confess your evils, let us help you rid all the guilt from your wretched lives."

Some believed the words of the fanatic and did turn in order to confess. Those of any station were publicly executed as heretics, with robes, hooks or fires. Florence became frail as art and any alternate view was torn violently from the minds of their creators in the torture chambers of the Catholic defenders. The streets lost their color as all turned to black and white with only the brave willing to dance with the grays. Life within the flower began to wither; the nectar it once produced was no longer allowed to flow and nourish all the creators who were supporting themselves as well as the others internally.

After the events in the Piazza della Signoria, there still lingered inside most of the citizens that need for expression. When Marianna and Sandro Botticelli tried to bury Gale di Anti's scorched body, the Dominicans refused to allow it, citing the old man as a heretic. His body was taken by the inquisitors and all of his remaining works that could be found were gathered and torched. This act of changing history by denying any memory of Gale di Anti's life as a mentor to the greats of the

Renaissance was the most blatant act of cowardice that Savonarola committed. This and other mistreatments ignited the majority to begin the events leading to the overthrow of this insanity and to place the guidance of Florence back into the hands of the de Medicis, even though Piero was the reason for Savonarola's rise to power in the first place.

The undercurrent of dissent that Botticelli had weaving inside him, gave the artist resurgence and a belief in The Five Gale di Anti had brilliantly portrayed. He started to read Dante's 'Divine Comedy', as he saw mysticism as the answer for his salvation. One evening, Sandro saw The Five in the moonless skies over Florence. He was sure the face on the Magician was his as the five Arabians rode through pillars of Jupiter and Saturn on their way to the constellation of Scorpio, where all is forever changing from one life into another. A place of continuous metamorphosis as one mistake is changed into another ability.

He saw the Emperor secure the boundaries of the expanses as his Empress planted the seeds in her fertility of spacious soils. The Fool in a chariot of stamina played amongst the stars in a pageantry of un-possessed imaginations as the High Priestess' inspirations seduced the Magician. In the skies all was possible, for there was nothing remotely similar to the defecations that were so prevalent in the kingdoms of ignorance. There in the skies along with all of the freedoms, existed all of the excellence in the divinity of artistic expression, all in the glory of life itself.

Botticelli's vision started to be breathed into the same air that the others of foresight began to embrace into their lungs and into their hearts. This revival was displayed on the stage of the second opera with the Chorus singing a similar feel to Handel's Gloria. Art was asked to expand into the horizon so eloquently displayed in the vision upon the nighttime skies in the wondrous mind of Botticelli. All the masters of all the disciplines could be seen in this fortress of sanity singing to the glory of the creators inside every one of them, a moving performance that soared the spectacle into the eternal consciousness of every free spirit in both audiences.

Then a tender Aria filtered through the extravagance as the Empress could be seen singing to her lover.

"I keep my soul pure by my devotion to the prolific. From my womb grows the extravagance of every creation. I bear your fruit as my husband is faithful to his duties. I warm your bed even though your heart longs for another. You cannot take from me what I so graciously give you. You cannot take my chastity for it is already in your possession. We meet in court as all the pleasantries of the Empire must be observed. We are seen as a pair in the highest ranks of the ruling class. But my lips remain damp for yours, as my shoulders tremble, longing for your arms' embrace, and my body lays naked under my garments that has no ability to shield my want for you.

"I will wait in the shadows of your life for a stolen moment, for it will be precious to me as it fills my eager desires. I will gleefully move upon your feathered bed in the manner of a common whore for you, as your physical satisfaction is my joy to give you. My love cannot be harnessed by what is thought to be of good taste and of the highest morals. I will be my husband's wife in the light of all those that cannot bear the dark, while I am of your service when I am called to your quarters. My devotion to you does not cheapen me, for it is pleasure I gain in my life from the love I have for you. I will forever know that your strength was partly nourished upon my breasts."

The Aria is then extended by the vibrant voice of the Magician.

"So beautiful you are my lady, my forgiver. I have not lied to you. My heart is given in earnest to the inspiration I receive from a younger and more pleasant seduction. I have you when my frailty comes to call, for you shield me from the anguish of seeing myself in a truthful mirror. I may call to the other, but you are there to quiet the desire with your willingness and your patience. You softly keep me still as you perform your calming abilities on me and upon my person.

"I do harbor a love and devotion for you, although it cannot be maintained under more welcomed circumstances. I am sorry your husband's diligence to service leaves you so vacant that you allow me to pirate your affections, but I am advised by you that what little I can give is more than you can hope for. Perhaps you also are too devoted to your idealism. Whatever the circumstance may be that keeps you running to my bed, know I thank you in all sincerity for the comfort and privilege your affections offer."

The two join the other for a duet of an intriguing libretto.

"The intimacy we share is our guarded secret. There is not a soul that needs to know. We wave away any earthly shame, for those kinds of inhibitions sour the bliss we both enjoy. Our desires may be different before we lay together, but when we breathe in unison, there is only one desire that remains. We move together on clouds so soft that mist is created by heated caress and passionate flame. We join in a sweetened interlock that melds our very hearts. When there is no distraction, what is being created feels luminescent.

"We dance every step as two of a single movement, in perfect balance and harmony. Two notes that tremble together, that reach the ear as one. A blended sound that enters the torch of passion with a fuel of softened sighs, as Angel feathers fall upon our bodies with a fragrance of the richest oils. We coil within the love we express, in an inconsumable flame that lights the experience with a heightened awareness of this bliss we create together. There is no call that can be heard as our ears belong to the moment. Our eyes are blind to all but us, as our voices sing together."

The pair floated away as the Fool appeared in the beams of the Sun that filtered through the lush forests.

"If I let my mind wonder on that particular branch, I begin to see the outstretched arm and frail fingers that have been elongated by the passage of the ages. It seems to be pointing at the fragment beam with a new hatch of butterflies swarming without a direction. They are not of this grove, for they have been transported from one distant imagination to the imagination that is acting itself out at this almost present moment. The beam masks itself in the appearance of a light through a broken passage to the beyond and before that kind suggestion, as the wings of the butterflies are less resilient but far more transparent.

"I lock myself to the fragmented beam as it appears to be wavering in favor of changing shape as well as texture. A moment before it turned to shadow, the light became organic as it was captured by the transparency of the whole realistic illusion. All that is left ahead are the butterflies and their beyonds that are left behind. The branch no longer points to the beam, as both no longer resemble what I had imagined in that particular past. In the future there will be more pasts that I will explore, as I may have missed an important article in a past exploration. Or perhaps my future will not resemble a past transparency. I thank my mind for the seclusion it gives me from what is considers rational thought, the exclusion of a point that can only numb the point of having the power of imagination, the freedom of pointlessness."

The Fool's solo ends with a harp flowing upward in a retarded de-crescendo that disappears in the space just as the voice of a true baritone begins to sustain a long, clear and heavy low D. The contrast to the Fool's tenor perfection instantly changes the mood from one of playfulness to one of sober conformity. The Emperor's lament is full of duty, honor, and their tragic circumstances.

"I defend the realm with courageous stamina that allows my subjects craftsmanship. They are the glories of the possibles and the disbelievers of the impossibles. They are free to expand upon expression and to grow stronger than I will ever be. They guide my resolve to duty with compassion and loyalty to our state of being. My honor is their masteries and my pride is their growth, as I refuse to come down from my birthright of servitude to their brilliancies.

There maybe things I neglect in life like myself and those who I choose to adore. My strength is constantly growing as my wife drifts further away. My son is born to follow me, though I seldom give him time, and my daughter drifts like an illusion with wisdoms superior to mine. I ride the borders of the empire with my braveries by my side, as we consistently protect from the disruption of our faith, while life goes on around us within creative grace. I am a man of service, a leader who supplies an enduring peace. As excellence expands itself into the horizons beyond this seed, I am a man of service; I am a man who believes.

My gift is unbendable and my life is given without contempt. I will not judge the actions or philosophies that are the result of my station, for they will grow to a maturity that has been the result of all the enlightenments that are created in our unified genius. Without my support, these creations would never exist. I understand the gifts I give and the prices I personally must pay for their never-endings. I sacrifice my freedom, for the yoke I wear as a crown is loaded with the eternities my subjects are creating. How could I forsake the paradises that will be for more than a small moment of pleasure?"

The dignity of the Emperor is defined with a splendor of self-sacrifice as he acknowledges the fact that those he loves are free to live their lives in search of what they require, even if it means disloyalty to him personally. He cannot demand the same things he cannot give, for he honors his service far more than he honors his own household.

As he and his braveries leave the stage, a mist appears and from it in her abundance, The High Priestess can be seen. She walks slightly above the ground as her long black hair flows along her shoulders that are slightly exposed as her white gown seems almost sheer as it is held up by what looks like the most delicate of straps. Her body is proportioned in the most feminine of ways, as it supplies every invade-able mind with an uncontrollable seduction of the most primaly supplied. Her voice is of the finest quality in the Mezzo-Soprano range as she sings about her knowledge of how to seduce creative instinct.

"My power is less than subtle, my power breathes on it own. My power can enchant the most impotent, while it enhances the most powerful of providers. I can glance at a single theory and leave it with millions of practitioners. I am the lover of every triumph and the consort of every minor attempt. I seduce the faint of spirit to fly above their dreams. I stop the most resilient with the fantasy within a calm that they forgot to employ. I give myself without deceit as my seductions go further than the simplest of all requests, though there are the weak that attempt to keep me forever.

I am a drifter, for boredom is in constant supply. I understand my frailty, although I would rather leave than sustain the same mood. What good is a creator if it is not supplied with all outcomes? How could its work be sublime if it had no knowledge of ulterior motives? How could it understand the simplicities of life itself if it was not supplied with the observations of how barren all is without them? I am Inspiration, but I inspire every possible spectrum of all the rainbows of emotions. I am lost, just as I am found.

My heart cannot remain with one. My frailty is never being able to stay in love with one. My sadness is watching as they let me go. I can smile though, because they will never forget the experience we shared, and they will forever have the ability to love another as they love themselves. I know that inspiration will forever be with them because they will see life for what it is, the extravagance of continued inspiration. The glory above all glories. The ability to feel, the ability to experience, and the ability to be forever involved. I am seduction for I am life and I will always be loved eternally even though I may become a sweet memory."

As she ends, a large troupe of dancers start the Grand Adagio of the Creator. It begins with the orchestra in an andante tempo that has a mixture of reverence and foreboding as the Chorus is also present. The Magician moves through the congregation in what seems to be an over crowded Chapel. He sends to the heavens the beginning stages of a Tessitura of astounding resonance with startling moments of high sustain and emotionally draining librettos, as the Chorus and ensemble of dancers react in perfect echo of his every phrase and every motion, as if he is painting the whole movement at the moment. The Emperor, The Empress, The Fool, and The High Priestess also react in accordance to The Magician's will.

"Without me there would be emptiness. Everything you see I created. There would be nothing to be aware of. So what good would consciousness be? Most of the world neglects my creations; they use my brilliances without any praise at all. They cry because of ignorance as they see the beauties I have spawned as trinkets or light sparkles. They are aided by my pathways both physical and philosophical but never bother to question the intent behind my efforts. They praise the supposed God that they pretend to know while hardly noticing the God that walks in their midst.

If I sin according to their sterile judgments then they notice what makes me their peer. Though that is not how they see me as they deny their own shortcomings, they see me as far less than their personally annulated Sainthoods. They try to walk a righteous path that constantly is too hard to maintain. That is because of a simple reason, I have never created such a thing. They do not see The Five inside themselves because they become one of the four supporters. They glorify a part of themselves as they deny the presence of the others.

If they become The Emperor, they will find themselves fixated on one aspect of life. Duty to the cause will be how they reward themselves with honor. They will work their lives away and in the end find themselves tragically incapable of understanding themselves, others and the glory of the entire experience of life. Their power will bore them as their treasures lack originality, and their legacies will be collected by the dust fields that are destined to thirst forever.

If they become The Empress, they will become barren and overused by the ones they have nurtured. They will not learn how to take from another as all take from them. They will never leave their preoccupation for they truly believe that they were born to supply and be used. Few will remain by their sides unless nurturer breeds nurturer which can be seen as a crime against individualism. Once the obvious happens, the fertile soil will die from overuse and be eroded away to be collected by the dust fields and be destined to thirst forever because the last drop will not be taken, it will be given away.

If they become The Fool, they will never find an end to their travels. They will wonder through the places in their minds that will never cease to call. They will refuse to rest from their needs to play and their minds will never learn how to find the stillness within contentment. They will forever find forever in the eternities within the eternities, as they will overlook their exhaustions until they will collapse in their own collages. They are destined to repeat their illusions as these visions will become star dust that is collected by dust fields that will forever thirst for a committed conclusion.

If they become the High Priestess, they will forever journey as they will be forever pursued. They will love deeply but far too quickly as lust ignites the Nova flash that is destined to forever burn out the quickest. Their lives will reach all the heights of all the emotions as well as the darkened and forgotten caverns beneath. Their hearts will never rest in the mid regions on the terraces of life. They will become emotionally drained and spend their last years away from any temptation of deep involvement in life. They will refuse to drink from the passions of life as they are collected by the fields of dust that forever thirst for a patent love.

In my life I am the Emperor because I refuse to dissect parts of myself in order to be the creation of another's perception of who I am or who I will become. I will not compromise who I am for any momentary excitement. I will protect my principles, my borders from any hostile, disguised, or kind attack, for I possess the wisdom that I could be an ornamentation on the table of a being or of a concept.

In my life I am the Empress because I understand my abilities and talents. I will always give them nourishment in order to grow to their fullest. I will forever be willing to learn for I will never become arrogant, for I learn from my frailties that I too will forever remain a student. I will grow stronger as I will appear passive, but my gentleness will always be the result of my strength, though some will ignorantly assume it comes from weakness.

In my life I am the Fool because I will forever play in my unbridled imaginations. I will forever think of the beauties yet to be found, and I will forever toy with my seriousness when I mistakenly think life has betrayed me. I will ask questions as an innocent as I acknowledge the openings of a new personally unexplored region. I will learn through my imagination what could possibly be, and I will imagine that through my gifts I could become the discoverer of the new.

In my life I am the High Priestess because I will always be inspired by my involvements in the glories of life. I will not be a shy lover that refuses to take my chances in the intercourses of life. I will forever be passionate as I lust for the entire experience within the involvement. I was born to make love to life, and I will forever be faithful to the continued inspiration it gives me in return.

I am the Magician, The Creator, for I understand that I am the one who must be kind to the others inside me. I will insure they will be balanced and well cared for. I will never be dissected by anything that is meant to betray me, for I will never betray myself. I am the Creator. I am the one God in my Life, in my awareness."

The whole magnificent illusion within Gale di Anti's masterpiece 'The Five' came to its conclusion as the ashes of the whole extravaganza began to fall from up above the Piazza della Signoria, as the Finale in all its luster and formality could be heard in its earnest.

As the ashes hit the ground at center stage a different fire was beginning to be lit. This had only three vanities that were about to be burned. Father Savonarola, Fra Domenico da Pescia and Fra Silvestro were positioned at center stage as the rest of the Ensemble sang and danced around them as the fire was lit for the execution of the three who were being burned alive for being heretics. Florence was liberated as the three could be seen crying out in agony as their legs were being incinerated while the singing could not totally submerge the screams.

CONFORMITY

As you feel a dream come true while being, you weave your golden thread through the tapestry of the dense thickness of living miracles. Between the grown and the promise, your delicateness hides itself from the view of those that can handle just so much. They salt the flavor of the soup to taste, for their stomachs have soft digestions that cannot tolerate the new or the exciting. Your golden thread appears finely at the edges and the crests of the unfolding. These are the exact moments where perceptions begin to dance in the imaginations of those that still hold tightly to the railings.

Their grips are dependent on how they see themselves in the panorama. They may let go easily or may clutch to what they determine is reality tighter than ever before, but they most assuredly will be swept away. This fact is due to your continuous stitching, as well as the continuousness of all the multitudes who weave with different threads and intentions. The grand tapestry will never be finished as long as there are those who feel the need to express beyond where miracles dance in the imaginations and come to life in perception's infinities that thrive far from the railings.

The only commonality that can be considered stable is the expression itself as it alternates while adapting to the changing atmospheres throughout the tumbling ripplings of the current. Those who remain attached to the railing react as they squeeze their judgments tighter and tighter, as they hold on to the material power the railings give them; the false sense of station as they feel they view all the foolishness before them while forgetting they are being squeezed themselves against the walls of their own perceptions. Those that seldom notice the self crushed along the railings, weave masterpieces that are followed by the inspired. These inspirations fire a new forge that forms astounding ventures into the territories of the unknown, which are the only areas left to grow into.

It is the masters of originality who first weave into areas untouched before and it is their perceptions that are the only worthwhile to explore. These individuals have a similar trait; they need to go much further than ineptness, much further than the practical, much further than the lifeboat of fear, and much further than a moment ago. The only true tragedy is when these emancipators of imagination are cut down by the weapons of conformity. It is those at the railings who wish to be the pallbearers of a stagnant coffin that find comfort in the conformities that destroy the brilliant eternities of unchained imaginations.

The lesser in intellect use all of the malfunctions; jealousy, greed, perversion, gluttony, vindictiveness, cowardice, and disregard. They hold themselves up by use of the railings at the edge of inspiration. They lack everything required for personal identification, while they subject themselves and their narrowness on the defenseless and the young. They will be swept away by their need to expose themselves as the inefficient and the incapable. Their supposed power will pay for the niceties of life, because they will never receive the genuine gift of the highly prized tenderness of the one true glory, the simplicity of love. For they cannot see the beauty in the freely given, and they will remain forever ignorant of the beauties that they continue to crush inside themselves.

I was in the complete; I was in the extraordinary of what was before me. Those that also sat in this audience were fed perceptions from two stages that bounced imaginations into each other that then shattered into crystals and shards of multicolored expressions that shined through in an unending explosion of expressions and excitements. We were in the hands of captivations that molded us into the various and the universal, as we experienced the frail, the frightening, and the flagrances of our lives both now and then. I could see in my breathlessness the beauty I held within myself. I could see my capabilities, my capacities, and my captivations at this very moment. And I could see my futures in my personal optimisms, in my personal orientations and in my personal originalities.

I could feel the accuser in my life, see the witness against me and hear the judge pass judgment on me for the crime I committed, although I had no true understanding of the law that was being enforced.

"I sentence you to constant self-denial for the crime of trying to be yourself. And may God have mercy on your unmemorable life as well as your unused soul."

All three spoke as one, as all three used the same voice, as all three were me. I felt as though I was a masterpiece thrown into the Bonfire of the Vanities with the rest of those in both audiences. All of us were mere creatures of creation by just another creator, who would be carted away by the ones that grip to the railing in their robes of the legions who defecate on anything that searches beyond the ordinary. I was being stretched between conformity and inspiration as I wondered if I was salting the soup to taste. Do I have the strength to explore within the depths of my originalities, or am I, too, fastened to this seat I sit upon in this theater that had once been agreeable to the perception I had come here with?

There was a sadness that I felt due to the fact that I was not alone in this paradox. It seemed to me that everyone else in this first audience, were as close to the edge of decision as I was. I was willing to jump into the depths of myself even though I knew I would never grip the familiar railings again, but still the uncertainty of what would be shaped stalled my advance into myself. Suddenly, the stage began to show me that I must be willing to write the opera of my own design.

When 'The Precursor and The Creator's' last note melted away, the audience on stage rose to their feet and applauded with an enthusiasm reminiscent to the crowds along the thoroughfare as the hero returns from the feat. The whole stage was a vision of triumph and glory, as Carl Scherer and Gabriel Mechant were at center stage in the midst of the ensemble. Angelique and Wilhelm joined the composer and the librettist as the Viscount and the Grand Duke walked towards them. After a long while, Leopold raised his arms to silence the masses and then began to speak.

"Never before have I seen such a performance, this work will not only entertain its audiences, but will continue the debt of what transpired during the time of Father Savonarola. We must stay open to the views of masters such as Mechant and Scherer, for it is vital that we all share the knowledge that can be found in their insight, as well as their opinions.

"I would like to publicly thank the both of you for honoring Florence with this first of many performances, and I give you my word that I will be in the audience when it opens at La Scala; thank you."

The theater erupted again as Leopold and the other dignitaries openly congratulated the pair and the rest of the ensemble.

As this was happening, the displeasure of the Catholic Clergy present was obvious. They left the theater without comment as it became quite apparent that the topic of the opera, along with Bishop Joel's disappearance could be considered the definition of bad taste. Carlo Giorgio hurried himself towards them, as he understood how the whole could be interpreted. Pope Pious the VIIIth was not openly favored by the more conservative branch in the Papal state of Tuscany, and Carlo understood how the politics of the Catholic Church worked. He realized that the opera was in jeopardy if the support of the Catholics was not granted.

As he was noticed by the group, a priest stopped his advance as the rest left the theater. "Carlo, you will not be heard by the Bishop. Your presence at this time acknowledges the fact that we are not in favor of an open defiance of a true follower of the faith. Savonarola will be forever thought of as a hero to the Piagnoni as well as the Dominicans and the Franciscans, even though the Jesuits remain definitely against him. You cannot overlook how Erasmus stood firm as Luther divided the Church.

"What happened in 1497 in this city was not a witch hunt; it was Savonarola's intention to prove that there can only be one creator, God himself. This story you have involved yourself in speaks of countless creators. These kinds of humanistic views are contrary to the teaching of the Lord and therefore the teachings of the Holy Church. There cannot be and will never be a creator other than God the Father. His children must follow his word in order to be granted redemption and eternal salvation. The views you have associated yourself with are the views of non-believers, and therefore will be eternally dealt with as such. I will pray for your soul. Good bye, Giorgio."

As the Priest left the theater, Carlo followed slowly behind him until he began to walk alone into the night of Florence. It was evident to the audience I sat in, that the administrator understood that the grand opera of 'The Precursor and The Creator' had most likely just finished its last performance in a Papal State. Its topic might become too controversial for any future performances in any theater that was in the jurisdiction of a predominantly Catholic viewpoint. This meant that the opera could be destined to failure because it most absurdly would be banned from the region where Classic Opera was born, although the Americas and London were still possibilities, but Bishop Joel would most assuredly object.

"Willy, come back with me, we must see how Camille is. Your work on this project is over and you know that there will be others in your future. It is time for your family to recover from the blows it has suffered during the last seven months. Your mother is in Paris and I am sure she would find a great deal of joy as she watches you step into the future as a Count. If we left tomorrow we would be back in time to celebrate your birthday together."

"Yes Papa, I will go back with you, Camille needs all of us at this time," Wilhelm assures the Viscount, as the two of them return to the main room where the post-performance engagement is taking place.

"Madame Beauvie, your husband's story will create a great deal of controversy, was that his intention?" Leopold asks Angelique.

"Leopold, I am sure I am not aware of what controversy you are referring to," Angelique responds.

"The Church will find the topic not open for outside discussion, as they are in enough turmoil with how much of a grip on conservatism is appropriate. What has been referred to as the age of enlightenment is now being left as the pendulum of change is swinging back in favor of their resistant point of view. The Vatican will always be the slowest to conform to new thought. This opera will open old wounds and pour the salt of the next enlightenment upon them while the Council in Rome will do all that is in their power to stop that eventual outcome."

"Leopold, do they still have the power?" Angelique asks naively, the first such occasion so far in the whole event.

"You are suffering, my dear, from the ailment most of us suffer at our particular place in society. I have to balance all the dishes in the air, that is my duty as leader of this Grand Duchy and a diplomat in these times, that is why I can see what you cannot. The Church has incredible power, for they occupy the minds of the ignorant. I am a Catholic, but that does not mean I believe in the Church. However, there are those in the same position as I am in other jurisdictions that are entirely the puppets of Rome.

"These personalities do not have the strength of their own convictions to guide them. They have been softened by their pillows and by the strokes of their egomanias. The Church finds such leaders easy to corrupt and even simpler to threaten. This extravaganza may never again play in continental Europe. It could find its fortune elsewhere, but I am sure that was not the intention of its composer or its author. I am sad to inform you, Madame, that you may also suffer from the comfortable insulation that comforts the ones I speak of. "

"I am not a practicing Catholic, Leopold; I assure you that the Church does not have reins on me," Angelique responds with a touch of wasp.

"Perhaps not, my dear, but when one forgets that the world they created has been created right in the middle of another's empire, it will inflict injury and therefore must be extracted. Power can be brutally subtle, Madame Beauvie, and pushing one's views into the ears of the defiantly deaf will not last long as the hand swats the irritation away. This opera, though highly intelligent, has made the fundamental mistake of overlooking the political situation and the philosophies of the times. This, I assure you, is the mistake of political amateurs or those who think they ride in the chariots in the skies far above the lowly mundane realities. I am sorry to inform you that this theater is not in an ideal meadow where it will be allowed to grow tranquilly."

"My, I must admit that idealism has again seduced the easily pleased. I wonder if my husband and his partner are aware of these circumstances. Tell me Leopold, would you come and watch a performance in London?" Angelique asks as she smiles at the Grand Duke.

"Madame Beauvie, I would be honored," Leopold answers as he graciously bows.

Angelique then leaves the Grand Duke's side and wanders through the reception until she finds Gabriel. They can be seen by Leopold talking as they slowly leave the festivities behind them in the manner of two thieves leaving ever so nonchalantly from the robbery that is still in progress. The two dismiss themselves from the gala and find a comfortable open carriage to silently steal themselves away from the obvious disappointment.

The stars brilliantly play in the skies above them as their twinkles grant the pair instant wishes far from the circumstances on the stones of the realities the pair in the carriage so roughly navigate over as their escape will be simple, although the details will most assuredly follow them like the wolves that chase the chariot of the god Thor and its other occupant, the Sun. No one is immune from their outcome.

The next day, Wilhelm left the Palazzo Corsini and Florence to accompany his father, the Viscount, on their mutual journey to Paris and their responsibilities to Camille. Herr Scherer was complacent in his good-byes to his lover and protégé, as the composer had accomplished a new thickness to his arrogance. Gabriel and Angelique were also of the same mood as the young Count-to-be; they could also feel the time had come to leave the place of birth of the spectacular production and take it away from the places of its certain demise. Scherer, in his style, went along with the decision to leave as the three believed that Paris would be the appropriate place to rest and plan the next performance and its location. Carlo Giorgio was persuaded to accompany the three, and he in turn, secured the majority of the ensemble's promise to pick up the opera wherever it opened.

The four traveled to the coast and secured passage on a boat to quickly take them to Nice where they stayed for a few days until they completed the journey to Paris. When they arrived in the city, political unrest greeted them as King Charles was curtailing the civil liberties of the citizens, and the lower classes were continually creating disturbances in retaliation. Even though France was a Catholic nation, it was not a Papal State, so the Church could not use its persuasive powers to quell the unrest. The House of Bourbon which included Wilhelm, Camille, and of course, their parents, was losing its grip on the railings of power.

The press was being curtailed and at times completely silenced if they wished to express any alternate view other than the message of the Bourbon's. The performance in Florence of 'The Procurer and The Creator' was not reported on publicly but in private it had done exactly what Leopold had suggested it would, it had added to the discussion of what art is and what treason is; an interesting occurrence when one considered what France was gripped with at the time.

Madam Angelique Beauvie was in glory once again as she was forever in the company of Gabriel Mechant and Carl Scherer, who were seen as folk heroes for their opera. It was seen as a compelling view of how oppression could destroy the legacy of the individual, and therefore, human beings as a whole. Copies of the libretto mysteriously began to surface and were read and discussed all through the overture of the second wave of the French Revolution.

Charles the Xth was in a binding position when it came to the topic of the opera and the connection his family had in the production of it. The Church still enjoyed influence when it came to the Monarchy, so much so, that in 1825 Charles passed the Anti-Sacrilege act which meant that the death penalty could be administered to those who dared to engage in blasphemy and sacrilege towards the teaching of the Church. He decided to not publicly notice, thus taking the position that the powers that be thought the opera and its topic was nothing more than a commoner's ignorant pastime and unworthy of intellectual thought. This proved to be an intelligent tactic as the opera itself was never performed in the weeks ahead. All it created at the time was an illusion of a far away possibility that was incapable to solidify itself as another rallying point.

Gabriel still enjoyed the worship he was receiving, though he understood fully that the Catholic Church still had more than the opera as a reason for their fixation on him and the others who were in London at that particular time. The French police interrogated all of them using the Bishop as the central reason for their inquires, however, the mysterious appearance of the libretto in a booklet form was the real reason for the minor inquisition. Treason was still a crime, even though the Bourbons were certainly losing the grip to the thrown, and the trick of leaking material was a well played card in the streets of Paris that was used many times before.

Even though all this intrigue was playing in these scenes of Gabriel's life, he was still drinking heavily, and most of time he was despondent; a fact that could simply be seen as his morbid reaction to the plight of his mistress, Camille. Gabriel had not yet gone to visit her at Chatham, perhaps the paramount reason for this was the fact that this whole entanglement had started there months previously. Or, it could be that he was certain about the vision that awaited his arrival there, a scarred, boiled over reminiscence of the once untouched purity of idealistic male fixation. Life is mostly cruel to the living portraits of the beautiful idealistic illusions, for even they must survive the aging process.

On June 29th, in the mid afternoon, a distraught Wilhelm burst through the front door of Gabriel and Angelique's Paris apartment with the intention of confronting his sister's seducer, but all he found was an old man so drunk that he could barely see coherently.

"Who is there?" was Gabriel's only reaction to the noise coming from the hallway. As Wilhelm entered the room he could see the half clothed man in an arm chair clutching an almost empty bottle of cognac.

"My sister is dead!" Wilhelm screamed at Gabriel as the younger man cried uncontrollably.

"She died?" Gabriel asked solemnly as the bottle slipped from his hand.

"She died giving birth to a dead premature deformed gargoyle you gave her to carry as you most assuredly wrapped both of them in your fallacious disease."

"She was pregnant?" Gabriel responded as he tried in vain to stand as his drunkenness kept dragging him back into the throne of his bitterness.

"You killed her intentionally even though no court would ever be able to convict you for the crime of stealing the purity of the defenseless. You knew all along what kind of spell you could weave in her heart. You are a master of corruption and a devourer of youthful ignorance."

"Watch your words Willy boy," a more awake Gabriel warned. "I loved your sister and I would have welcomed the child handsomely in my childless existence. Look at me you fool, and see what I am without her. I am lost, and I will never recover from her death, and I will never smile again, for the child I never knew existed, has taken away any future happiness that might have been possible, away from me."

"You are an obvious liar. They are using your name in the gutters of Paris as they try to overthrow my cousin as you did by sliding under the sheets of my sister's bed. Without question you satisfied her momentarily but she was beginning to see other pleasantries in much younger eyes than the bloodshot pair that you blindly see with.

"Your glories are bought for you by the way you move a pen on a bare piece of paper, but you are nothing but an imposter, as your personal behavior can never equal the words you run together with extraordinary brilliance. How could a pig like you ever produce more than a grunt?"

"You little... Willy, let us not forget how you enjoy having your ass fucked by your surrogate father. You are young and you have already learned how to keep your ass tight by use of your smugness. Your man is through with you Wanda, you do not seem to understand that you are getting too old for him. Surely you are aware of the fact he always has at his disposal ten year olds to satisfy his repulsions," Gabriel says as he regains his feet. He then feebly lunges at the Count missing him while crashing into a table that he uses to steady himself. Wilhelm reaches for a dueling foil that is upon the wall next to its twin. The Count turns the sword on Gabriel as the older leans back while the edge is directly pointed at his bare neck.

"Wanda, are you growing testicles?"

"Hold you profanities within, Mechant; I am not willing to continue to engage with an old cliché."

At that moment Gabriel moves towards Wilhelm as the young man slashes the sword in fear. He then drops the foil and gasps as he realizes that he has cut Gabriel from his neck downwards to his upper chest. Gabriel feels his wound and then looks at the blood that has quickly coated his hand. He then bends down and picks up the foil and points it at Wilhelm as he says without any apparent pain;

"My boy, you came here to get my attention, I must tell you that you have succeeded."

Mechant then pierces both shoulders of the stunned and then plunges the point deep into the heart of the convicted. After Wilhelm falls along with the discarded sword, Gabriel finds another bottle, returns bleeding to his throne, and quietly says;

"This fiction took my life in the beginning and now in the finale I no longer have to act. What a pity, there is not a single soul to hear my last words. But then again no one ever heard a single word I ever said, for I was never allowed to be truthfully understood."

He then drinks until he can no longer lift the bottle as his throne of bitterness becomes another crimson sacrifice while he bleeds ever so silently to death.

Again the lone voice of a boy soprano hangs in the air suspended between the reality played out on stage and the perception that floats into the audience. We begin to hear a faint whisper of a non-distinguishable sort that adds an element of unjustified judgment as one voice is worthy of remembrance, and the other is lost in the moment. I feel myself being taken by the event on stage to an illusionary courtroom of unbendable bias. I find my seat in the jury box while evidence is being given by the prosecutor. I then notice tragically that the defendant, Gabriel, has been muzzled. I stand in unison with my fellow jurists and shout 'guilty' as the head of the defendant falls to the floor and rolls towards a street gutter where it falls into the storm drain with the others who have been severed as they are swept away by their faults found in the human environment.

I feel surprisingly clean as my biased morals wash away any disfavor I have in my duties of upholding human decency, even though I am fully aware that, at times, the two concepts have very little to do with each other. I find myself back in the audience as I realize that I harbored hate for Gabriel, and I am happy, in a way, that he died so coldly. I then start to think about Camille and her brother as my compassion for them secures my redemption as a person of true moralistic ideals. I take some notice that my personal beliefs may be entirely arbitrary, although they are undeniably self-serving.

I feel I have regained my senses as I sit more comfortably in the audience while I continue to watch a portrait of the outcomes of indecency. Suddenly, I see myself on a high pulpit as a bonfire is burning below me. I hear my voice praising the destruction of opposing viewpoints as I quiver in the sweet stench of my grip on the lifelines of those I hold in contempt. My words light the flames under the heretics in my life as my heart and soul can be seen escaping from my hollowness. Suddenly, I feel my forgiveness as my tears fall on my contempt and I let go of the railings inside of me as I find forgiveness for the Gabriel that is a part of me.

How dissected am I when I am swept in the same torrent of human polarities as I witness the severed portions of myself falling into the storm drains of the various lives I have led. I am Gabriel, Wilhelm, Camille, Angelique, and Scherer, as well as the other characters in this opera that has been so cleverly disguised. I now notice what it has always been, a portrayal of the parts of my unbendable self. I now understand what my dilemma has always been. I have not learned how to conform to myself, and that is the only true conformity there can ever be.

Later that day, when the front door of the apartment was being opened by Marta, a heavy smell of liquor rushed into the hallway past her, Angelique, Scherer and their bodyguards. There was an impending feel of tragedy that also mingled with the distasteful aroma. The bodyguards halted the advance into the apartment as two of them went in alone. One came back to the party and told them not to come in. Scherer in his arrogance refused the request and pushed himself past the guards and into the apartment as Angelique and her maid followed behind.

"Damn fools!" was all Scherer could say when the bloody room was introduced to his eyes. Angelique screamed in horror as Marta and a guard went to her aid. They took her away from the scene as a trail of urine could be seen behind her. Scherer and the remaining guards all had a shocked look upon their faces.

"Get a doctor for the woman; she will need someone to help her through this. While you are at that chore, the police should also be notified."

Scherer ordered the men as it was obvious that he was in deep thought about what the ramifications of this incident would mean to him. As the room was vacated by the guards, Scherer looked at the slaughtered pair in their separate pools of drying blood, went over to the side table and poured himself a glass of wine and then toasted the dead while saying,

"You both take from me my burden while give to me glory in return. I thank you both for your sacrifice to my wellbeing. To you Willy, I thank you for the gift of your brilliance with orchestrations and melodies, your garment of genius fits me perfectly. And, dear Mechant, I thank you for the gift of a full writer's share of the opera's receipts and a welcomed return to London as the disappearance of the Bishop has finally been solved. Again, I thank you both. Where would I be without your involvement?"

He drinks his wine casually as he bows ever so arrogantly at the two. Scherer then puts his glass back on the side table as his smile leads him out of the room. Behind, a silence begins to chew on the lives that have ended, so Scherer's pretence can be well nourished like any other vultures' vulgarity.

When the police arrive, Scherer remains in their presence and successfully keeps them from questioning the distraught Angelique. He later leaves with an inspector while Marta is left with the Doctor and a nurse as they all attempt to quiet Madam Beauvie. A dosage of opium and sherry relieves her from her misery while the corpses have been removed and the cleaning of the death room has commenced by two cleaners brought and left behind by the mortician. The nurse remains in the bedroom while the Doctor and Marta speak in the pantry.

"I will notify her parents and discuss the fact of the case with Dr. Mousseau at Charenton; he will want to aid you in your Mistress's care. She will be despondent and I think her sadness may give her thoughts of harming herself. I do not think it would be wise to leave her alone. I will send another nurse to aid you in the watch over her. The dosage I just administered to her should be repeated at six hour intervals, for a day or so. I will return in the morning to examine her again. Good evening."

"Good evening Doctor," Marta says as she helps the man with his overcoat. After he leaves, she goes and checks on the progress of the cleaning. She then walks back to the front door of the apartment, opens it and looks around the corner for the guards.

"Gentlemen, could you please help us?"

"Right away Marta," is the answer given, as three of the gentlemen file inside the apartment.

"What do you need us to do?" asks the Captain, and Marta motions for them to follow her. When she re-enters the room, she says,

"Please Frances, could you and your men remove the carpet and the chair, the both of them will not be needed anymore."

The stained carpet is rolled up and carried out and then the chair is the next to leave while the blood is being removed from the floor. The room is restored to its original cleanliness except for the obvious hole in the picture that the removal of the piece of furniture and the ornamentation has left. When the guards return, Marta walks in before them saying,

"Put these replacements in the appropriate spaces."

The guards have another carpet and chair in their possession and once the carpet has been laid down and the chair has taken the place of the one before, the cleaners and the guards leave Marta as she returns the fixtures to their appointed perches. She even hangs the foil back on its hooks next to its partner on the wall. She then smiles as a sense of normality returns to the space that has been covered in a thick surrealism as Marta defies the moment with a sweet, patient denial. She pours some wine into a glass and toasts eerily in the same fashion as the one before her.

"My daughter returns to me and I am assured that she will be mine alone until death discovers that I must be repaid in the afterlife for my duty to repentance. I will no longer be the afterthought."

The deaths in the days after supplied the boulevards of Paris with more fuel of descent as the thought that Gabriel Mechant was killed by a distant cousin of King Charles enraged those who reacted before gaining the entire truth. The fact that the two were involved with the same opera and somehow connected to the disappearance of Bishop Joel would quell another determination for the outcome. But for the purposes of creating hysteria, Mechant being murdered by the King had a very favorable sound to it as it added an undercurrent to the events of July 1831.

Scherer was returning to London as the police in Paris had been in contact with Peal and his office. Apparently, new developments about the Bishop had come to the attention of the Paris inspectors, and the return of Herr Scherer had a great deal to do with it. Angelique was still very fragile although she was, at times, her old self. On the afternoon the day before Scherer was scheduled to start his journey back, he came to visit her one last time. She met him on the terrace of her apartment where Marta had prepared tea for the both of them. A week had gone by since the occurrence and a genteel manner was employed by the both of them.

Scherer was led to the terrace by Marta where he found Angelique alone. After Marta closed the doors on the pair, the pleasantries began.

"Carl, how good of you to come to see me. I hope you are coping well."

"I will survive this, but you Angelique have lost more than I. Are you returning to your usual health?"

"In time I will adjust to my losses. The Doctor has taken good care of me, Carlo has been ever so kind, and of course, Marta remains steadfast in her loyalty to me. I have been told that you are returning to London."

"Yes, I will be leaving Paris tomorrow."

"Will you be staying there for long?"

"Well Angelique, it is my home."

"The Bishop may have something to say about that, Carl."

"I think I have solved that problem as well."

"Interesting, could you be more specific?"

"I think that in your condition you should leave this to me. You must be more concerned with continuing with your improvement in health. These details may be too much for you at this time. Trust that I will clean the entire mess for the both of us."

"Carl, I may be slightly beaten, but that does not destroy my memory about your lack of talent in the areas of deceit. Of course you are capable of covering your tracks but you do it with such distastefulness and predictable clumsiness. Perhaps I should be the one employed for this delicate procedure. Of course my record for such things is quite masterful, do you agree?"

"Angelique, your husband is dead, that means, as you so often said before, your voice has been silenced. I think that our tenure together has been severed along with your vocal cords. I no longer have to be polite to you, Madam, you have lost your grip on reality and you do not see that you have fallen backwards to a time when your words had thunder in them. I apologize in all sincerity, but I can no longer hear you."

With that he begins to laugh as he starts to leave.

"Before you go, you pompous ass, I should tell you that there are entire stories and librettos that wait for your scores. You could continue to write with your collaborator for years."

Angelique then stands and walks toward the composer, and strangely whispers,

"Gabriel's words are not dead, he can write from the grave. You would be making the mistake of a lifetime if you refuse to investigate my voice and the words it speaks at this very moment."

"You are insane Angelique."

Herr Carl Scherer says coldly as he then turns and walks defiantly out of the woman's life.

As soon as Carl walks out of the apartment, she finds Marta.

"Have a carriage readied, then come and help me ready myself, I own my dear friend Pierre a visit."

Marta begins to smile as she hurries to fulfill the requests. In a while, the carriage door is being opened for the again radiant Madam Beauvie as she enters alone with her typical grace. As the horses are coaxed to move by the driver who is sitting next to Frances, the Captain of the guards, four other guards ride alongside, with the Captain's horse following behind as it is led by a tether that is tied to the baggage compartment.

When they reach their destination, four police officers walk towards the transport and along with the five guards already present encircle the Madam as she walks through the doors into the foray of the main Paris police detachment. Once inside, Angelique is greeted by Inspector Pierre Legard.

"Madam Beauvie, this is a pleasant surprise. I must comment on how well you look when one considers the difficult time you are experiencing."

"Inspector, as usual you are the epitome of graciousness. I hope my visit here has not come at a particularly busy time."

"There is always time for you, Madam."

The Inspector says as they start to walk down the hallway while they secure more privacy with every step leaving the escort behind to wait.

"We will be able to talk privately once we are in my office."

"Thank you, Inspector."

As soon as the door to the office is closed behind them, Angelique embraces Legard tenderly.

"It is good to feel you again Pierre, I have missed you terribly."

The Inspector kisses Angelique passionately then walks to his desk as he begins to speak.

"It has been months since I rescued your husband and his German friend from that mess they repugnantly created last October. The German's plaything died in the cell of Mosseau's sanitarium without any care or concern. I held my words, Angelique, as I promised I would. Now you appear boldly in my detachment at supposedly a tragic time in your life. Tell me, why do I think that our past love affair is not the reason for your visit?"

"My husband is dead, Pierre, there is nothing that can separate us anymore my love. You have always been well informed, you know I have been traumatized by all that has happened in the months since I have seen you last. I am still not at my best, but I must make a future for myself as I spend the present regaining my strength and composure for that future. We have always worked well together, Cherie, that, you are certain of. I want to welcome you back as my lover and I have a gift for you that will prove my loyalty."

"I am well informed, apparently your body has been active these past months, do you intend to continue to add to your lengthily list of indiscretions?"

"I will gladly answer that question my darling if you first tell me how many have been added to your list. We have never been puritans, and those garments would be misfits for us as they would never hide our hypocrisy. No Cherie, I am certain that neither one of us would wander from our beds, unless of course, you have an attachment. Do you? And could she compare her vileness and techniques to mine?"

"You know the truth about me, Angelique. I would rather bed the professor than chase the students, as age is required to complete the duty with perfection when youth stumbles while usually being infected with short attention spans. There are no particular involvements at this time, so very little adjustments would be needed in order to find space for you.

This gift that you mentioned, what would that be?"

"Would your superiors be excited if you solved the disappearance of Bishop Joel as well as the deaths of Count Wilhelm and my husband?" she says as she smiles and sits on the Inspector's desk like a wrapped Christmas package anxious to be opened. Legard stands up and moves towards the woman and starts to unbutton her top until her still very firm breasts are exposed. He puts both of them in his palms and lifts them slightly higher as he looks at her face intently.

"They would be very excited, as I am beginning to realize that I, too, am enjoying that particular feeling. Perhaps we should consummate our agreement."

"You will feel, Cherie, that my entirety agrees with you most warmly."

The two then embrace as the desk is used as the structure for the purpose of signing the partnership. We watch the pair on the stage as music again fills our ears with a melody layered with a harmonic element that makes the feel of the movement seem stale and uninspired. It fits perfectly with the vision upon the desk of an old seductress making the same over used potion she has made throughout the whole performance.

The Inspector can be seen happily tangling himself in her web as her skills of deception have him believing he is in the paramount region of lust. He obviously feels his hands and his fingertips are fortunate enough to touch the mounds, valleys, orchards and streams of well used fairgrounds where admission is paid for by committed sins. Venus will never starve as there are an abundance of fools who are happy to be manipulated. Venus will never lose her grip on the only heads that matter to the ignorant and Venus will never grow old in the eyes of those that prefer idealisms and their instant intoxicants.

Eleven days later, Herr Carl Scherer is arrested for the murder of the Bishop of Normandy as he enters his London estate. He is taken into custody by Scotland Yard as the carriage is stopped as soon as it passes the front gates. Peal opens the door and greets the Grand Composer in an irreverent sarcastic demeanor.

"How good of you to join our party Mister Scherer, I thought you would be happy to end this ordeal for the lot of us. This gentleman to my left has been sent by the Paris Constabulary. Inspector Legard, this is the man of the hour."

"Herr Scherer, I am very fortunate to meet you. I am sure you will enjoy the tour we are about to take."

"Now Pierre, you will spoil it for him."

"I apologize, Inspector, I should remember my manners."

"Pierre, a trivial faux pas. And I am sure you remember Jonathan Broadfoot, the Times writer."

"Good to see you again, Herr Scherer."

Broadfoot says as he smiles and bows.

"Shall we begin, Scherer?"

"Inspector, I do not find this event amusing and I am certain that you are stepping over the wishes of those who employ you."

Scherer says in his usual arrogant way.

"You are right, tunesmith; the King himself told me that he wished to see your face when we nailed your arse to the wall. You know he has a wonderful sense of humor, especially when he is relieved of nagging irritants. I have noticed that you enjoy being an irritant."

"Now wait a minute, I told the Paris police about everything, you are making a terrible mistake," Scherer spills as his usual nature is beginning to crack. Still, he is forced to walk towards the lake and the gardens in between the two households.

"Pierre, could you inform this person about all the information gathered in Paris?"

"I would be privileged, sir. You must understand Scherer that your account of the events seems to be contrary to what can be described as, how should it be said - believable.

You have stated that the deaths in Paris were due to Wilhelm Gunner's vengeance towards Gabriel Mechant. You say that Mechant seduced Camille Gunner and that was the motive for him to murder the Bishop."

As the group descends down the hill and towards the lake, Scherer is shocked to see Viscount Gunner waiting to join the crucifixion.

"Good day, my Lord, I hope we have not kept you waiting," Peal asks.

"No, I find the summer warmth very fitting for this particular outing, and I assure you Peal, that I will relish it in its entirety."

"Indeed, please continue, Pierre," Peal says in agreement.

"As I was saying Herr Scherer; this account of a motive is very thin. You see, the Viscount's children had also made statements, although their accounts were subject to a wavering of certain particulars that have recently been made clear in a miraculous fashion. Madam Beauvie has finally come forward."

Scherer's face begins to whiten as his mouth opens in surprise.

"We now believe that the motive had to do with the opera and the homosexual encounters you and the young boy had been having for years. We feel that you infected the mind of Wilhelm with your perversions when he was very young and as he grew older, the morally weakened boy continued being controlled by your destructive spell.

You were caught in the act of one of your many perversions by Bishop Joel on the night of his disappearance. The boy's Grand–Uncle then escorted you out of the Viscount's home and as soon as the two of you walked past the first set of hedges up on the hill there, just outside of the house, you killed the man."

"No, no, it did not happen that way. Mechant killed him, I am innocent. Beauvie is insane," yelled the very frightened accused.

"How dare you slander the poor woman? Shut your mouth and listen, Scherer, or I swear I will gag you. Believe me, man, you have said far too much and I have no more patience for your repugnant hollow arrogance. Please carry on, Legard," Peal said in the extreme voice of authority.

"Yes. You then carried the body to the lakeside where you rowed him in that boat and threw him into the lake. I have been told that it is very deep."

"Okay Charlie, turn the boat over," Peal tells his constable, as Legard continues.

"Look, Herr Scherer, under the side of the interior of the vessel, can you see that stain, right there? We believe it is the blood of the Bishop. Look at the rope; it is not the same rope that was there on the night this boat was used in the effort to conceal the body, is it?

"It was wondered why the retaining wall was constructed until we learnt that there used to be garden nymphs there. Seven but we could find only six in the shed close to the working buildings and stables.

"We know it was not Mechant that murdered the Bishop because he always used the small cottage on the other side of the lake for his rendezvous with the young Camille. He was much more sophisticated in the art of sodality than you, Messier. He would never have let his indiscretions be discovered, he was not drinking heavily, and therefore, he would have remained extremely careful.

"No, it was you that had the most to lose with an opera pending that most assuredly would have rejuvenated your dying career. With the brilliant Gabriel Mechant writing the libretto, and the young genius of Wilhelm to steal from, you knew this would be your only chance to reach the upper floors of artistic acceptance. That is the motive that is most convincing. Inspector Peal, is the main event about to commence?"

"With pleasure, my friend; okay, Charlie, let us watch you go fishing. I have a feeling that there is a big surprise waiting for the piano player."

"Watch, Herr Scherer, this part will be very exciting for you. You are about to be reintroduced to a very intimate acquaintance of yours, who will also join with us as we all denounce you. I hope you find this as enjoyable as the rest of us do," Legard recites in the continuing grinding tone of sarcasm.

The boat is put into the lake as the constable joins a fellow officer as he begins to row it towards the middle. Another boat can be seen rowing from the other side as three swimmers also move to the same location. The swimmers are the first to arrive as one of them can no longer be seen as he most assuredly has started to swim to the depths. Soon, he reappears with a rope that he then passes to one of the other swimmers, who then it turn gives it to the Constable as he arrives.

"We left the treasure where we found it earlier, minstrel. We thought that you would want to see how unfriendly the water is to a dead body," Peal adds with the same source of contempt that has followed Scherer throughout these travels.

As the men in the boats pull on the rope, Scherer begins to cry openly. The others with him are certain now that the man is guilty as they see his tears as the admission of the crime and the end of this part of it. Scherer does little to console himself and nothing to try to hide his crumbling. The man of stoic resistance to anything that could be described as gentle is now finally without a handkerchief to hide behind.

The body of the Bishop is raised and put into the boat along with its anchor as it is then rowed back to shore where the men are waiting. When it comes to shore, the pale and blotted body of the Bishop can be seen with missing parts of his ears, toes, fingers and face vividly describing how the fish in the lake have been gathering extra nourishment. Next to the banquet, the nymph can be seen with the word 'Lust' cut deep into it.

"That is the rope that once served to tie the boat, is it not Messier? You used it to tie one of your sins to Bishop Joel. How ironic," Legard eloquently observes.

"A wonderful phrase, Inspector. May I quote you in the book I have been writing about this case?" Broadfoot asks, while the Viscount turns swiftly and looks straight at the writer as Legard answers,

"Certainly."

On the morning two days later, after a quick exercise in a courtroom, Carl is being dragged to the gallows. He is gagged as his eyes are filled with terror. The Viscount and the two Inspectors are in attendance, and in the crowd Jonathan Broadfoot can be also seen talking to those around him.

A hood is placed over the head of Scherer, the noose is then tightened and without a chance to breathe, the body is dropped in such a fashion that it is certain that executioner's apprentice has not had the duty of administering the quick judgment.

"And that is all that needs to ever be said about this subject again," the Viscount tells the Inspectors and the others close to him on the podium as he looks directly at Broadfoot.

Two days latter, the writer is found murdered, deep in a dark London ally, an incident that the London Constabulary quickly rule to be an unsolvable robbery that tragically went wrong. A small obituary appeared in the London Times three days later, and with that, nothing else was ever said.

SHADOW

Fully involved in the spiraling illusion where my noble occupation is retrieving what little there is that may have a faint hope of leading to a portion of reality. I kindly ask the porter in the wind which cycle or updraft would better serve my unknown purpose. The answer drifts in the drafts of the other words that are launched by the constant array of points unsharpened, and therefore, unable to stick in my unstable memories. That is where I began my search, in a vain attempt, that these recalls so strictly placed on the shelves of my past school libraries, may hold any reliability. Even though I began my effort with the knowledge that should it be found, it would be shredded from overuse.

I notice that up there, close to the burnt out candle, the flick of an eyelash hints that an oasis is close. I feel my toes blend into the sand that they struggle through in the attempt to take me to the place where I can become a vision for some other unidirectional journey. As I come closer to my intention, the sand swallows my feet, leaving me without the means of quick transport. Being a noble fool, I crawl to the location where my lips will feel the moisture of an oasis that will aid me in passing my words outside of this turbulent tunnel, as it funnels my collections of thoughts into the universes that rely on my unreason and their fogged-out magnifications.

I understand nothing as I have been a witness to a celebration in a well aged dream. I think I have circulated throughout the stew, though I will admit that I have been stirred. I am a spice or a potato or a rancid piece of meat, for when I am chewed, my delusions in this simmering spiral will do little to still the discoveries found in this passage of passions. I feel the rest of the ingredients in this covered pot have no more of a hold on their discoveries than I do. I feel comforted by the fact I am not alone in this illusion so skillfully played on the stage. I have one chill left to describe, though. I cannot be certain where the stage is. Is it really before me, is it in me or have I been chasing it all along?

I have found a small piece of rationale. Could the answer be that I am a voyeur? A transparent survivor from the illusions I contend with on a consistent basis? Perhaps I enter these sorts of theaters because they open their doors to me. They need to have me participate in their irrational behaviors with what seems to be rational occupations, for the ones whose lives were created in order for me to find a moment of solitude in this giant audience, I always seem to be in need of. This audience I am in helps me to secure myself, as I alone cannot find why I need to stay here until the end.   Something inside this place, inside this storm, speaks to my personal puzzlements and helps me unfasten my personal paradoxes. Here, I can see myself in the illusions of another that flies in the flocks throughout and within this very wide audience.

On Sunday, July 25th, 1831, twelve days after the execution of Herr Scherer, Inspector Legard is greeted at the front door of Madame Beauvie's residence by Marta.

"Inspector, I am happy you are here, my Madame has been anxious to see you. Please go out on the terrace, it is in the shade and a pleasant breeze is coming from the Seine. I will bring you some refreshments after I tell the lady you have arrived."

Legard casually walks out to the splendid vantage point that looks out upon the beauty of Paris. The breeze is welcome as the heat and dryness of the season has made comfort hard to find and more difficult to preserve. He sits after beginning to enjoy a freshly lit cigar just as Marta brings a small sampling of the household's appreciations for fine cuisine and the best French wines that can be offered. She pours the gentleman a healthy taste of the merlot and hands it to him as he sits back in the chair like a stallion who has just demolished the field.

"Please Inspector, relax and enjoy, my lady will be with you in a moment."

"Thank you Marta, I will."

Marta then leaves the terrace as the lady of the house appears a second later. She smiles at Pierre as she closes the doors behind her. Legard stands and opens his arms as Angelique glides perfectly between them. They kiss very passionately before they begin to exchange a single word.

"Mon amour, I am so happy to see you. I have rested myself so much that if I had to entertain boredom any longer I swear I would…"

"Silence Angelique, I am back and I desire to taste more than your food and your drink. I am sure you have heard how Herr Scherer confessed to a majority of his crimes and when he was put to death, along with him went all of his lies and comments about those he encountered in the last few months."

Angelique kept kissing his face and lips as he was talking to her. With every word about the demise of Scherer she became more amorous with him.

"Mon amour, for saving my honor, all I have at my disposal I give to you. Anything you want, need or desire. I promise I will fulfill your every word and your every command. Come with me, my bed is soft and I am ready."

She then leads the man through a different set of doors that opens upon her boudoir. She quickly closes the doors behind them and then starts to undress her old lover as he touches her face with a gentle caress that has the certainty of many more to follow.

As the two fall into their familiarities, out in the streets of Paris the talk of revolution is starting to fail as it attempts to balance between outrage and action. King Charles is losing his grip on the control of the throne as it is very apparent that he has long ago lost control of the lower classes of Paris. As Angelique rewards her accomplice well into the evening, the shadows of the street lamps spider web the boulevards and walkways in a way that does little to contradict the action of the Black Widow on top of her victim as she embeds her fangs deep into Legard's jugular.

He lies there as she skillfully wraps him in a silk cocoon for the purpose of a future meal or means to another of her well planned devourings. He will always be appointed to a duty in accordance to her wishes, desires, and yes, even more minor chores. After all, a woman of station cannot be expected to become overwrought on more than a few occasions in her entire lifetime. It is in bad taste to be distasteful in public. That is why a refined person employs those who are indeed quite good in the talent of secretive service. Anyone who understands power understands the hidden filth behind it, and at times it is amusing when the falling become incapable to continue to hide it.

The following morning the pair were still together in Angelique's bed as she was sleeping contently with her arm around her lover's shoulders. His eyes opened slightly as he smiled upon seeing her hand dangle before him. He moved his lips closer and kissed each finger in a tender romantic way as she smiled and purred, "I love you."

He turned around and he kissed her with an embrace of loving intention, his lips were still on hers as the first few words filtered out.

"Angelique, I have deeply loved you for years and I realize that this may not be the time for you to establish a firm answer, but I cannot wait any longer. Marry me my dear. It is time that the both of us stop running from the truth our muffled hearts have been longing for. Marry me, Madame Beauvie."

"Yes Cherie, of course I will. With all that has passed, my love for you is the only thing that remains in place."

They start to roll happily under the duvet until they stop in the middle to continue with the more intense part of the mutual decision. Their love affair had been ongoing for years and her frailties were always mended by the soft encounters the two would spoil each other with when she was in Paris or he found time away from his duties.

He was always a notification away, as he was the one that managed to eliminate the circumstances that came close to grounding her consistent flights over the walls of containment and common practice. She became known for her skills under the covers because she practiced diligently with her two partners, Gabriel and Pierre. Of course, she entertained others, but never with the same energy that she put into her passions with the two. Gabriel was her addiction, but Pierre was the only man she ever truly loved.

There were many others of both sexes, but there always was a motivation behind her seductions. She bestowed on the easily manipulated a physical pleasure that always made them enormously satisfied but forever longing for another taste. Gabriel was the only one she had ever known that had shown boredom in her bed. Perhaps, he knew that she would never love him fully. Perhaps, he could only love pure perfection, a commodity not easy to find and even more difficult to acquire.

As the morning grew older, Angelique left her bedroom to secure breakfast for them. "Marta, Pierre wants to marry me and I have accepted."

"Finally the two of you have seen the pledge of sanity; I promise you that he will make you happier than you ever have been. He is a real man, not a boy pretending to be what would be impossible for him to attain on his own. Inspector Legard is a general far too smart to ever fail his intellectualism. I promise that he is what you have always needed."

"Make us a grand meal as I bring him his paper. Has Le Moniteur arrived yet?"

"Yes, on the table where I usually put it."

"Quick, cook; we are both weak from our festivities."

Angelique then returns to her room as Pierre is still lying on the bed with a look upon his face that sings of true contentment. She jumps on the bed and straddles him as she looks deeply into his eyes. "I will be a faithful companion, mon amour, I will allow you to remain in my heart as I do trust you emphatically. I will ease your tension and chase away anything and anybody that comes close to breaking the tranquility you are feeling at this instant."

"Life will not leave us alone, my beauty. There will be moments where tranquility will not serve the requirement. We are predators in the jungle, and we know how to accomplish the task at hand. Comfort will consistently reward us for our diligence to never fall into an unfulfilled need ever again."

Soon the door is knocked upon as Marta rolls in a large tray of well cooked food and other complements. She smiles as the two hold one another. She rolls the tray into the proper position, curtsies and leaves the two to complete their morning vows to one another. The coffee is poured as Pierre opens the newspaper and says, "My dear God. The fool."

"What?" is the only response that Angelique gives as she has begun to eat.

"The King has signed into law what has been termed the July Ordinance. The citizens will not stand for it. The man will abdicate before the week is through, I am certain of it. I will have to leave soon and return to my detachment."

"You will return to me?"

"Of course, by this evening you will again be in my arms, my beauty. I am going to marry you, but I am still a police officer and there are orders I must follow. The day will not end well, and if revolution cannot be avoided, my jurisdiction will become the military's problem. I promise you, the men in my command know I would never put them between the King and the people in the streets."

"But your duty is to stop chaos."

"You are testing me, teacher, you are well aware that chaos will never be stopped if the police protect the one who caused it. That is why the throne employs soldiers. We both know they are the most ignorant, for it is a soldier's duty to react to an order, not to think about it. I am a different breed altogether; for I am paid to think, then react."

"I am sure Viscount Gunner's wife will find a small bit of solace in the fact that the House of Bourbon will hold the throne through their romantic ties with the House of Orleans. She will be treated with the highest respect. I hope in some way it will compensate her for our mutual tragedy."

"Romantic ties? Amusing Angelique, I am sure romance will be forever a dream to those that have been raped by power. It is the type of lover that never learned the meaning of the word 'no'."

"Cherie, I am aware of many exceptions to your theory."

"Yes, you are right. But is it not funny that the exception helps to avert the eyes from the rapes that are occurring down the hall and in the rooms where the decisions are actually being made."

"You have always appreciated my sarcasm, mon amour," she says as they kiss before Pierre begins to dress. He leaves her apartment as she is in a mood that has yet to be observed throughout this treatment of the story. She begins to sing as violins can be heard in tranquil accompaniment. The temperament of the performance has somehow avoided the circumstances that would be the realistic outcomes of the losses this woman has suffered.

There is no logic being portrayed on the stage between these curtains. How can she simply bury all that has occurred in a shallow grave that in our minds casts a scent that entrances the wolves, rats, mites and other grave robbers whose chore it is to devour the excrement flushed through the bowels of life? We watch as she is capable to still glow from her never escaping physical beauty but somehow her flaunting has the appearance of the worst of repugnancies. Our view becomes difficult to witness as it is a vision of how ugly denial can be.

She is able to rejoice as the city of Paris and the country of France is being cast into darkness, while she is sure of the outcome. We are then faced with a question that has been taunting us from the beginning. What from the outset of our diligence to this undertaking can be considered sanity? What part of this delusion was real? How long have we been left inside the sanitarium we were taken into? And why did we not heed the warning given in the first four words, 'madness is a quaint genteel'?

We are unable to leave at this juncture; the exits are no longer clearly indicated. Are we in the cage of the mongrelized or are we in the same cell as the dying corpse? Perhaps we are still in the groups that wonder by these appearances as we mock those that could not handle the distortions found while breathing. Are we still so unaware of how short the fall is between our conceived height and their gutters of swirling visions? I will tell you that I am no longer sure if the gutter is below me or as close as a wrong step in my perceptions.

Later that afternoon, Angelique is alone in the front room writing at the desk when she is heard to say, "Slow down, you are going too fast again, the pen does not fill itself. Now you had just said…, 'and the hearts are vanishing from the chests of…,' go on."

Again, she begins to write. She looks calm with her task, and at times, she makes comments.

"I like that."

"Where is the period, after time, or after worn?"

There is no one else in the room as she gives every indication that someone is dictating to her. A soft voice slowly hums along with a fragmented melody a piano is playing. The two glide together in an often distracting way that seems so close to an edge of a symbolic chasm that is sure to be bottomless, where those that have fallen before float in place for a while before they hurtle down once more.

Marta comes into the room with every attempt to not distract the apparent interchange. She smiles as she lays a tray of tea and assortments on a table close to the desk. She then turns, but before she leaves, she kisses Angelique on the forehead. Angelique softly says, "I love you, Mommy."

Marta leaves the room in silence as the pen moves swiftly from left to right and from page to page. A few moments later, the pen is perched in its stand as Angelique moves towards the tray and pours two cups of tea. She prepares both, one with milk and one with honey. She brings the sweetened version to a chair in the corner and lays it on the table to the side. She then goes back to fetch the other cup and saucer and walks while drinking as she stretches to relieve the cramps in her shoulders that have be placed there by her long vigil at the desk.

"Where are you about to go?" Angelique asks as she looks at the vacant chair. "You must really believe in the gullibility of those your words are meant for."

"I know, you always answer the question the same way. You have a very creative mind, perhaps after all these years you could put together a new set of words that would be more interesting to listen to. Why do you give your work all the originality, why not keep a bit of it to change the way you personally look at things?"

"You are hopeless, my dear. Yes, stop failing yourself. We have worked closely for years, but still you react in the same childish way whenever my patience has come close to being worn thin."

"You have explained your outlook on these matters in similar terms before. Why do I bother having these conversations with you, all we ever accomplish is the acknowledgement that we are both solidly encased in our immovabilites?"

Angelique then returns to the desk, sits and readies herself to begin writing again. "Now what is next?"

She dips the pen in the ink well as the page and the tip begin the dance again. She writes in a fury, never stopping to think, the words waterfall out of her in full form and phrases. Every page lies still as it is used until every space has accommodated the thoughts that need to be expressed. She reacts to the sentences in various degrees of facial gestures, smiles and laughter as well as frowns and sighs. She writes as if a true dictation is occurring, but the oddity of the scene makes one think that the pages have very little to do with coherence.

Myself and those that surround me share the same emotion, I am certain of it. The fully formed tragedy that we are intently watching must be the result of a mental sickness. Syphilis in its darkest style could be the culprit. There does not appear to be any other rational explanation. The words, "…write from the grave" were used before in reference to Gabriel. He is the one who must be dictating to her. He is the one her mind will never sanction a death for. This chilling emotion that moves me has the added feel of sympathy for a woman I have come to know and feel for.

Later, as the evening was beginning to push away the sun, there were sounds of coming turmoil that could be heard from the woman's terrace. She stood and watched the streets below her as Marta was close by. Chanting began, 'A bas les Bourbons!' and 'Vive le Chartel!' These were the familiar signals that the stamp of defiance was starting in earnest. She turned to Marta with anguish so perfectly sculpting her face, "Pierre, where is Pierre, Mommy?"

Marta held the sobbing creature in her arms as she rushed her inside and away from the whip coming from the horizon of a new hysteria that would be the next chapter in the French Revolution. The night was spent in Angelique's bed where Marta continued to hold the despondent woman as Angelique danced between rest, sleep and tears. Marta's voice remained calm and composed as her words defined her loyalty and love for her mistress.

"Settle my dear, there is no need to succumb to your coldest fears. Your mother is with you as I have always been and where I will remain. We will see the sun again and your Pierre will return once this foolishness has run itself dry."

By the mid morning the two had both been sleeping for a few hours. The sun was up, but the sounds from the street did not have normality to them; the activity was not of the same degree as would be expected for a Tuesday morning. Marta was the first to notice, and her expression foretold that the apparent stillness was the warning that rest would be a limited commodity and tranquility would be in short supply.

When Angelique opened her eyes, Marta's face was the first thing she saw. The smile that Marta was wearing was mirrored by the younger woman.

"Stay still my lady, rest more. I will leave for a short while to do some marketing and when I return I will cook you a splendid morning meal."

"I will not leave my duvet," Angelique answered as she turned and fell back into her sleep. Marta then left the room and, in a short period, the apartment. When the older woman walked down the stairs there were no guards any longer. The street was still except for the odd conversation that she overheard while her trip to the market was the only purpose that completely involved her intentions.

When she got to her destination, the owner's son was beginning to close the shutters. Marta hurried in as she was greeted by a very concerned man.

"Marta be quick about it, gather what you need. I will not allow you to stay in here for very long. There is hardly time enough."

"For what, Monsieur Chapdelaine?"

"To leave this area, Madame. The Revolution is about to enter its next stage. The rumor is that the Garde le Royale are about to be called to duty, and that means the battle lines are being drawn once again. Please, Marta, take what you need. Pay me when this chapter has ended. Hurry!"

As the light from the windows was being blanketed out by the closing shutters, Marta filled her bags quickly with the essentials needed to secure enough nourishment for more than a day or so. She gave Chapdelaine more money than what the goods were worth, kissed his cheek and said, "Stay safe, my friend."

She then ran out of the store, down the street towards her duty once again as the store keeper said to his son, "She is one of the beautiful people in these ugly times."

Marta guided herself through the filling streets as the factory workers, laborers, office workers, unemployed and others were gathering in darkening storm clouds of rage and non-compliance. Their chants were the thunder from these turbulent crowds who were no longer silent as their rights to existence were being trimmed yet again.

They did not resemble the hedges that stand in perfect rows because the earth's nature refused to comply with the images of structure so redundantly placed in the supposed creativities of the landscaper and his employer. They held onto the appearance of a weed in the garden that had gotten out of hand because its determination to thrive had not been yanked out by the roots of its own convictions.

Marta was not stopped or harassed as she made her way clear of the storm front as it most assuredly would soon confront its opposition, the unmovable mountains that stood stationary at their posts of sentry to protect those in the valleys of privilege behind them. She found her destination at last when she saw the fact she feared so vividly; there were no guards in sight. She knew that they had their own families and loved ones that they had to protect first and foremost. But the stairs to the doors of the apartments could easily be used if the stores did not hold enough for the looters. And then there were the other possibilities that remained when an entertaining trauma starts to visualize the atrocities that a drunken mob can commit on the innocent and those of a particular gender.

When Marta entered the apartment, she fastened tight the locks and other obstacles that would make the front door difficult to open. She then noticed Angelique again at the desk writing in her hurried motion. The older lady smiled and made her way to the kitchen knowing that her mistress was again occupying herself. There was time to prepare a morning meal and there would be time to later find the appropriate prescription to help Angelique when she begins to disintegrate as the day progressed with its explosions and its reactions.

The tray was prepared in the same fashion, it was rolled into position in the same way and the kiss was laid on the forehead at the same destination for the same lips danced together in their appropriate angles. All was similar, even the cup and saucer were in their proper proportions as they were delivered to the same table next to the same empty chair. Angelique sat and ate her meal silently though, as she did not appear to have new words or old phrases to use to push away the strange silence. There were strange glances at the vacant chair, faint smiles and the oddly placed kiss that was sent in its direction, but the scene was bare without her voice in an apparent discussion with the chair and its invisible companion.

After she finished with her meal, the voices and the commotion that came from the streets finally passed words through her lips.

"I cannot stop the interference, they will have their way and the rest of us will have to bear with their need to complain about the position they find themselves in. All we can do is continue with our efforts and perhaps that will blow away the sounds our ears are not accustomed to."

She regained her position at the table and again she began to write without a stop for a correction or a thought. The pen filled the pages with the same intensity that was witnessed when this peculiarity surfaced for the first time. Her facial expressions started to expand on the words she was writing in the same way they had done before. Her beauty could not overpower the image in front of us as it was sadly clear that the woman was again supplying her incoherence with an outlet.

As the afternoon became heavy and began to fall into evening, the streets below the terrace echoed with the sound of hooves as the cavalry and foot troops began to take position a hundred meters or so down the boulevard. A large group of Parisians were milling around and sporadically throwing cat calls and obscenities at them. Though the opposing forces were well entrenched, it was the commoners' ranks that were fattening. The troops held their guns pointed at the crowd while all the citizens held was their defiance that now had a visual target to aim at. Around six-thirty that evening, a tense calm eased a silence through the scene, but the feeling was that the sudden breeze of the coming twilight would feed the fire below the surface.

Angelique could be heard above the street's tension as she began to scream, "Pierre, Pierre, come home to me! Please, Pierre I need you! Please Pierre… please!"

Those that were close enough to hear her every word looked up towards the terrace and then lowered their heads as they knew in their hearts that lives would be sacrificed that night. The street fell into the shadow of the event above and beyond the terrace as the tears of extreme pain could be heard as they were cast into air by the painful crying that could be heard by any ear that dared to listen.

In the apartment on the other side of the terrace, Angelique was being held by Marta as her hysterics had more than passed the surface.

"Leave me alone, Marta… take your arm from me… let me move freely, old woman!" Madame Beauvie ordered her servant in a tone that had not been heard before. Marta complied but tried to embrace the despondent one with her words.

"Angelique, Pierre will return. Look at the boulevard, see for yourself what is about to happen. Pierre is at his post, not in the exchange that is readying itself below."

Angelique's tears were held as she ran onto the terrace to see for herself, but as soon as she met the railing the fighting began below. Marta ran to her side as both women watched the troops being attacked by the mob with cobblestones, roof tiles and anything else that could be thrown through the air. Gun shots were first fired in the air in order to warn the attackers to move away from their directed defiance, but the crowd did not stop. On the contrary, they advanced holding clubs, sticks, knives, and other forms of weaponry until the soldier's guns were lowered and the next series of bullets were cast into the crowd.

The women ran back into the apartment as Marta clutched Angelique's arm in an attempt to take her mistress away from the windows and into the back rooms of the apartment. Angelique pulled the older woman back towards her and then slapped Marta across the face, landing her on the floor.

"I told you to not handle me, Mother!" Angelique said in a menacing tone that served the threat so vividly. "Mother, or should I say my father's whore, your female bastard has had enough of your directions. You lie about everything and I have the same venom in my fangs as you. Your calm approach fools no one any longer, look around, old bitch, we are alone with each other for the first time since you powdered my vagina in order to feed me to the snakes that you never could control on your own.

"My father was faithful to me, not you. It was me who he protected after he impregnated you. All you were then was a servant. Look and see, you still have a servant's garment holding in your fat. I lost my whole life because of you and your ignorance. All my words were stolen by that puppet I married. He was the great writer, but all he could ever achieve on his own was an erection. I called him 'my voice' as he tore my legacy apart while you conspired with him, as the both of you made sure I kept producing in order to feed your never ending gullets."

Marta righted herself as blood appeared at the side of her mouth; she walked towards her daughter and looked her straight in the eyes. "You ungrateful… you still cannot understand what I gave you. I knew you were a genius, I knew you were destined to write extreme triumph. Your father left me money to protect you with, enough to have kept me comfortable for years. I could have left you long ago, but you always seemed unable to be left alone. Your writing was the only friend you ever had. You still talk to him, you still listen to him.

"Mechant stole your writings and published them in his name, but he paid a heavy price for his plagiarism. He did love you, Angelique, but he knew how much of your spirit he tore from you. Camille was you to him when the both of you believed in magic. I know he failed at being a man, but his name on your work crushed his own spirit and his hollowness grew larger as the space became too much for him to ever fill on his own."

"Why are these words new to me?

"Because you loved to play with the fools you overpowered in your life. They would lay lifeless as you became the cat who enjoyed torturing to death the mice you captured. You enjoyed your cold nature and you will only listen to me now because there is so little left."

Angelique backs herself onto the terrace where the fighting below is magnifying. Marta goes out and yells, "Please, come back inside, please Angelique, it is not safe out here."

Madame Beauvie begins to spin herself around and around as she holds her hand tightly on her ears trying to stop the sound of madness that is circulating through the smoky air above the spasms of France.

"Stop screaming at me, stop tormenting me, stop, please, stop!" she loudly pleads, as she falls violently to the tiles that are patterned upon the floor of her balcony. She encircles her arms around her head as she takes cover from the turmoil both outside and inside her mind as she cries in sweeping sobs. Through her dressing gown her legs are exposed and blood can be seen trickling from fresh wounds and scrapes on her knees. She looks down towards her legs and she screams in horror at the blood as it begins to branch out slowly.

"Let me help you Angel," Marta kindly says, as she bends down to help the hysterical up. But what Angelique sees is the face of a demon as it smiles at its captured while it opens its mouth to apply the fangs to her neck that would secure the death and the coming meal in the never-ending fires of Hades. As Marta comes closer she is greeted by a backhanded fist that sends the woman to her back and her shoulder to the heavy metal leg of the terrace table. She rolls to her side as she groans in pain, while Angelique has risen to her feet that hold her dangerously above the fallen Marta.

With the sound of guns, horse hoofs, screams of death parading upward from the battle grounds below, Angelique grabs at the long grey hair of the old woman and begins to drag her into the front room of the apartment. Once inside, Marta's journey ends in the middle of the room on top of a rug that has been displaced because of the procedure. Once that has been accomplished, the bloody legged predator straddles the prey, hitting her face over and over again, while with a completely composed, almost sympathetic voice, she explains, "You are tired Mother, it is time for you to rest."

Angelique reaches to the chair close by and a pillow is then swiftly pressed down on the face of the next sacrificial offering to the god of the unbalanced. She holds the instrument with the force of duty as she recites, while Marta thrashes beneath her, "I can no longer ask you to stay with me, for I notice your sadness can no longer be hidden. My love for you is a lie if my weakness means more to me than the joys of life I keep you from tasting. Opening the gate to freedom is the hardest thing imaginable, for the simple reason that I would witness your disappearance. I would remain full of fear to what I would learn about myself and the paradox is that the only comfort I have ever depended on is here inside this cage. The gate is now wide enough to see the dreams that await you. Please, as you go do not shut the gate on me as I have done to you. I may see a dream beyond the hinges that asks me to follow, though I will remain here where my weakness promises to remain faithful. My life will never be the same without you, while my cage is now freshened by the air of the unexplored. Go, my dream come true, I have overused you."

As she ends her speech, she removes the pillow from the face of the demised and then she lies next to the shell, holding it close to her. "Mother, I will be fine without you. Do not worry any more. I can feel you are in the presence of the trinity as your youth has been restored and your virtues have been mended. I have been selfish all these years but now I have repaid you for all I have taken from you. Heaven and its paradises have been given to you by your very thankful child. And peace will remain eternal, for there are no distastes that will ever bother you."

She then holds her dead mother even closer, almost morbidly, moving the corpse on its side. After she is through with her kisses and embraces, she stands and moves the body to the chair, where Angelique makes her mother appear to be just sleeping. A quilt is rested on top of Marta as her daughter begins to sing a familiar folk song. Her voice is drowned out by the continuous battle that dances just beyond this pirouette. The ballet possesses a beauty in its execution and a coherence in its gravesite. Even the Chorus in the background adds a shroud to this spliced eccentricity.

Angelique leaves the room, returns with a dampened cloth that she cleans the blood from her legs with, and then in turn, she wipes the bruised face of her mother with the cloth, now soaked in blood. A crimson mask starts to take shape on the lifeless expression of the damned. Once the face has been coated with the color of an open wound, Angelique smiles and begins to sing again. She drops the cloth to the floor as she sits next to it with her head in the lap of the lost.

She stays there for a few moments, then goes to find a brush, some makeup and perfume. She starts to brush her dead mother's hair and applies color to the face that creates a clown-like appearance. The flowery scent is scattered behind the ears as Angelique begins to speak.

"She looks beautiful. Tell me, would you dance with my mother when the orchestra is through with this disturbing nonsense they are playing at the moment? How could anyone feel the rhythm in all that clutter? I could never understand it. Well, it will be through soon," she says in reference to the battle that is still raging in the boulevard. She begins to dance as her stained dressing gown is fully opened, revealing her small linen slip and her tattered knees.

"Yes, this one is more to my liking. Dance with my mother, Virgil. Stop and enjoy yourself, your seriousness at times is such a bore. Let's join the others on the terrace, closer to the party, come, let us mingle and laugh."

She moves herself gracefully through the open glass doors out onto the terrace moving as though being led by a true courtier. She smiles at the others she can see in her mind while they smile back as all are enjoying the festivities.

"Thank you Virgil for joining the rest of us, and Mother, you look so young tonight," she says as she sees the enchanting sight of the two of them finally enjoying the evening. Wine and other complements are on the banquet tables surrounded by those that require nourishment as the well oiled service staff helps them gather what tempts their palates. The elegant gowns flow magnificently as the handsome charming men in uniforms or in formal attire entertain the well kept ladies with wit, humor and polite trivial conversation.

Below this abundance, the night is not being held at bay as all the streets lamps have been smashed and the web they create with their shadows has been swallowed by the darkness. The spider has vanished and the fighting has stopped. The silence of a cold stone spreads itself through the streets and begins to climb the walls toward the event upon the balcony. Angelique stops dancing as she notices the music has run itself out. She feels the wind and tastes the bitter air. She stands in the darkening as a petrified look begins to scavenge away what little delight is left.

She moves herself quickly into the front room where she lights candles that cast moving shadows upon the clown in the chair. Soon, a fire is lit in the fireplace and the few pieces of dried wood that can be found in the apartment are piled at the edge of the hearth. Angelique closes the doors to the Grand Ball Room and the circumstances that are playing themselves out down the same walls that have been concurred by the silence that occurs as all begin to notice what they have just done.

"I have never scolded you for your temper tantrum in the Duomo," Angelique says as she begins to burn what has turned out to be her manuscripts. Page after page she watches them burn as she performs this maneuver with grace.

"Do you know what is written on these pages, dear Virgil? They are your words and the excitements they sing about. Sit down close to Mommy and watch me punish you for your little outburst. When you first talked to me, you were so sweet and kind. Remember how you always comforted me when I was sore from Gabriel's attentions? You slid into bed with me and touched me with such tenderness that I felt I was being worshiped. My head would spin and my heart would outpace the fastest falcon.

"In the Duomo though, you lost your mind as you screamed at the victims. What good did you think you were doing, there were few that wanted to hear you vile judgments? Your hatred for the Church torments you and I am forced to keep your pen steady when you become enraged. But when you feel compassion I can feel the pen move me as if I was a feather. Oh, master, why have you begun to use me to kill for you? You torture me when I refuse to be the instrument of you lowest treachery. How could you, and after all the beauty that I helped you give to world?"

She then goes to the bookcase and begins to throw the plagiarized volumes of the works of Gabriel Mechant into the fire.

"Look how your words slowly burn in the flames of Hades. A bonfire of your own vanities, Virgil."

She then leaves for a moment and soon returns with a small jewel case in her hands. She lays the case near the fire and then goes to the desk and brings the large pile of filled paper back with her. She sits close to the fire again, this time she leans comfortably on the same chair that holds her mother. She reaches for a bottle of wine, fills a glass with the liquid, and pokes at the fire, making sure that the books upon it burn evenly.

She then stands with the glass in her hand and begins to dance around the room as she blows out the candles with the perfection of a well practiced choreography. She takes more books with her and returns to her place in front of the fire. As she places another book on the flames, some more pages and a piece of wood, she again speaks to her company, this time however, the only light that is cast into the room is from the fire. The light dances with the shadows as they both play tricks on the faces of the masqueraded, one who remains speechless and one who spills words that seem to vibrate through the room.

"I love how the fire can calm you. It moves differently tonight, do you agree? I think it is reading all the words I wrote for you. There is something I never told you, master. At times I changed your words and blended them with ideas of my own. I found it very amusing when my voice fooled everyone into believing that a parrot has the ability to think. I was thinking all the time. When you, sweet Virgil, refused to listen, I found your weakness. You can dictate, but you are unwilling to hear. You went to your grave wrapped in your self-made shroud of arrogance. What a fool you are. You could never see how I used you. Your words are impure, for I tainted all of them in any way I saw fit.

"Go ahead and laugh at me. Of course Gabriel played the same game on me. Tell me master, which one of us wins? Mommy won nothing. Look at her, she has been thrown into the audience and forced to watch from the highest seat in the balcony. The other players are out of the competition, too. It is just you and me left now, even my love, Inspector Legard, is gone. He can thank his stale duty and his rotten honor for his inability to compete any longer. No, we are the only ones left, but I cannot see anything of value left to play for.

"You, my dear, have been dead for such a long time that even life itself cannot be the reason why you still remain involved. Why stay here any longer, the flames are all there is left and when they die out, this room will house only dead spirits that never found comfort while they lived. Open the door and leave, I so desperately want to be left alone."

She turns in silence to watch the fire as it burns away her life's work. She pours more pages on it as she can see inside the flames all the souls of her dreams she held so close, burn in her personal hell. She lays another piece of wood and the rest of the manuscripts into the holocaust as she sighs because she knows that along with her talent's departure, Virgil has finally been exorcized. She opens the jewel case and removes the same knife that was used in the Bishop's murder.

"I hope that in this place of burning souls, you, Bishop Joel, are present. I confess to you that I stole your life. I confess to all that it was my hand that felt your last breath. If there is mercy for me, please cover me with it. It was Virgil's hate that was the motivation, while I was the child that could not stop him. This time I take full responsibility," she says as she stabs herself in the chest. She falls instantly as the blow has been perfectly aimed at the heart, a motion she had seen her husband use many times before.

As the light continues to play games with the faces, the pages burn quickly in the fire. At that moment, the front door is broken through. Pierre enters the room with an expression of horror carved deeply on his face as he sees the last embers of the burned words begin to rise up into the chimney where they soon meet the blackened sky. Their dance entertains Paris as the city lies bleeding.